LIBERIA;

OR,

MR. PEYTON'S EXPERIMENTS.

EDITED BY

MRS. SARAH J. HALE.

AUTHOR OF "WOMAN'S RECORD," ETC., ETC.

> Thus doth th' all-working Providence retain
> And keep for good effects the seed of worth;
> And so doth point the steps of time thereby,
> In periods of uncertain certainty.
>
> DANIEL.

NEW YORK:
HARPER & BROTHERS, PUBLISHERS,
329 & 331 PEARL STREET.
FRANKLIN SQUARE.
1853.

PREFACE.

> "Two hundred years! two hundred years!
> How much of human power and pride,
> Of towering hopes, of trembling fears,
> Have sunk beneath their 'whelming tide!"

In 1620 the first African slaves were brought to Virginia. In 1820 the first emancipated Africans were sent from the United States to Liberia.

If a superior intelligence, while contemplating, from the serene heights of the mansions of the blessed, the movements, the tumults, and the aimless activity of the inhabitants of the earth, had observed that one little ship taking its solitary way across the ocean, laden with emigrants returning, civilized and Christianized, to the land which, two centuries previous, their fathers had left degraded and idolatrous savages, would he not have thought that, of all the enterprises then absorbing the energies and hopes of man, this, regarded by so large a portion of the few who were cognizant of it as a wild and hopeless venture, was the one which promised to the human race the largest portion of ultimate good? And who can doubt that, in thus providing a home of refuge for "the stranger within her gates," our beloved Union was nobly, though silently, justifying herself from the aspersions of oppression and wrong so often thrown out against her?

What other nation can point to a colony planted from such pure motives of charity; nurtured by the counsels and exertions of its noblest, wisest, and most self-denying statesmen and philanthropists; and sustained, from its feeble commencement up to a period of self-reliance and independence, from a pure love of justice and humanity?

The aim of this little book, imperfectly as it has been carried out, is to show the advantages Liberia offers to the African, who among us has no home, no position, and no future. These advantages have not been exaggerated. The endeavor has been to present the unvarnished reality; to be as exact and accurate as possible, and rather to err by keeping within than going beyond the bounds of truth.

For the few incidents in the history of Liberia that are mentioned, the writer is principally indebted to the author of "The New Republic;" the little memoir of Lott Cary is taken from "A Plea for Africa;" the accounts of the productions and climate of Liberia are derived from the most authentic sources.

Philadelphia, June, 1853.

LIBERIA;

OR,

MR. PEYTON'S EXPERIMENTS.

CHAPTER I.

A TRIAL OF FIDELITY.

It is a noble constancy you show
To this afflicted house; that not like others,
The friends of season, you do follow fortune,
And in the winter of their fate, forsake
The place, whose glories warmed you.

JONSON.

THE Peytons were among the earliest settlers and largest landholders in Virginia. Their plantation stretched along one of the southern branches of James River, called Rock Creek, although, but for the overshadowing of its grander neighbor, it might well have been dignified with the name of river, for there are many celebrated streams that are neither so deep nor broad as that known simply as Rock Creek.

The family mansion, a large, substantial stone

building, with a piazza running entirely round it, was built some years before the province of Virginia became a state, and its wide hall and winding staircase of dark mahogany, its deep window-seats and broad fire-places remained unaltered, although here and there a few of the modern improvements or additions might be traced. It stood upon a hill once covered with a forest of cedars, but they had long since been cleared away, excepting a grove of them which clustered down one side of the hill and along the creek, and gave their name to the place. Cedar Hill was celebrated through all the country round for the hospitality, liberality, and true benevolence of its high-minded owners. They were the great people of that part of the world, and were sometimes called the "royal family;" but few royal families can claim as much real respect and true homage as was rendered to the Peytons in the esteem of all their neighbors.

For the last few years the shadow of grief had been resting on Cedar Hill; for first the head of the family, whom years had seemed only to mature and ennoble, and in whom no trace of infirmity had yet appeared, was suddenly summoned away, and in the two following years Mrs. Peyton saw her eldest son lying in the fresh glory of his young manhood by his father's side, and her daughter's husband, dear to her as her own children, was brought by his desolate widow to wait with the rest for the final resurrection.

A gleam of sunshine had fallen on them when, a few months before the story opens, Charles, Mrs. Peyton's youngest child and only living son, had brought home a bride, a being who seemed the incarnation of hope and gladness. Bright, joyous, and restless, she shed the light of her happiness through every dark corner of that saddened house.

It seemed to Mrs. Peyton that Virginia was a living blessing sent to cheer them after the great sorrow that had been crowded in the last few years; and even her widowed daughter, Margaret Fairfax, felt the influence of the sunny nature Virginia was gifted with, and could better endure the mirth of her fatherless children, and watch with greater calmness the daily unfolding of the latest blossom of their love, on whom a father's eye had never rested, who had never known the great happiness of a father's love and care.

But already that transient gleam had passed away, and for days and weeks Virginia had been the quiet, and sometimes, for hours, the almost motionless tenant of a single room. Sitting by the bedside of her young husband, who was stricken by a slow fever before the moon which had shone upon their bridal had waned from the sky, she watched him with the intensity that could only be felt by one who was conscious that her all of earthly happiness was in imminent peril. There was but little that could be done for him—to moisten his parched lips, to bathe his fevered forehead or hands, to arrange his pillow, and give him from time to time a little refreshment or medicine, was all that he required; but in these little offices Virginia jealously refused all assistance, and, watching him night and day, slept only while he slept, and waked with his slightest motion.

Her cheek soon lost its color and roundness, and her eye its light, but she persisted in saying that she was neither tired nor sleepy, and neither Mrs. Peyton nor Mrs. Fairfax could gain resolution enough to insist on her leaving her husband, while they felt how precious every moment that she had passed with him might soon become to her; for the physician had the day before announced to the family that there was but little, if any hope, of a favorable termination to his illness. It had been a long and exhausting one; and, now that the fever was conquered, or had worn itself out, he feared that there was not strength enough left in the patient for him to rally.

Margaret had promised her brother, in the early part of his illness, that if there were any doubts of his recovery, she would inform him of it; and leaving to Mrs. Peyton the sad task of acquainting Virginia with the physician's opinion, she went to her brother's side to fulfill the promise she had made to him. It was a hard task she had to perform, but Margaret Fairfax was never known to shrink from any duty, or to put aside any cup her heavenly Father held to her lips. The whole family were accustomed to rely almost implicitly on her judgment in all times of difficulty, and Charles, who was some years younger than herself, regarded her with a degree of love and respect that might almost be called reverential.

Her sad duty was performed with the greatest tenderness, and Charles, looking the thanks he was too weak to speak, whispered to her to read to him from the Psalms.

After she had finished, he asked if Virginia knew his danger.

"I believe she does," replied Margaret; "I left her with mother."

Just then Virginia walked into the room, and the sad question was answered—a soul so despairing looked out of her deep eyes, and intense grief had given to the almost childish countenance, for she was but seventeen, such an expression of sternness and solemnity, that she seemed almost transformed. She bent over her husband, and pressed her pale lips to his forehead.

"Dearest," he feebly murmured, "Margaret has

been reading to me; but if you could, I would like your voice to be the last I shall hear on earth, if I must leave you so soon, Virginia."

Margaret turned to the fourteenth chapter of St. John, and Virginia, as she read the blessed words, felt insensibly sooothed and comforted. Lulled by her sweet tones, Charles fell asleep. At first his sleep was troubled, and every few minutes he would open his eyes, and fix them on his young wife's face with an anxious, searching gaze; but gradually he grew quieter; and at last, when Virginia laid aside the Bible, she could not help imagining that his slumber was deeper and more natural than any he had enjoyed through his whole illness. She wanted to call Margaret or his mother, but refrained for fear of disturbing him. Occasionally they glanced into the room; but seeing him asleep, and Virginia's face turned toward him with the paleness and almost the immobility of a statue, they went silently away, knowing that perfect quiet was the only medicine for the invalid in his present state of weakness.

Thus passed away the night; as the morning light was slowly breaking into the room, Charles opened his eyes; in answer to Virginia's glance, which looked the question she could not speak, he said, "I feel better, dearest; it seems to me that I must be much better; but I am yet very weak."

He spoke in a whisper, and Virginia had to bend low over him to catch his words; but, faint as it was, a watchful ear outside had heard it, and the door was softly pushed open as a dark face thrust itself in and turned anxiously to the bed. Charles caught the earnest look and smiled in reply. The whole expression of the troubled countenance changed as if by magic, and then disappeared.

"Keziah has gone for your gruel," said Virginia.

"Mast'r Charles is gwine to get well," said Keziah to the eager questioners in the kitchen; "I seed it in his face the very moment I opened the do'; besides, I had a dream about him last night, and know'd as soon as I woke up he wouldn't die this time."

"What was your dream, aunt Keziah?" asked half a dozen voices.

"Oh, go long, chillun, and don't speak another word to me; don't you see I'm too glad to talk, and I must make this gruel this very moment; he's mighty weak, but he'll get well."

Keziah was a privileged character in the kitchen and out of it. Few of her fellow-servants ever ventured to oppose her, and it would have been useless if they had been inclined to attempt it. To say that her will was iron, is to give but an inadequate idea of it, for its strength lay not only in passive resistance, but in active exertion, and so not another question was addressed to her by the chattering group, all full of anxiety to hear about Mas'r Charles, and devoured by curiosity as to Keziah's dream. In grim silence, which certainly did not look much like gladness, the gruel was made, and most carefully arranged on a waiter. A little boy, who seemed to know what was expected of him, came running in from the garden with a freshly-gathered bunch of flowers. Throwing aside the gaudier ones, Keziah selected some English violets, a half-blown rose-bud, and some geranium leaves, and arranging them in a champagne glass, with a taste no one would have imagined lay hidden under such harsh features and an expression so forbidding, she placed the simple but fragrant bouquet on the waiter, and proceeded to the sick-room.

For the first time since his illness, Charles observed the flowers, and with evident pleasure; for the first time, too, he seemed to relish his breakfast. These symptoms of amendment could hardly have given greater pleasure to Virginia than they seemed to produce in Keziah. She strove in vain to retain her usual grim composure; but the broad smile, which seldom appeared in Keziah's face, yet when it did, produced a general illumination in that abode of gloom and sternness, was now a fixture there for several minutes.

"I wonder why the doctor does not come!" said

Virginia; "he said he would be here before this time."

She was very anxious to see him, that he might encourage the hope newly sprung up in her heart; her next thought was to impart her good tidings. Bidding Keziah remain, for the first time for many weeks she left the sick-room of her own free will, and hastened to find Mrs. Peyton. She met her in the hall; and telling her as connectedly as she could that she thought, she hoped Charles would get well, he was so much better, and asking her to go and see if it were not so, she flew in search of Mrs. Fairfax.

The overseer, Mr. Burke, was with her, but Virginia did not see him. With an exclamation of "Oh! sister Margaret!" she leaned her head upon Mrs. Fairfax's shoulder, and burst into tears. Mrs. Fairfax, who already seemed to have been agitated, terrified by Virginia's sudden appearance and great emotion, could hardly support herself. She sank upon a chair near her, and, with a voice hardly audible, asked,

"What is it, Virginia? what have you to tell me?"

"Oh, he will get well—I know he will get well—he is so much better."

With great difficulty, Mrs. Fairfax controlled herself. She neither fainted nor wept, though she felt for a moment that if she could yield to her feelings, they would be more endurable; but so much was depending on her, and there was a crisis full of such great terror before her, that she nerved herself with all her strength to meet it. When Virginia wiped away her tears, Margaret was smiling upon her, but it was a smile so tremulous and sad that she exclaimed,

"Do you think I am deceiving myself, sister Margaret? Do you think it impossible that Charles should recover?"

"No, dear, I have never thought him so ill as Dr. Parker seemed to, though I did not say it, as I did not wish to excite false hopes; I will come and see him directly."

"What is the matter, sister Margaret?" Mrs. Fairfax hesitated. With an air of impatient authority, Virginia turned to Mr. Burke.

"Something is the matter — what is it, Mr. Burke?"

"Why, ma'am, they say the negroes are rising all through the country."

"It may be only a false rumor," suggested Mrs. Fairfax; "don't be alarmed, Virginia; I will take some immediate measures to ascertain the truth."

Virginia did not look in the least alarmed; the blessed hope of her husband's recovery so predominated over every other feeling, that she could hardly dwell long enough on any other idea to realize it.

"There must be some truth in the report," said Mr. Burke, "even if things are not so bad as I have heard; for Dr. Parker stopped outside the big gate to tell me that he could not come here this morning, as he was taking his wife and all his family to Somerton; he told me all the neighbors were going, and that, if you could, you ought to go too."

"But Charles can not be moved," said Virginia.

"So I told him, ma'am," replied Mr. Burke, "and he seemed to feel very much troubled about it, and said that, as soon as his family were safe at Somerton, he would come back if he could, and see him; but it is more than ten miles there, you know, and the roads are very bad."

Just then the hasty tramp of a horse was heard, and in a moment, without knocking, a young man walked hastily into the room. After the usual greeting, he said,

"I have come, cousin Margaret, to take you and all the rest of the family to Somerton. My mother is waiting in the road for you. We knew cousin Charles was too ill to take care of you, and we could not go by without stopping to see about you."

"Charles is too weak to be moved, cousin Frank," replied Margaret, "and we can not leave him, of course."

" In a case like this, when the danger is really so great, for we have heard the most horrible rumors of deeds the negroes are committing all through the county, and it is said they are marching on here in great force, don't you think it better to run the risk of injuring Charles, than that all your lives should be sacrificed ?" said Frank Lee.

" It would kill him to disturb him now," said Virginia, with an imploring gaze ; "I am certain he could never bear that long, hard ride ; but you know we are not sure the negroes will come here, even if it is true that they have risen."

Margaret agreed with Virginia that, to escape an uncertain danger, they ought not to sacrifice a life so precious to them, and that, in Charles's debilitated state, he could not endure any agitation or exertion.

Frank Lee urged every argument in his power to induce them to join him. He said all the neighbors through the whole country were flocking to Somerton, and that they would be necessarily left alone for the present, till each one had seen that his immediate family were safe. He wished, at least, to take Mrs. Peyton with him ; but, on being informed of the circumstances, she resolutely refused to leave her son. Mrs. Fairfax hesitated about her children ; but her oldest son, a brave little boy of eleven, begged so hard not to be separated from her, that she told Frank Lee he need wait no longer—

trusting themselves to Providence, they would live or die together. Frank left them most unwillingly, promising, if possible, to return the next day.

They decided to keep Charles in ignorance of their situation, and Virginia returned to his sick-room. Something flurried or excited in her manner seemed to strike her husband, but he made no remark about it.

All the active duty fell, as usual, upon Mrs. Fairfax.

"Can we depend upon you to remain with us, Mr. Burke?" asked she.

"Of course, ma'am, I would not leave you entirely unprotected, though I think it would have been better for you to have accepted Mr. Lee's offer; it seems almost like tempting Providence to stay here."

"We certainly have no right," said Mrs. Fairfax, "to expect you to expose your life for us, and if you think the danger is so great, I hope you will not suppose it necessary to remain. One person can do but little in such a case, and—"

"Oh, Mrs. Fairfax, do you think I could leave you now; don't speak of it again, I beg of you," exclaimed Mr. Burke, vehemently.

Mrs. Fairfax had trembled inwardly lest her proposal should be accepted; for, though she had not wished to show it, for fear of inducing him to remain against his inclinations, she could not help feeling that even one strong man was a great protection and safeguard.

It was settled, therefore, that the house should be shut up, excepting the front entrance, where Mr. Burke stationed himself to keep watch and ward. But it was no easy matter to fasten the house securely. The outside locks, and bars, and bolts on a Virginia house in those days were so little used, that, when needed, they were almost always found out of order. In this instance they succeeded tolerably until they came to the rooms that had been occupied by Charles before his marriage, and then even Mrs. Fairfax was obliged to give up in despair. The negroes about the place, all in the state of the greatest excitement, were crowding about the house, talking, advising, and trying as well as they could to help Miss Margaret, whom they all looked upon with a feeling amounting to veneration. She selected some of the most trustworthy, and told them to guard certain points that were the least protected, and give her the earliest possible notice of the approach of those she dreaded so much to see. She called Nathan, one of the older and most trusted servants, a man who had been "born and raised" in the family, and upon whose judgment and fidelity she felt she might rely, and told him to take his position on the top of the house, from where he could see far over the surrounding country.

"You will stand by us, Nathan, will you not?" asked she.

"Till I die, Miss Margaret," he replied.

The day wore away. The last rays of the sun fell on Nathan, patiently watching from the house-top—on the groups of negroes about the lawn, flitting and changing like the figures in a kaleidoscope—on the figure of a man on horseback, riding swiftly along the highway to Somerton—and they lighted up with gleaming radiance the three monuments that rose like columns of snow from beneath the grand old cypress-tree at the foot of the garden.

Mrs. Peyton stood at the window, looking in that direction, her favorite place of late years, and watched the pale, unearthly light that radiated from those memorials of the departed. "Oh! if I had wings like a dove, then would I flee away and be at rest," she softly murmured. An arm gently encircled her, a stately form bent over and kissed her, and the mother and daughter stood in a silence full of eloquence, gazing on the spot where each had laid the strong arm on which they had leaned so trustingly, the courageous yet gentle heart, that would have shed its last drop of blood ere harm should come near them.

"Mr. Burke has gone, mother," said Margaret,

calmly, after a few moments; "the negroes brought so many tales, each one more dreadful than the other, that I suppose his courage gave way. He took Argyle, Charles's fastest horse, and is a mile or more on his way by this time; he met Polydore, and sent him back to tell us."

"Yes, missis," said an immense black man, full six feet and a half high, and large in proportion, but with a countenance as amiable and simple as a child's—"yes, missis, I was clar down by the big gate when Mas'r Burke came ridin' past, and he told me to come right straight to you, and tell you he was gwine for help; he didn't think he should be back for some hours."

"No, he will never come back," said Margaret; "I saw, some time ago, he was getting more and more alarmed."

"I seed Mas'r Burke a riding off," said uncle Nathan, putting his head in the door; "but don't be frightened, Miss Margaret, nor ole missis either. I'll take his place at the door, and send one of de little niggers up on top of de house. No one shall harm either of you while I am alive."

"I believe you," replied Mrs. Fairfax; and both mother and daughter felt a sensation of security they had been strangers to before. Nathan's manner was so earnest and devoted, that they could as soon doubt themselves as him.

"I am afraid, mother, we shall have to tell Charles our situation. He hears the commotion outside the house, which I can not prevent, and the little bustle within, so unlike our usual stillness lately, and he has been insisting on knowing the cause. I dread to tell him, for any agitation must be so injurious to him now!"

While they were consulting as to what had best be done, a message came from Virginia, begging them to come to Charles, who was insisting on being dressed. They hastened to him, and found that he had partly guessed and partly discovered, by questioning adroitly his young wife, the alarming state of affairs. He insisted on going with them to Somerton. No arguments nor entreaties were effectual in changing his resolution. He thought only of their danger, and would not admit that there was any to himself.

By this time night had come on, cold, dark, and starless. Margaret drew aside the curtain, and showed him the thick darkness that seemed to encompass them. She reminded him of the wretched roads, and of their doubly defenseless state if met by the armed negroes on the way at night.

"Wait only till morning," said she, "and we will do whatever you wish. If we only considered ourselves, and not you, we should be safer here, I think, to-night. There is not a servant on the plantation who does not seem anxious to prove his fidelity, and Nathan is a host; Polydore has found a gun, and is marching up and down before the door, just as he saw the soldiers keep guard at father's tent during the last war."

"If I had only known this in the morning," said Charles, "you would all have been safe now!" and his eye passed sadly over his wife, and mother, and sister, who returned his glance with looks of calmness and assurance, that sadly belied their fainting hearts.

"Ah! you can't deceive me," he continued, smiling sorrowfully. "You are not so brave as you wish to make me believe. I know very well that, if I were not lying helpless here, you would all be trembling, and crying, and clinging to me, especially you, you simple little deceiver," turning to his wife, whose lips trembled, but who could not trust herself to speak.

"Margaret," he went on slowly and with difficulty, "you have thought too much of me; think now of yourself, of your boys, our precious mother, and my wife. If you really think that it would be safer for them to wait till morning, I will consent; for myself, I feel that the delay would be harder to bear than any exertion."

They decided to wait till dawn. A sleepless night was passed amid frequent but groundless alarms. The least noise sent all the little negroes flying to the house with tidings of the approach of the enemy; but the gray dawn came slowly on, and no destroyer's foot had yet trodden the path to Cedar Hill.

There was great bustle and confusion around it. The carriage-house, with all it contained, had been burned just before Charles's illness, and no one had thought yet of replacing their loss; so a large covered wagon stood before the door, in which Keziah was carefully arranging a bed. As soon as it was ready, Charles, partly dressed and partly enveloped in a wrapper, was brought down by Polydore and laid upon it. He fainted from over-exertion and excitement as his head touched the pillow, and it was some time before he revived. Virginia took her seat by him, supporting him to prevent him from receiving too rude a jar in their progress. Then Mrs. Peyton, Margaret, her two youngest boys, and their nurse joined them.

Nearly all the negro men, and many of the boys, were assembled in a group on the lawn, and Nathan was marshalling them in battle array. Such arms as he had, he had distributed to the most efficient of them; the rest he had told to look out for themselves, and, consequently, pitchforks, hoes, and rails figured largely among their hastily-collected weapons.

"What's dat you have dar, Orful?" asked Nathan of a boy, whose real name of Lord Orville, given to him by some novel-reading damsel, was changed to Orful by his companions.

"Tongs, uncle Nathan, and Peter he has de shovel —couldn't find nothin' else, you see."

"Oh, go 'long, you didn't look; you niggers are too lazy for any thing. Take your place there at de tail of de line; you hear?"

With great difficulty Nathan arranged the curious assemblage in two lines—one to walk on each side of the wagon. Polydore was to march at the head of one column, while Nathan took command of the other, and superintendence of the whole. Philip Fairfax, mounted on a spirited pony, with some difficulty reined it in that he might keep by Polydore's side, into whose charge he had been especially given, for between these two a most devoted attachment existed, that dated from Philip's babyhood. It began by his always preferring to be carried about, during a long period of great feebleness, by Polydore's stalwart arm, and then, as he developed into a sprightly, intellectual child, he never felt that he had half enjoyed any fairy story, or tale of giants and magicians, till he had related them to his patient listener, and heard his exclamations of wonder. The only fault Polydore had in Philip's eyes was an unfortunate facility in going to sleep, and often he would have to be waked up in the most interesting part of the story, and kept awake by the most energetic means till it was finished. Since Philip had left off fairy stories, and taken to history and mythology, this propensity had greatly increased.

"Laws, now, Mas'r Phil," Polydore would say, "I only shets my eyes to hear better, you see." But five minutes after he had uttered this justification, he gave such convincing evidence of the depth of his slumbers, that even Philip could not doubt their reality. He had been trying to teach Polydore to read for the last two or three years, and to see the intense earnestness with which one threw his whole soul into the work, and the easy complacency with which the other gave himself up to be instructed, would have amused any one.

But now Philip's mania for instruction was forgotten, and he rode silently by Polydore's side, whose heavy tramp kept steadily up with the pony's dainty prancings, and who, with eyes glancing with unusual restlessness, and lips closed with strange firmness, was mentally resolving, at the first alarm, to catch Philip in his arms and escape to the woods with him; for Mas'r Phil was his idol; he loved him as well, perhaps better, than any one in the world. A native African, and separated from all his own family, he had but few else to love, although for Keziah he cherished an attachment as yet unrequited. In fact, it had but once burst the bonds of silence, and then was received with such an energetic "Shut up! I don't want to yer none of yer nonsense!" that the poor Polydore had since worshiped in the sleepy depths of his soul.

At last the cavalcade was in order. The wagon moved slowly through the heavy roads, and Nathan, riding at the head of the troop, looked with no small satisfaction on the train he had managed to bring into something like marching order. Suddenly an expression of vexation appeared on his face; the light from a blazing pine knot, held by one of the impromptu guard, had fallen on a yellow turban that was resolutely forcing its way through the crowd, throwing all into confusion as it passed.

"Dat's Keziah—I knowed she'd be coming," muttered Nathan; and, in truth, at that moment Keziah's gaunt figure and grim face appeared, unmoved by all the commotion she had left behind her.

"Go right straight back, Keziah," uttered Nathan, in a commanding voice; "we don't want no women folks."

"You attend to your own niggers, and I'll take care of myself," was the curt and decisive reply.

Nathan was not a man who readily gave up what he intended to do, and therefore, from his not insisting on obedience from Keziah, it may be inferred he knew the hopelessness of the undertaking.

Keziah had good cause for all the gratitude and devotion her conduct displayed. Ill treated from her earliest infancy, first by an unfeeling mother, whose punishments were all so many ingenious tortures, and who had twice been prevented by her master from killing her own child, having hung her up once with her head down, and at another time being caught dashing her up and down against a pile of bricks; afterward falling under the power of a harsh and capricious owner, who, with a dim perception of her capabilities, and vexed at not knowing how to avail himself of them, determined, as he said, "to beat her sulkiness out of her."

He could not have chosen a worse course.

Every week Keziah grew more obstinate, perverse, and sulky; at times a strange fire gleamed in her eyes, like that which may be seen in a newly-encaged wild beast; and if the mutterings of her restless lips could have been understood, she would have been guarded like some savage animal. The fell purposes she was nurturing in a soul tortured by desolation and cruelty into crime had not yet matured themselves into action, when, providentially, her whole life was changed, and with it, as if by magic, her character developed itself in feelings and acts before strange to her heart. As some deep valley, made damp and unwholesome from the dark shade of the overhanging trees, leaps into beauty and freshness when the sun's rays fall unobstructed upon it, so great and entire a transformation did happiness produce in Keziah.

Charles, when a mere boy, was sent by his father to Keziah's master on an errand. As he was leaving, she crossed his path, returning to the quarter after one of the severest punishments she had ever received. Every nerve thrilling with agony, she walked with difficulty. Charles could not help perceiving that something was the matter. His look fell compassionately on her. She raised her eyes, full of a dumb yet fierce despair, and met his kind glance. A sudden impulse seemed to tell her that here lay her only chance of salvation for this world or the next. Moved by an irresistible impulse, which she always declared came, not from herself, but the Lord, she stood for a moment, and, stretching out her trembling hands, exclaimed,

"Mas'r Charles, will you buy me?"

The words were few, but the attitude and manner were so imploring, so full of entreaty, that Charles, with a heart full of generous and kind feeling, could not withstand it.

"Yes, Keziah, I will," he replied, and rode off.

All the way home, his thoughts were dwelling upon his promise and upon the means of fulfilling it. He felt that he had done wrong in having made it unconditionally, but since it had been given, and given to one so helpless, every high and honorable feeling in his boyish heart forbade him to retract, or even to repent of it.

He informed his father of what he had rashly bound himself to do.

"As it is your own promise, my son, and made without consulting me, you must suffer the consequences yourself."

"Yes, sir."

"There is that new horse I promised you when you were fifteen, and your birth-day comes next month, I believe."

"Yes, sir."

"And the rifle your brother intended to give you."

"Yes, sir."

"And the watch your mother has sent to England for for you."

"Yes, sir."

"If you give up these, I can let you have the money to do as you please with it."

Charles had had little opportunity in his life to cultivate the Spartan virtue of self-denial, the corner-stone of so much that is noble and elevated, and even *his* generosity was put to the proof, as all these long-desired possessions were slipping from his grasp. "He that sweareth unto his neighbor, and disappointeth him not, though it were to his own hinderance," rose in his mind, as if some guardian angel were whispering it there.

"Yes, father, I must do it, for I promised Keziah; besides, I can do very well with old Roanoke and my gun; the watch is the hardest thing to give up," and Charles sighed.

"Do as you think right, my son," said Mr. Peyton.

"Could you go over to Mr. Carpenter's to-night, father?"

"No; but I will go to-morrow."

And, in due time, a miserable-looking figure, barefooted, and with but one poor garment and no bundle, stood in the broad gravel-walk leading to Mr. Peyton's front door.

"There, Charles, is your purchase," said he, smiling. "Go tell her where she is to stay."

Charles led the way across a broad lawn sloping gently down, then through a grove of trees carefully cleared of underbrush, and then, winding his way among a cluster of whitewashed cabins, he came to one a little larger and more carefully built than the rest. An idiot boy was basking in the sun before the door; within, an aged, infirm, but happy-looking woman lay in the bed.

"This is Mammy Katy's cabin," said Charles;

"she nursed us all; but she has been bed-ridden for the last ten years, and now we nurse her. You are to stay here for the present. You need not go to work in the field till you are quite well;" for Keziah's languid step and heavy eye showed clearly that she had not yet recovered from her severe punishment.

Fortunately, the management of Keziah was left entirely to Charles. She had learned his sacrifices for her, and her devotion to him knew no bounds. She begged to be allowed to wait upon him and attend to his wardrobe. Her uncouth figure and coarse hands seemed but ill fitted for any in-door work, especially the needle, but no shirts could have been more neatly stitched or elaborately made than Charles's. The work she put upon one would have made three in the ordinary way.

Her habits were peculiar. It was asserted for a long time that she never slept nor ate. But Charles, having investigated the matter, discovered that her only meal was a late but very substantial supper, and that she slept on the stairs, or threw herself, with no covering nor bed, on the floor in the passage leading to his room, or, if any one in the family were ill, near their door, so that, at the slightest noise, she was up and wide awake, to render any service that might be required.

It was almost wonderful to see into how much

responsibility and trust Keziah had gradually worked herself, and her influence over the other servants was hardly less than that of the master or mistress. Nathan was almost the only one who did not stand somewhat in awe of her, and even he never ventured to thwart her when she was bent on any object.

So, much to Nathan's discomfiture, Keziah, grasping the handle of a well-sharpened carving-knife, the blade of which was hidden in her dress, headed the march; and doubtless, if she had been put to the proof, her yellow turban would have been, like Henry the Fourth's white plume, a guide to the hottest of the fray.

The morning light came slowly on. At every breath of clear, bracing air, Charles felt renewed vigor, and, ordering the covering of the wagon to be put back, he lay gazing out on the earth and glowing sky he had never thought to see again but with spiritual eyes, and felt that he could almost realize the emotions of the widow's son, as, at the gate of Nain, he rose and looked around on the crowd whose mourning was changed into wonder, and on Him whose heart was ever open to our sorrows, and touched with a feeling for our infirmities.

He felt so tranquil in his helplessness, so full of trustfulness and hope, when, having no power to do any thing for himself, he had placed himself, and all those who were dear to him, in the keeping of Him who is mighty to save, that he had no room in his heart for fear. Repeating aloud David's speech, "The Lord that delivered me out of the paw of the lion, and out of the paw of the bear, He will deliver me out of the hand of the Philistine." "Do you remember, mother," he continued, "reading that to me when I was a little boy, and how much I liked it, and repeated it so often that father and brother Hamilton called me 'little David' for a long time."

His mother smiled sadly, and whispered to him not to talk, for it might disturb Virginia.

There was little danger of that, for she had fallen into a sleep of perfect exhaustion, and her slumber was so profound that Charles was at first alarmed, so like death were her pale cheeks, her eyes sunken with long watching and tears, and her lips lightly parted, through which, so gently did her bosom heave, no breath seemed to come.

He turned from his young wife to his mother and sister, and saw, in the cold, truth-telling light of the morning, lines of care and sorrow that had been newly traced in the last few weeks. A feeling of passionate love for them—love that would have held life cheap if his death could shield them from one pang or fear, mingled with a conviction of his great weakness, swelled his heart almost to bursting.

Turning for consolation to the sky, that whispered to him of all-embracing love, and the green earth, that murmured in its thousand voices lessons of hope and faith, his eyes fell on the rude guard that marched steadily by the side of the wagon. In whatever direction he looked, he met only glances of affection and encouragement. Different voices, all familiar to his ear from childhood, called out to bid him, in their untutored but heartfelt words, to be of good cheer, they would defend him with their lives. He thanked them by a look, and, leaning back on his pillow, fell into a train of earnest thought.

What had he done for these men, that they should devote their lives so willingly to him and his? His parents had been faithful to the great responsibility they took up with their lives, his sister was untiring in her efforts for the improvement and education of her family, but beyond a general feeling of kindness and interest, he could recall nothing that would account for such fidelity. Excepting in the case of Keziah, he could remember no instance of self-denial that could excite their gratitude.

"Hereafter, if God spares my life, it shall not be so," thought he; "I am rich—as far as this world is concerned; I have nothing to strive for—my lines are cast to me in pleasant places—I will devote my life to them who are now so willing to offer theirs for me. I will make it my chief object to see how best to promote their interest and advantage, and may God help me to a right decision."

With a few words of earnest prayer, he looked again on the dark throng around him, letting his eyes rest on each face, that he might impress it, with his vow, on his memory. One of them stepped close to the wagon, and in a whispered voice said,

"Please, Mas'r Charles, would it 'sturb Miss Virginia if we sung a little? We can hold out so much better if we can sing."

"No, a cannon would hardly disturb her now," replied he; "sing, if you wish to."

And the voices of the motley crowd rose in singular harmony in the clear morning air. The most delicate ear would have been puzzled to detect a false note, no matter how varied or intricate the tune might be. The songs they sung were principally the joyous and triumphant hymns heard only at a Methodist camp-meeting, and especially suited to encourage and animate persons in doubtful or hazardous situations.

Keziah was indignant at this interruption to the stillness that had prevailed. In angry tones she demanded silence, but in vain.

"Mas'r said we might sing," shouted Orful, from the farther extremity of the line.

"Mas'r Charles said so," echoed Peter.

"Keziah," said Charles.

The faint whisper of that voice reached the ear to which it was addressed through the confused murmuring around. Her great love seemed to quicken all her senses. In a moment the yellow turban was stretched over the side of the wagon, that Charles might communicate his wishes with the least possible exertion.

"You know this is the only road till we reach Derrick's cross-roads, four miles off. So, unless the people are already on their way toward us, they can not hear us; if they are, no noise can harm us. It cheers me to hear them sing."

"Sing away, boys," said Keziah, with a condescending nod; and again the strange harmony rose in the air. Even the horses seemed to feel the inspiriting power of the music, and moved more rapidly.

The favorite melody of "The old Ship of Zion" was just commenced, when a trampling of many horses was heard. A silence full of horror and dread fell over those in the wagon. Charles grasped his mother's hand, and threw himself over the unconscious Virginia, as if to shield her with his body—it was all he could do. Margaret clasped her infant closer to her breast, and threw her arm around her little Harry. She cast a glance of agony on Philip, whose boyish face was the calmest there.

"I am not frightened, mother—don't think of me," said he, in reply to her look.

"Polydore, take care of him," exclaimed Mrs Fairfax.

"Yes, Miss Margaret, I will," was the reply.

These were the only words spoken. Keziah strided on far in advance of the rest, and, if it should prove to be the enemy approaching, woe to the first man that should cross her path. No womanish fears, no feminine tenderness was in her heart, but the fierceness and pitilessness of a lioness fighting for her young.

Nearer and nearer came the sound of hurrying hoofs, and, as all strained their eyes to catch the first glimpse of the approaching crowd, each heart grew stiller and more resolute, excepting that beating in the breast of the young Lord Orville, who, shaming his illustrious name, stood trembling fearfully, while the tongs clattered in sympathy in his hands. At last he fairly turned, and, fleeing for safety, hid himself behind the trunk of some fallen monarch of the forest. Peter, with uplifted shovel, looked in supreme contempt on the base flight of his whilome companion in arms.

"Hi! I allers know'd he no count," said he, and stretched his short neck to see what was coming.

"Oh, glory! glory! if it ain't Mas'r Frank and all de rest on 'em."

Orful heard the shout, and, peering over his rampart, saw, to his great relief, a crowd of the young men of the surrounding country, who, having attended to the safety of their own families, were on their way to escort the defenseless inhabitants of Cedar Hill to Somerton.

Learning that all was quiet in the neighborhood, and that the threatened disturbance had nearly passed over, Charles dismissed his faithful defenders with earnest expressions of thankfulness, and left them to return home under the guidance of Nathan, while the family pursued their way to Somerton, to wait there for a more settled state of security, and to give Charles the repose he needed after so much excitement. Keziah accompanied the family, being unwilling to trust her young master to other hands until he was quite recovered.

CHAPTER II.

THE FARM.

Oft expectation fails, and most oft there
Where most it promises.

SHAKSPEARE.

The Peytons remained in Somerton about two weeks. The excitement which the necessity for exertion had produced in Charles, seemed to have a wonderfully favorable effect in enabling him to throw off, with much more facility than would have been possible under other circumstances, the languor produced by the long and debilitating fever.

Obliged by the necessity of the case to leave their large plantation with no overseer but Nathan, and he having been hastily intrusted with the office with no direction but the general one, to keep every thing in as good order as he could, Mrs. Fairfax dreaded the return.

"We must expect to find the greatest confusion," said she, as they were on their way back to Cedar Hill. "The servants seem to have looked on this time as a kind of Saturnalia, and to have done whatever they pleased. Dr. Parker's family found their store-room and smoke-house completely emptied of their contents, and Mr. Carpenter, Keziah's old master, you know, found every article of furniture or clothing he had left in his house had either been stolen or spoiled. Mrs. Carpenter, poor old lady, was more distressed at the appearance of her floors than any thing else. It was the labor of her life to keep them well-waxed and bright, and they were so cut and marked that it will take weeks of hard rubbing to make them look decently. I have not seen Keziah so pleased since you recovered as she was when she told me about it, for those floors had been a source of torment to her for years. She told me that there was not one in the whole house that had not caused her a whipping."

"When mother told her she ought not to rejoice over others' misfortunes," said Virginia, "she said, 'I know that, missis; but I've not got clar of de ole man yet; I has tough fights with him sometimes, and dis time he's got the upper hand. I's glad in my heart, I is;' and she laughs whenever she thinks of it."

"How did the Lees find their place?" asked Charles.

"That was kept in very good order," replied Mrs. Fairfax, "for the overseer remained there.

He said he had lived with them more than twenty years, and would not leave them at a time when they most needed him. But Frank did not know that he intended to stay, or he would not have consented to it; he expected him to follow them almost immediately."

"Well, if the old house is left standing," said Charles, "I don't think we have any cause for complaint."

"Complaint, no!" exclaimed Margaret; "when I recall the feelings with which I last passed over this road, and my sensations now, I can hardly realize my happiness."

Virginia had caught a glimpse of the white-covered wagon, which, laden with groceries for the family, toiled slowly after the carriage, and interrupting the flow of reminiscences, that were as yet too painful for her to dwell upon, she broke forth into the "Old Ship of Zion." After doing full justice to as much of it as she knew, she amused herself and her more thoughtful companions by singing little snatches of all the songs she could recall, until she was stopped in the midst of "Home, sweet Home!" by the opening of the big gate.

"How dy, Polydore?" said Charles to that servant, who was busy cutting down a lightning-struck tree near the carriage road.

"How dy, Mas'r Charles?" replied Polydore,

coming forward quickly to shake hands; "I'm mighty glad to see you again, and Miss Margaret, and the chilluns, and ole missis, and Miss Virginny too," shaking hands with each one.

"I've got a new Bible, with big print, for you, uncle Polydore," called out Philip from his seat by the coachman.

"Thank you, Mas'r Phil," said Polydore, with a look of intense delight.

"How are things going on about the place?" asked Charles.

"Couldn't be better," was the reply. "Nathan's 'bout the best driver I seen in all my life. He makes the niggers stan' roun' like dey was sent for."

"Have you heard any thing of Mr. Burke?" asked Mrs. Fairfax.

"Yes, Miss Margaret, dey say he so 'flicted with havin' been took so by sprise, and flyin' off dat er way, dat he's gone clar off, whar he come from. I reckon we sha'n't see him no more."

From the roadside gate to the house was a distance of about half a mile, and when the arrival of the family was made known, in that mysterious way by which all news travels, the progress of the carriage was greatly impeded by the troops of busy idlers who flocked around to welcome them back.

At length the coachman succeeded in bringing

his horses harmlessly through the swarm of little negroes, who had seemed bent on immolating themselves in the triumphant progress of "the family," as their kindred spirits throw themselves beneath the rolling wheels of the car of Juggernaut, and, having surmounted the last gentle slope, the old mansion arose before them in the massive homeliness so dear and familiar to their eyes.

"See how fast aunt Abby is walking," said Virginia; "I thought she was entirely too dignified ever to hurry about in that way," as the short, rotund figure of the old housekeeper appeared on the piazza, giving directions and uttering exclamations of joy at once.

"You, Peter, tote some light 'ud in the dinin'-room, this minute. I'd ha' been all ready, missis, but I didn't spect you till to-morrow. Ben, run and tell Apphia I'm comin' to give out supper directly. Oh, Miss Margret, I'se so glad to see you, and the chillun too! Bless 'em all!" and she kissed them heartily.

Keziah now came up, having alighted from the wagon, and, by the aid of her general efficiency, fires were soon lighted in the different rooms, and an abundant supper—a Virginia supper—prepared for the once more happy family.

In going over the house, and examining it thoroughly the next day, Mrs. Fairfax was astonished and delighted to find every thing left untouched, except by aunt Abby's careful hands.

Before her promotion to the office of housekeeper, Abby had been the especial attendant of Mrs. Peyton, who, when she became too stout, and burdened with the weight of too many years, to move as readily as she had once done, showed her opinion of her integrity by giving all the keys of the house into her care.

"Why, aunt Abby," said Mrs. Fairfax, "how did you manage to keep every thing so safe?"

"I jes' lock all the do's, Miss Margaret, and I ses, nobody but me and Nathan is to come about the place. Dey all wanted to come and help me put every thing straight, but I ses no; I don't want none of your help. I knows what I am, but I don't know what you are; so get away with you. And Nathan, he's kep 'em right tight to work. But, bless your heart, Miss Margaret, dey didn't need no keeping; dey never worked half so well in all dere lives."

Charles found that this assertion was true. He accounted for it—not by the idea that his servants were better than those on some of the neighboring plantations, who had showed themselves unworthy of trust, nor by the flattering thought that more indulgent treatment than they received elsewhere had awakened more noble qualities, for there were many planters around, who held the reins of discipline with a looser grasp, and whose easy tempers led them to pass unnoticed over faults that Mr. Peyton would have punished severely; but their religious training was more carefully attended to than usual, and besides, the principal ones among them were, without exception, persons of tried integrity, fidelity, and Christian principle. There is nowhere a more sympathetic or imitative race than the African, and by working skillfully on their feelings, Nathan, who possessed something of the "wisdom of the serpent," had contrived, with little difficulty, to induce each one to perform voluntarily his daily task.

As soon as things had fallen into their usual routine, Charles began to reflect upon the best means to repay the debt of gratitude he owed to his dependents, and, at the same time, to fulfill his vow. He consulted his sister about it.

"There are some to whom I must give their freedom," said he; "I should as soon think of keeping my own brother in unwilling bondage, as those to whom we owe so much. But what shall I do with them or for them afterward? The best plan I can think of is to place them on a farm. I have some very valuable land lying on Rocky Run, about three miles from here. I think I might manage to settle at least ten of them on it, with a prospect of making a comfortable subsistence, if they are only industrious."

"A very important if," said Margaret Fairfax. "Judging by the free negroes we see around us, the probabilities are that they will degenerate from honest, faithful servants, into idle, degraded, and worthless men, a burden and a nuisance to every respectable person near them."

"If I thought that, of course it would prove an insuperable objection to my project; but how can I believe that a man who has stood the test of the ordeal through which Nathan, and Stephen, and Polydore, and many others of our servants have passed—not only this last trial of their fidelity, but the countless temptations they must meet each day—should become like those who have grown up in ignorance and idleness? I can not imagine that they would ever become a burden, much less an injury to society."

"They may not, brother," said Margaret; "but who shall answer for their descendants? Many of those we see around us received their freedom as a reward for their good conduct; and if they have not degenerated, is there an instance where even that could be said of their children?"

"Yes, Margaret, I think there is," said Charles; and after a few moments of thought, he mentioned two or three who had vindicated their claim to the title of freemen by their industry and uprightness.

"Is there any other way I could take, my dear sister," continued he, "to elevate my people to the position in which I wish to see them placed?"

At that time Liberia was unthought of, or existed only in the minds of those far-sighted enthusiasts to whom it owes its commencement. The question perplexed Mrs. Fairfax, so that she remained for some time without replying.

"There certainly ought to be some other course open in such a case as this—some way not only to free our negroes, but to place them in a situation where the superior position and cultivation of the whites will not react upon them, so as to deprive them of the hope, and, with it, of the wish to elevate themselves; but, I confess, I do not see any other. What do you say to sending them to the free states?"

"I have thought of that; but, besides the climate being so ill adapted to them, they are not regarded there with the same kindness and toleration as with us. The tie that unites us to them—the only possible tie, it seems to me, between the two races, has taught us to regard their necessities as our peculiar care. We are so familiar with their habits of improvidence and indolence, that it does not strike us with the same feelings of surprise and contempt that it does the thrifty Northerners. Besides, I would like to keep my people near me. After they have been taken care of by our family so long, I would not like to have them suffer, even by their own fault. We hear of a great deal of suffering in those Northern cities, especially among the negroes."

"Yes, that is true," replied Mrs. Fairfax; "that I know from observation. You remember my taking mammy Betty to New York with me, when Philip was a baby, and that she was persuaded to leave me. I remained in the city several months, and heard nothing of her. Indeed, I never expected to see her again; but one day I received a message, imploring me to come to her. I shall never forget the horror and misery of the places through which Mr. Fairfax and I had to pass in order to reach her room. We found her sick, and almost starving, and pure pity, if nothing else, would have forced us to take her back with us. Poor mammy can never bear to hear of the 'big norrard' since. To be sure, that is only a single instance; but I have heard of many others."

"We hear of them, and see them constantly at the North. No, Margaret, I have great hopes that I shall be successful in this plan; and if I am, I know many other planters who will follow my example, for there are but few that are not troubled by the present state of our relations to our servants

And when the slaves see that by their good conduct they may hope to attain freedom and respectability, who can tell how great a stimulus the prospect will be to them?"

Mr. Peyton was generally distinguished by great calmness and coolness of judgment; but the warmth and earnestness with which he entered into this project for repaying the great debt he owed his bondmen, kindled a degree of enthusiasm in his heart that made him set aside all doubts and misgivings as unworthy his design, and the people who were to carry it into execution.

"I am working with pure heart and hands," thought he, "and it seems impossible that I should fail; but if I do, it shall not dishearten me."

When Nathan was informed that his master intended to bestow upon him and all his family the great gift of freedom, together with enough land to render him independent, partly in recompense for his past services, and partly, Mr. Peyton said, that the neighborhood might have no cause to complain that he had thrown his people upon them for support, he could hardly believe the good tidings.

He hastened to impart them to his wife, but soon returned with a more anxious face than he had often been known to wear.

"My ole woman say, mas'r, how will Junius do

'bout his learnin'? He's mighty fond of books, and would be a preacher one of these days, if he can go on. He's been studyin' Latin, and Greek, and Hebrew, and I don't know what else, with Mas'r Philip's tutorer, and he say he's the best scholar he has had for a long time. But if he has to work on a farm, he must give up studyin'."

Mr. Peyton knew that Junius was a boy of uncommon abilities, and he had given the tutor permission to teach him, but he had no idea he was so far advanced.

"I will see Junius myself, Nathan," replied Mr. Peyton, "and if I find him so good a scholar as you say, I will do the best I can for him."

For Mr. Peyton to promise was almost the same that it is for other people to perform, so Nathan went away quite satisfied.

Mr. Peyton found that Nathan had not exaggerated about his son, but that the acquirements of Junius were so great as to appear wonderful when compared with his slender advantages. He was never more perplexed. "What shall I do with Junius," thought he, "if, by my connivance, he fulfills the promise of his boyhood, and becomes a learned man? What position in America can he occupy?" Then the question arose, "Is it right to stifle the yearnings for knowledge in any human soul, particularly when the knowledge can be obtained without the violation of any duty?" Every feeling in Mr. Peyton's generous heart said no.

It was then resolved that Junius, freed with the rest of the family, should remain with Mr. Peyton, and, fulfilling the duties of his position, that of assistant waiter, he might devote the rest of his time to the improvement of his mind, with all the assistance he could obtain from the tutor or Mr. Peyton's library.

Essex, an old family servant, the head waiter and butler, was next informed by his master of the happiness in store for him. He was a true Virginia servant of the old school. His courteousness and suavity of manner, his dignified politeness and ceremoniousness, might have put Beau Brummel to the blush. "The first gentleman in Europe" bore himself with no more stateliness and consciousness of his high position on the mightiest throne in the world, than did Essex when, with a wave of his silver waiter, he ushered the high-bred ladies and gentlemen of the "Old Dominion" to their seats at the table in the dining-room of Cedar Hall.

"Have I ever disobliged you, master?" asked he, with a magnificent bow and flourish of his hand.

"No, Essex, you have always been a most faithful servant."

"Is it Madam Peyton's wish that I should leave you?"

"My mother wishes you to go, as it will probably be for your greater usefulness and happiness; but, on her own account, she dislikes very much to part with you. You were father's body-servant so long, that she has become strongly attached to you."

"That will do, Master Charles. If I could forsake the family I was born in, it would not be while my old mistress needs me. If I decline into an invalid, or become supernumerary afterward," with another flourish, "you can turn me off, if you please. For myself, I do not approve of novelties. As I came into this world, so I go out of it. And, if you please Master Charles, don't speak the word to me again."

Another bow—another flourish, somewhat more deprecating than the others—and he was gone.

Amused and gratified rather than discouraged by his vain attempt to make Essex understand the value of the great boon he offered him—an offer Essex evidently took as a slight to his services, and a civil way of telling him he was no longer needed—Mr. Peyton continued his efforts with unabated zeal.

The next person from whom he experienced any opposition was one of the last from whom he expected it. Ben, the coachman, a bright mulatto, and a man full of energy and ambition, in his own way, after consulting his wife Clara about accepting his master's proposal, came to him with a positive refusal.

"If it was to work about hosses, now, mas'r, I wouldn't say no, for that I knows all about, and likes better than to eat my dinner; but I never know'd any thing about working on a farm, and never 'spect to. 'Pears to me like a mighty coming down, to go to field-work after I've been raised in the house. Clary thinks so too."

"But the land will be your own—a very different thing from working for a master."

"I'm much 'bliged to you, mas'r; and ef it was any thing else but going on a farm, I'd 'cept your offer; but, 'deed, I couldn't do that for nobody"—for Ben possessed the negro passion for horses to its fullest extent.

"But, Ben," continued Mr. Peyton, "think that you can be a free and independent man."

"Yes, Mas'r Charles, I told Clary so; and she said it didn't make no difference to speak of—a nigger's nothing but a nigger, whether he is free or not."

"I am afraid Clara dreads the hard work that may fall to her lot, if she leaves her comfortable home here," said Mr. Peyton. "Call her to me, Ben; I will talk to her about it."

She had been down to the quarter administering a dose of medicine to some child, by Mrs. Fairfax's orders, and, summoned by Ben, she soon appeared, slowly emerging from the clump of trees, and ascending the slope that led to the house.

"Hurry, Clary, hurry; mas'r's waitin' for you," said Ben.

"I am hurrying; don't you see I'm running as fast as I can?" replied Clara, changing her leisurely movement into what might be called rather a brisk walk, if the epithet brisk could be applied to Clara's graceful, swaying motions.

She was a picturesque-looking object; and, gazing upon her then as she crossed the lawn, the imagination would be irresistibly carried away from this land of universal activity, useful inventions, and angular movements, to those Eastern climes, where the sun and the genial soil do all the labor, and their spoiled children have but to receive and enjoy. With just such a gait of stately languor—regal in its indolent repose—might Pharaoh's daughter have walked, amid her attendant maidens, along the rush-bordered Nile. Tall and slender, with beautifully-moulded limbs and bust, small hands and feet, softly-rounded features, and large, deeply-fringed eyes, in whose dark depths the gazer might fancy he could discover terrible capabilities of passion or feeling, or infinite powers of love and tenderness, she was yet only a gentle and affectionate woman, very vain, and very fond of ease and enjoyment, but, in the main, faithful and true-hearted.

She had been generally employed about Mrs. Peyton's person, and, as Charles Peyton supposed, dreaded the hardships and privations of a life of labor on a farm. But she had accompanied her mistress on two journeys to Philadelphia; and the fine dressing she had seen among persons of her own rank there, with their opportunities for enjoyment, had struck her so favorably, that she had been since very desirous of returning. She told her master that, if he could get Ben a situation as coachman with some of his friends in Philadelphia, she would be very glad to help him as much as she could by sewing, but that nothing would make her consent to undertake the farm. Mr. Peyton would not agree to this proposal, and therefore, with many misgivings, Ben decided to remain a slave.

Another surprise was in store for Mr. Peyton.

"I shall make the same proposal to Keziah that I have done to Nathan and the others," said he, "but I do not suppose she will accept it."

"Oh, no, certainly not," exclaimed Virginia; "I should not wonder if she felt even more hurt than poor uncle Essex."

But Keziah embraced the offer with an irrepressible delight most foreign to her nature. Mr. Peyton could not prevent a sensation of disappointment, for he had felt convinced that Keziah loved him too well to leave him. She instinctively divined his feeling.

"I belong to you all the same, mas'r; and if you ever want me, speak the word, and I' come from the farmost ends of the arth; but I's born to be free, mas'r; I allers know'd it. Some niggers born for slaves—heaps on 'em fit for nothin' else; but this chile ain't one of them ar people."

And she turned to go away; but quickly changing her mind, she returned, raised her eyes, generally downcast and brooding, and fixed them, with a searching look, full on his face.

"Mas'r Charles, next to God Almighty, I love you; and you taught me to love Him the best: if you want me to stay with you, I stay."

"No, Keziah," replied Mr. Peyton, the momentary feeling of disappointment having passed away; "probably you will be of more real service and advantage to me by the good effect your industry and honesty will have on your companions on the farm, than if you spent your life in my service."

To carry out this attempt to free his servants, and teach them self-reliance, Mr. Peyton selected ten of the best men upon his place. Nathan, with his wife Sally, and a family of six children, and Polydore, with his patient eyes still fixed on Keziah, who possessed a strange power over the docile giant, were among the most prominent of the band.

Mr. Peyton himself had built as many cabins as were needed, and furnished them with the articles that were absolutely necessary. The rest they were to obtain by their own exertions. But many a millionaire has begun with less.

During the first year they worked the land for Mr. Peyton, as he wished to ascertain if it were sufficient for their support.

With the conscientious Nathan as their overseer, and animated by the desire of proving themselves worthy of their liberty, all faithfully performed their part in the common task.

Even Polydore seemed more thoroughly awake, and no longer took advantage of the opportunity offered, by being appointed to drive a cart or wagon, to enjoy a stolen slumber, while the sagacious animals chose their own gait and direction. There was a story still current, that one night he had waked up to find himself fast in a swamp, ten miles from home, which he had left at sunrise to obtain a load of wood. But no such disaster befell him now. Perhaps Keziah's rebukes, sharp and decided, though rare, had some effect.

He had selected a cabin close by hers, and employed all his leisure time in assisting the severe mistress of his soul in cultivating a little flower-garden she had planted; for, great an anomaly as it might seem, Keziah was an ardent admirer of every thing beautiful or lovely in nature.

The farm proved so much more profitable the

first year than Mr. Peyton had expected, that he was much encouraged. Distributing the proceeds among the laborers when he gave them their freedom, he asked them whether they preferred to work the land together as they had been doing, or to have it divided into lots.

As they all relied greatly on Nathan's judgment, they decided to continue the first arrangement. Keziah opposed this decidedly, but, overruled by numbers, she yielded.

The second year was not so favorable. In Mr. Peyton's frequent visits to Rocky Run farm, he found Nathan often sad and disheartened.

"Every thing is gettin' behin' han', mas'r," he said one day. "The niggers won't work; if dey has de least ache or pain, dey nusses demselves mos' to death. Keziah's de best man in de lot, and she keeps Polydore pretty well up to the mark; but de rest—dey work one day, and rest two."

The result proved that Nathan's complaints were well founded. Instead of making more than enough for their support, as they should have done, they found themselves in debt, and some of them had to apply to Mr. Peyton for relief.

The next year matters were still worse; they had tasted the pleasure of an indolent life, and were not inclined to resume their old habits of active exertion.

Few men naturally like a life of labor. It was first inflicted as a curse; and though obedience often transmutes it into a blessing, yet people generally, white as well as black, count it a happiness if they are elevated above the necessity for exertion.

It was easy for Mr. Peyton's freedmen to work enough to satisfy their consciences, and to procure a part of what was necessary for their subsistence, and often a great part; for it is wonderful, to those of many wants, how little will suffice to satisfy those whose only desires spring from their animal nature. And they knew they had an unfailing resource, if sickness or distress came upon them. Mr. Peyton never refused them what they really needed, both for the sake of past services, and because he did not wish to be the means of burdening others in the community with the care of his people. But he marked, with bitter disappointment, the downward progress of what, in his sanguine visions, he had depicted to himself as the Utopia of the colored race. It needed no prophetic eye to see that the children trained in indolence and self-indulgence would probably, when his restraining influence and willing aid were withdrawn, become the pest of the neighborhood by their thriftlessness and dishonesty.

By the end of the third year, Nathan's patience

was worn out. He came to Mr. Peyton with the proposal that the land should be divided.

The reasons that he gave were, that the labor fell principally on himself, and those of his children who were able to work, Polydore and Keziah; yet the others expected an equal share of the profits, and were inclined to find fault with him, on account of the falling off in their crops; and if he managed to lay up any little store for himself, the rest evidently thought that, as long as it lasted, they had as good a right to it as he, and would come to him very much as they would have applied to a master, only with more freedom and importunity. The African is naturally generous, kind-hearted, and yielding, and Nathan often found himself unable to refuse, though, in the end, he was the greatest, perhaps the only real sufferer; for the rest, without hesitation, went to Mr. Peyton when other means failed; but Nathan had determined that nothing but "extreme extremities" should force him to do that.

"If I can not support myself and my family after all that Mas'r Charles has done for me, I don't ought to be free;" and so his family often, during the third winter, lived for days on hoe-cake. Sometimes his oldest boys would succeed in catching an opossum, or some rabbits, which made a welcome variety in their fare, and fuel could always be obtained for the trouble of collecting it from the neighboring forests.

Yet, even in this, Nathan's patience was put to a hard trial; for, being naturally what the Northerners call "a fore-handed man," he laid in quite a store of wood, "light 'ud, back-logs," and all, before the cold weather came on. The first stormy day in winter, hearing a clattering and commotion outside his house, he opened the wooden shutter, which served also for a window, in the back of the cabin, and saw a number of little busy hands helping themselves liberally from his wood-pile. "What are you doin' dar?" he asked, in no gentle tones, while a disposition to run was clearly visible in the greater number of the little depredators; but a commanding "Stop! you hear?" kept them in their places, standing silent and abashed, with rolling eyes, and teeth, whose pearly brightness lit up occasionally some dark, chubby face, as, notwithstanding the awe in which uncle Nathan was held, an involuntary giggle would break forth.

At length one of the smaller ones took heart of grace, and said,

"Daddy sent me, uncle Nathan; he's got de rheumatiz, and mammy has to stay to take care of him. He said he knew you'd give him some wood."

"Well, ax me nex time; now take it, and be off wid ye. What you doin' yer, Jack?"

"Mammy's sick; she got de spine in her backbone dreffül bad; she got it working so hard in de tater patch, and now de doctor say she mus' lie in bed ever so long. Daddy's nussin' de baby."

"All he's fit for," muttered Nathan; but, touched by the singular nature of his mother's illness, Jack also received permission to go home with full arms.

One by one, each of the little throng came forward with his excuses, which were "no excuses," and his humble request, which, backed by the chilling rain, and raw, gusty wind, Nathan found irresistible.

It rained, and snowed, and sleeted for nearly a week, and by the end of that time Nathan's woodpile was, as he pathetically observed, "nowhar."

In this emergency, he went in to consult with Keziah, who, pointing triumphantly to her undiminished stock of fuel, said,

"She'd dare any lazy nigger to lay a finger on it."

"Yes, aunt Keziah, dat's all right; but, you see, I feels somehow like a father to dem all, and I can't see 'em suffer as long as dey are under me."

"Why don't you give 'em up, den, and go to work for yourself, as I wanted you to do at fust?"

"Dat's the 'dentical ting I've come yer about," replied Nathan; "let's hold a conference on dat very subject."

Just then a clumsy shuffling and stamping was

heard outside the door; then a knocking, which, being answered by a loud "Come in" from Keziah, Polydore appeared, leaving, after the custom of the Turks, though probably unaware of the existence of such a nation or custom, his shoes outside. Keziah's floor was not to be profaned by the mass of mud that Polydore gathered in his daily tramps; for, like the Hebrews of old, he was content if he could supply his wants from day to day, giving, literally, the morrow no thought.

"You've ben gone in de woods longer dan common," said Keziah.

"Yes," replied he, placing on the table several bunches of holly, with its red berries and glossy leaves; "fust, I had to tote home wood for myself, and den one and den anoder axed me to fetch some for dem, and I've ben as busy as dat ar bee missis used to preach 'bout till dis blessed minute. I fetched dat green stuff to you, for I know'd you'd like it to stick 'bout de room for Christmas times, and dat's comin' soon. I'll bring some more to-morrow."

"Have you had any breakfast?" asked Keziah.

"No," replied Polydore, with the reluctant, abashed manner of a child confessing a fault, and at the same time excusing it; "I hadn't no wood. It 'peared to me yesterday I had fetched home plenty for two days; but fust one came, and den anoder, and dis one was sick, and dat one was wuss, and it was all gone 'fore I know'd it."

"You and uncle Nathan is two blessed fools," said Keziah, with a sort of resigned contempt, as she went to work mixing a hoe-cake in the most scientific manner, and, after placing it in the hot ashes to bake, began making an *olla podrida* that sent forth a most savory odor.

While thus engaged, she kept up with Nathan a discussion of "ways and means." When they differed in their opinion as to the best course to choose, they appealed to Polydore, who would gladly have acted the umpire with impartiality and dignity; but his attention, distracted by the good things that were in preparation, he found it impossible, and, after chafing Keziah's temper to the uttermost by several *mal apropos* answers, he lapsed into a state of entire confusion, but placid satisfaction, and contented himself with clinching every proposal of hers with a "'Zackly so, Keziah," "Dat's all right, ole woman," until, soothed by his admiration, she resumed her usual grim composure, and placed the smoking viands before him.

To have seen the enjoyment with which Polydore fell upon these "creature comforts," would have given unalloyed pleasure to any benevolent heart. No fragments were left; but when Keziah had removed the dishes, she said,

"You know, Polydore, this is a very important subjec' Nathan and I are consultin' about, and we want your 'pinion."

"'Zackly so, Keziah; I knows dat. Drive ahead."

Thus adjured, she went on to tell him that the subject they were conversing about was no less than the advantages that would spring from a division of the property, each one cultivating their own farm, instead of working it in common as they had been doing. They were also considering what places they would prefer for their own share, if Mr. Peyton should approve of the division; for they still considered themselves as so much his charge, that they did nothing of importance without obtaining his consent.

They concluded that they would like to remain as they were, neighbors, as then they could mutually assist each other in their plans for improvement, and protection from the extortions of the indolent people around them.

All this was explained to Polydore, and discussed for his benefit, while he sat quietly on a section of the trunk of a tree, which, stripped of its bark, and carefully smoothed, filled well enough the place of an ottoman. It had a nice cushion and covering of bright chintz, which gave quite a brilliant look to Keziah's little cabin; but these only came out in pleasant weather, when visitors from Cedar Hill might be expected. When thus arrayed, Polydore never thought of occupying it, but now he had settled himself very comfortably, and, turning his head a little away from them, listened, apparently in motionless attention, to Nathan's calm, slowly-spoken arguments, and Keziah's pithy and decided remarks.

They finished what they had to say, and waited to hear his opinion. A lower droop of the head, and a deep, heavy breath rewarded their patience.

"He's dead asleep," said Keziah. "I believe in my heart if he was on de fiel' of battle he'd go to sleep with de bullets flyin' roun' him. But it don't make no defference—he'll do what we do."

"He'll do what you want him to do, Keziah," said Nathan, with a gallant bow; "de ladies is mighty powerful over our weakness."

Nathan was not much given to the vanity of complimenting, and Keziah appreciated his remark the more on that account.

After a few more words, Nathan rose to go, saying, "I'll tell my ole woman what we've been talking about, and de very fust chance I get at Mas'r Charles, I'll let him know how every thing is goin' wrong, and, to save my soul, I can't make it right; and I know he'll agree with us. You see, Keziah, I feel troubled 'bout my chillun. Naterally, dey ar as good chillun as ever lived, and we tries our best to larn 'em to obey dar parents, and to walk in de ways of de Lord. But we can't keep 'em from 'sociating with de oders; and dey larn such mighty bad tricks and words. If we have a farm to ourselves, we can live more to one side, you know."

And this conversation led to the proposal to Mr. Peyton that the land should be divided.

To this he readily consented. He saw that matters could not be much worse, and perhaps, when each one felt himself individually responsible, they might improve.

He had a long talk with the delinquents, to urge them to their duty. They all acknowledged their short-comings, and promised amendment; but when he placed several motives before them to incite them to improvement—among others, the increased respect with which they would be regarded—he always received this reply—varied occasionally in language, but conveying the same idea—

"Laws! Mas'r Charles, a nigger can't be any thing but a nigger."

The only resource he had, when reduced to this emergency, was to remind them that in heaven all distinction of race or color is unknown, and that they could hardly attain a state of blessedness in the other world without performing their duty in this.

But there were only a few on whom this argument seemed to produce any effect. It is a melancholy fact, that the external reality of heavenly things is but little felt, even by the greater part of those whose minds are trained to consider them from infancy. How, then, can we blame these ignorant beings, whose mental faculties lie almost dormant for want of exercise, if, having no earthly motives to stimulate them, they neglect the divine ones that are offered in their stead?

To do right, for the pure love of right, or the love of God, is a very difficult thing. Few know how difficult; for there are but few who have not some other helps to their upward course, in the approbation of friends, the increased esteem of their acquaintances, and the growing influence they must feel they exert in society.

These inducements can be applied but in a limited degree to the negro; and, with every earthly aspiration crushed out of his heart by the overpowering superiority of the white man in social and political advantages, it is no wonder he improves so slowly, or displays so little desire for intellectual cultivation.

The division of the land worked admirably for Nathan, Keziah, and Polydore.

All encouraging and assisting each other, their little places soon wore a look of thrift and comfort that gladdened Mr. Peyton's heart.

Their farms looked, amid the general decay and desolation around them, like oases in the desert, and, by contrast, served to bring out more prominently the improvidence and want of steadiness of purpose in the others, who had the same advantages.

Those only whose lives were regulated by their consciences and the word of God, were found strong enough to bear the trial of worldly prosperity. Those governed by lower motives sank, as soon as fear of their master's displeasure, or desire of his approval, were withdrawn, into a state of apathy as far as regarded every thing but their bodily comforts—and even those were reduced to a lower scale than before.

Mr. Peyton, though sick at heart whenever he thought of the failure of this experiment, commenced with such sanguine hopes, yet did not lose his interest in those who had once been his peculiar charge.

He labored earnestly to undo the evil he had unwittingly done to the community, by throwing upon it so many idle and useless people, who were allowing their children to grow up in practices of petty pilfering and vagrancy, which rendered them a nuisance to the neighborhood.

Every year of Mr. Peyton's life made his mistake clearer to him. Yet he was just enough not to attribute his disappointment to an inherent defect in the character of the colored race. Other people so situated, with so few inducements to self-improvement, might have worked much greater injury to society than they had done. He only felt that extreme caution was necessary before again taking a step that involved so much.

CHAPTER III.

LIFE IN A CITY.

'Tis all men's office to speak patience
To those that wring under the load of sorrow;
But no man's virtue, nor sufficiency,
To be so moral, when he shall endure
The like himself. Therefore, give me no counsel:
My griefs cry louder than advertisement.

SHAKSPEARE.

YEARS passed away. Another scheme for the improvement of the colored race, that seemed at first more uncertain in its results, and more difficult in its execution than Mr. Peyton's plan of the farm, had been commenced in weakness, and fear, and doubt; but, by the mighty help of Him who can make the meanest of His creatures do an angel's work, this little seed, when first put into the ground, the smallest of all seeds, was developing—slowly, indeed, but with a growth more vigorous and healthy on that very account—into a mighty tree, whose overshadowing branches should shed their blessed influences over a whole continent.

Steadily onward came the slowly-advancing legions along a path whose guide-posts and way-marks were the head-stones of those willing spirits who, with brave resignation, had placed themselves in the van, that they might meet the brunt of the battle, and bear the hottest of the day, and had laid down their lives with a martyr's willingness and a martyr's triumphant hope.

Mr. Peyton had been from the first deeply interested in the great plan of colonization, so far-reaching and comprehensive in its design, and he had tried to excite the same feeling in those of his servants whom he thought best fitted for liberty; but, as far as Ben and Clara were concerned, his labors were ineffectual.

A true type of many of their race, they would gladly have been free, if they had been allowed to exchange their easy, comfortable mode of life in the household of a Virginia planter for the greater variety and more easily obtained pleasures that would be afforded them in a city. A love of finery was also, in common with many other half-civilized people, one of their strongest passions, and the better opportunity they would have of obtaining and displaying it had no slight influence upon them. But a desire for freedom, for its own sake, was too abstract and intangible a motive to affect them.

Mr. Peyton was unwilling to expose their facile dispositions and unstable principles to the temptations a city life would offer them; and so time passed on, and they still remained members of his family.

At length an epidemic, often fatal, and generally supposed to be contagious, came, making its insidious progress through the land, and at one time every member of Mr. Peyton's immediate family lay struck down by the simoon of its breath. His mother and two of his children died, and only by the most assiduous nursing were the lives of the rest saved. Keziah, for whose assistance then many a wish was breathed, was far away, and the charge of the sick devolved on Clara and aunt Abby.

Clara's slow, gentle movements, her soft, light touch, and sympathizing manner, made her a great favorite at the sick-bed, and for many days she was in constant request. And yet her affectionate nature never grew weary, and she complied with the fretful wish of the convalescent with the same uncomplaining patience that she had displayed while they lay in the shadow of death.

"Is it still your wish to go to Philadelphia to live?" asked Mr. Peyton, when the family were able to leave their chambers, and dispense with their gentle nurse.

"Yes, mas'r; Ben and me would like to go very much, if you would let us," was the reply.

"Yes," said he, "you may go, if it is your wish;

I think you have well earned your freedom;" and he thought with a pang of his two fair boys, who had sighed out their last breath on Clara's bosom, and his cherished mother, who had had no other arm but hers to raise her dying head, and no other hand to wipe the death-dews from her brow.

"I shall go, as usual, to the North this summer," he continued, "and I will see if I can find a suitable situation for you among my acquaintances there."

"Can Americus go with us?" asked Clara.

"What! your brother? No, I think not," replied Mr. Peyton.

But Clara urged the matter with so much earnestness, that Mr. Peyton, his heart softened by his bereavements, felt unable to resist her plea for her only brother, a boy some years younger than herself, whom she loved with unusual warmth. He granted the request, on the condition that they should all remain with him one year longer. This he did, partly to see if their affection would bear the trial of self-denial and delay, and still more that he might train them more effectually for a state of independence. His first effort had shown him how much labor and patience were required for this purpose, and he now proceeded with more caution.

Ben and Clara readily acceded to this condition. Clara would have remained three times as long uncomplainingly for her brother, and Ben was very much in the habit of yielding to his wife's inclinations.

The course of the next year saw them fairly established in Philadelphia; Ben as a coachman in a gentleman's family in Walnut Street, with twenty dollars a month, Americus as waiter in another with fifteen, and Clara and her little girl in a house in South Street, where she was installed mistress of two rooms and a pump, with a coal cooking-stove in the kitchen, which nearly burned her fingers off, and drove her to the verge of distraction, before she learned how to manage it.

The next summer, when Mr. Peyton was passing through Philadelphia on his way farther North, he stopped for a day or two, that he might inquire after his freedmen. After dinner, on the first day of his arrival, Mrs. Peyton proposed a walk up Chestnut Street, to call upon some old friends.

It was early in the summer, before the streets get the deserted look, and the persons sauntering through them the faded, languid appearance they wear later in the season. Every thing was bright and gay; the streets were thronged with ladies in their fresh and delicate summer attire; airy robes were floating, dainty little boots glancing in and out, and bonnets, cloud-like in their translucent lightness, were decked with exquisite bouquets, mocking the eye by their close resemblance to nature's cunning work, till the passers-by might imagine themselves in some gay garden.

"What an elegantly-dressed lady that is before us!" said Virginia; "just notice in what perfect keeping every part of her dress is; that light, stone-colored silk, and white crape shawl, and tasteful white bonnet. I think I shall take her for my model. You know sister Julia wished me to bring her a fashionable shawl and bonnet, and I do not see any thing that pleases me so well. But how fantastically she has dressed that little child of hers!"

"It is the fashion, I presume," replied Mr. Peyton; "I have observed that they al llook very much alike."

A stylish carriage came rolling down the street.

"Look, Charles!" exclaimed Virginia, "there is Ben on the box."

The lady in front of them bowed. Ben smiled in return with an expression of familiar pleasure, and then, catching sight of his old master, his look changed to a whimsical mixture of delight and discomfiture. Pleasure at seeing those he liked so well, and that they should see his wife too, arrayed in her best, and doubt as to their approval of her manner of disposing of their funds, were about equally balanced. He had only time, however, to take off his hat with a peculiar flourish, meant to express a great deal, and to give Clara a significant look as he drove by. She turned to see what he meant, and her eyes encountered Mr. Peyton's.

"Oh, Mast'r Charles, I am so glad to see you!" she exclaimed.

"Clara! is it possible!" said Mr. and Mrs. Peyton in a breath. "Why, Clara, how fine you look!" continued Mrs. Peyton; "I have been admiring your dress for the last two squares. And this is your little Madge, is it? I should never have recognized her."

There was, indeed, a great metamorphosis. She had been a round, chubby, laughing little thing, dressed in a simple checked frock, and, except in the coldest weather, running about barefooted; and now she was thin and sickly-looking, with a closely-fitting frock that came hardly to her knees, and stockings drawn tight over her slender limbs, yet leaving them partly exposed; while gray boots, and a gipsy hat, with long blue streamers, completed her attire.

A consciousness that the surprise shown by her old master and mistress was not one of entire pleasure, prevented Clara from feeling perfectly at her ease. Yet she could not find it in her heart to be wholly sorry for the untimely meeting. She had often thought, when surveying herself in the glass on Sunday afternoon, previous to going to church, and taking her usual walk down Spruce Street—

"If mast'r or mistr'ss could see me now, wouldn't they be astonished?"

And astonished they were, even more so than Clara had anticipated.

"I thought Clara had more sense than to dress herself in that unsuitable way. I am sure Ben's wages can not support her long in that style. I must talk to her about it," said Virginia, as, after a warm greeting, they passed on.

"I wonder how this will end," said Mr. Peyton, musingly. "Judging by appearances, I am afraid I shall find I have made another great mistake. I will speak to Ben, and give him a little advice about his affairs."

Mrs. Peyton found Clara the next day, neatly and suitably attired, and busy with her sewing. She was alone, for Madge was at school, she said.

"What is she studying?" asked Mrs. Peyton.

Among a long list of studies, Clara mentioned music.

"Why are you having her taught music?" asked Mrs. Peyton; "will it ever be of any use to her?"

"Yes, mistr'ss, I think it will. A friend of mine, Miss Amanda Fitzwalter (and Clara, in her simplicity, showed evident symptoms of gratified pride in numbering Miss Fitzwalter among her friends) plays very well on the guitar, and sings most beautiful; and several white ladies take lessons of her. I thought if my Maggie could learn, she might give music lessons too—it would be more genteel than to take in sewing."

On giving her a little advice, and a gentle reproof as to her style of dress, Clara answered meekly that she had earned it all herself, excepting the shawl, which Americus had given her. The families her husband and brother were engaged in kept her supplied with needle-work.

"But have you laid by any thing, in case you or Ben should be taken sick?" asked Mrs. Peyton.

"Laws no, mistr'ss!" said Clara, with a wondering shake of her head; "me and Ben's never sick. White ladies think so much of gettin' sick! I never see one that they don't talk to me about it; but I don't know what it is."

"You may know one of these days, Clara," said Mrs. Peyton, rather severely, for Clara's flippancy had struck her disagreeably; but remembering her patient nursing, she went on to talk to her more plainly, and urge upon her the duties of economy and of desires suited to her position.

Clara listened without replying, but it was easy to see that her thoughts were wandering.

She was examining with a practiced eye Mrs. Peyton's simple yet elegant dress. At last, when

Virginia had set in every conceivable light the consequences of her folly and extravagance, in short, had given quite a good little extempore sermon, that she had been composing all the morning, Clara replied, "Yes, mistr'ss; I will try, mistr'ss; I really will. Ben and me will get along first-rate. But, mistr'ss, I would like to show you a new collar I've made myself, almost exactly like the one you have on"—and Clara went to the next room to find it.

While she was gone Virginia glanced round the room. It looked very neat and comfortable. The floor was covered with a nice carpet; there was a handsome sofa, and a bureau with a swing mirror, a marble-topped table, a few chairs, some gay colored engravings, framed and hanging about the room, with the portrait of a solemn-looking colored clergyman, in a white cravat and spectacles, with one hand resting on the Bible, and the other grasping a manuscript sermon; a few china ornaments over the mantle-piece completed the furniture and adornments of the parlor. A hasty examination of the kitchen, the door to which Clara had left open, showed the same orderly arrangement. The floor, the windows, the dresser, and the tables, in short, every thing that ought to be clean and bright, were spotlessly white. Mrs. Peyton remembered that the well-scoured appearance of the steps and pavement had struck her as she had entered the house.

"Clara was always neat," thought she; "but now she seems to have caught the Philadelphia mania for water;" and glad to find something to praise, she commended her, on her return, for the exquisite order of every thing around her.

Clara was very much pleased with the change in the tone of the conversation, and showed to her sometime mistress with no little pride all her comfortable household arrangements, told her how much Ben was liked in Mr. Westcott's family, and how well Americus was getting along. She expatiated on the comfort it was to her that they could all go to church together almost every Sunday, and hear so fine a preacher as Mr. Wiley, the man over the mantle-piece.

Mrs. Peyton listened with amused interest to Clara's artless confidences; it was impossible to keep up even the show, much less the reality of displeasure, against one so thoroughly good-humored.

"Then you like every thing here very much?" asked Virginia, as Clara stopped for a few moments in her outpourings.

"Yes, mistr'ss, 'deed I do; it is even better than I thought it would be; and I have so many friends"—

She was interrupted by the opening of the door, and a little black woman, round, plump, and consequential, with her chin thrown up in the air by the exertion of maintaining a proper dignity of deportment, entered with a roll of music in her hand.

"This is Miss Amanda Fitzwalter," said Clara, in some embarrassment, while Miss Amanda calmly seated herself.

"Ah! the friend you were speaking about," said Mrs. Peyton.

"Yes, mistr'ss," replied Clara.

"Oh!" said Amanda, with a shake of the head and an upward look,

> "What is friendship but a name,
> A charm that lulls to sleep,
> A shade that follows wealth and fame,
> And leaves the wretch to weep!"

This outburst took Mrs. Peyton by surprise, but she soon saw that it was only intended for effect; Miss Amanda having picked up those four lines somewhere, evidently thought this a good opportunity to display them. They were clearly not intended as an insinuation against Clara, who listened to her oracle in simple admiration, and with a blind belief in her that made Mrs. Peyton a little indignant as well as amused.

"I encountered Mr. Peyton a few moments ago," continued Miss Fitzwalter, addressing Clara, while Virginia wondered how she knew her husband, "and he reminded me that this evening is the last meeting for the season of the Philomathean Society, and at the termination they intend to have a dance. I promised him I would give my countenance to it."

"It is Americus, mistr'ss," said Clara; "he belongs to a society that meets in the evening and makes speeches. He speaks most elegant, they all say."

"What do they speak about?" asked Mrs. Peyton.

"'Most every thing, 'specially poetry and politics," replied Clara.

"Lately," observed Amanda, with her calm and measured propriety of utterance, "they have been debatin' on Foreign and Domestic Poetry. To-night the subjec' is, 'Which is the finest poet of Human Nature, Byron or Shelley?'"

Mrs. Peyton hardly knew whether to laugh or be indignant at the absurdity of the whole affair, and Miss Fitzwalter's pompous manner. She was almost ready to believe that the colored race were, as she had often heard, incapable of taking care of themselves, when she saw those to whom so much had been given—such careful, early training, so much religious instruction, and at last liberty—thus wasting their time and opportunities. When they might be vindicating their right to freedom, and also the capability of their race to appreciate and enjoy that precious boon, they were wasting their energies on every pursuit that could gratify their vanity, and losing sight of those means that could alone increase their true respectability.

Soon afterward, two or three more of Clara's friends entering, all handsomely dressed, and looking as though they had come to make a formal morning call, Mrs. Peyton took her leave.

When Virginia told Mr. Peyton the particulars of her visit, and the impression she had received from it, he did not agree with her as to the entire folly of the Philomathean Society.

"It is certainly better," said he, "than many other ways of passing their leisure evenings, and it shows some desire for intellectual improvement, and some power of application, for they must read and study to be able to make any speech at all. Byron and Shelley are not, to be sure, likely to be of any great use to them, nor will their studies of poetry bring about any practical result, I presume; still, there is a decided advance where mental enjoyments take the place of other pleasures. I met Americus a little while ago, 'encountered him,' as Miss Fitzwalter would say, and he is really very much improved in appearance; he has quite a stylish air, and seemed delighted with his new mode of life."

The next evening, Ben, Americus, Clara, and little Maggie came to report themselves to their old master. Mr. Peyton was very glad to see them so happy, and apparently so prosperous. He gave them a great deal of good advice about laying by a little store against "the evil day;" and they listened with deep attention, and made many promises, which Ben tried hard to keep, but which Clara and her brother forgot almost as soon as they ceased to fall upon their ear.

Americus looked a little confused when Mrs. Peyton asked him about the success of his speech. Ben answered for him.

"It went off most beautiful, mistr'ss; it's 'most a pity Americus ain't a preacher—he speaks so well. He's got all the big words ready for just when he wants 'em."

"Which side did you take?" asked Mrs. Peyton.

"Why, ma'am," said Americus, "Miss Mary, Mr. Patterson's daughter, told me that Shelley was an atheist, so, of course, I would not uphold him. I took Byron's side."

"Yes, mas'r," said Ben, "he spoke 'most an hour without stopping a minute. I never see how the words did come out of his mouth. I went sound asleep, for I was mighty tired—I'd been out till morning almost for three or four nights, driving the family home from parties—and when I woke up he was going on just the same."

And honest Ben seemed to take as much pride in his brother-in-law's achievements as if they were his own.

Mr. Peyton was gratified to find them so pleasantly situated. They went regularly to church, they told him; and little Madge went to Sunday school, as well as day school. If they had shown more forethought and prudence, more of Nathan's or Keziah's spirit, he would have felt fewer misgivings about them; but knowing the difficulties they had to contend against, and pleased to find they had fallen into no bad habits, he left them, hoping that his advice would have some effect, though he hardly ventured to expect it.

But their life was not all sunshine; and there were times when they wished themselves back under Mr. Peyton's protection, when occasionally the mighty arm of the law was found unable to resist the aggressions of the strong against the weak. Belonging to a race almost universally considered inferior, regarded as the pariahs of society, even when in outward forms justice was done to them, the spirit with which its enactments was carried out was often so oppressive, that they derived but little satisfaction from its decrees; and obliged to live apart, to eat apart, to enjoy themselves apart, and to come by themselves to that blessed sacrament in which believers declare that they are "one in Christ," while every attempt to put themselves on even a temporary level with those more favored is so jealously guarded against and resisted, it is wonderful that there is still so much good-will and kindness of feeling between the races, and that in the hearts of those on whom these customs must press so heavily there is so little bitterness or hatred excited.

Not long after Mr. Peyton left Philadelphia, there was an anti-slavery fair held there, and great feeling was aroused in consequence in relation to that much-vexed subject. In addition to this, an old feud between the lowest class of laborers and the colored race had broken out afresh in the suburbs of the city. All the watchfulness of the police was insufficient to prevent the perpetration of acts of fearful violence, in which the blacks were almost invariably the sufferers rather than the aggressors.

Americus had often seen a living proof of the savage ferocity with which these quarrels were carried on, in the person of a colored man, whom age and misfortune rendered venerable, standing at the corner of a street, with his tall athletic figure erect and motionless, his head bald and exposed to the cold winds, his sightless eyes touching every tender heart with painful pity. Though for years he might be seen standing in the same spot, the charity of the passers-by never failed to him, for it could easily be seen that he was no common beggar.

He had been many years before a maker and mender of shoes in a very humble way, and was so honest and industrious, that a good deal of the custom of the neighborhood in that line fell to his share. But unfortunately, after he had fairly established himself in his little business, many of the houses and shops around were rented by the whites, who, indignant at having colored people for their rivals, and often their successful ones, declared their determination to drive them from the street, or inflict summary vengeance on them. This poor man paid little attention to their threats. He could not afford to remove—it would break up his business, and ruin him entirely; and he had a family dependent on him. Therefore he kept himself as quiet as possible, and worked more industriously than ever. He could not have pursued a course better calculated to excite the malignant passions of the unreasonable and excitable people around him.

One night, after he and all his family had retired to rest, a gang of ruffians forced their way into his room, and while his wife and children were calling in vain for mercy and help, they made him blind for life.

Americus had often pitied and relieved him, and now, when the same state of feeling was showing itself, though not excited to an equal pitch of exasperation, he trembled lest a similar fate, or one even worse, might befall him or those dear to him. It was therefore with a feeling of no little fear that he prepared to attend a lady who had been spending the evening with his employer's family to her residence. If his natural diffidence had not restrained him, he would have told Mr. Patterson that he had heard that it was unsafe for a colored servant to escort a lady home at that particular time, for that, in the excited state of public feeling then, they were liable to be stopped and insulted; but he was very much afraid of being called a coward; and besides, as Mr. Patterson was unable, from the state of his health, to attend the lady himself, he saw no other way left, if she chose to walk.

His heart misgave him as she turned into Tenth Street, and continued walking for some distance in a southerly direction, and still more as the fire-bell had been pealing forth its summons for some time, its strokes indicating that the engines were needed in that part of the city. It had ceased ringing a few minutes before the lady had set forth on her homeward way, and they were passed by one engine after another clattering over the pavement on their return, with the usual noisy and shouting accompaniment of men and boys.

They passed quickly along, and Americus was in hopes that the rest of their way might be pursued without interruption, when suddenly strange and frightful sounds from one of the neighboring streets —oaths, imprecations, blows, hurried trampling on the sidewalk, with the sudden fall of some heavy body—startled the timid pedestrians.

The lady turned hastily to Americus, who was at a little distance behind her, and bade him come nearer.

"Some of the fire companies must be engaged in a fight," said she; "we had better turn into the next street."

But before they had time to do this, the combatants came rushing around the corner, shouting, fighting, and struggling in the most inextricable confusion. Some of the foremost of the crowd caught sight of the lady and Americus, and with a savage yell they sprang toward them.

The lady ran up the steps of the nearest house, the door of which was opened, as soon as she reached it, by the inmates, who had seen the disturbance, and were eager to afford her a refuge. They did not observe Americus, or were afraid to keep the door open longer, for it was closed as he approached it, and he was obliged to face the excited mob, whose passions having dethroned their conscience and overpowered their reason, now possessed the whole mass, and led them on to deeds that seemed rather the instinctive acts of ferocious and destructive animals than those of rational beings.

No one stopped to ask the cause of the onset on the unoffending man, still less to question its justice, and before he had time to collect his thoughts, Americus found himself the centre of the tumultuous crowd, and the recipient of blows and thrusts that fell upon him like a shower of hailstones. He was pushed down and trampled upon several times, and as often rose, terror and desperation rendering him hardly conscious of the injuries he received, and pressed his way through the throng.

Unfortunately, he happened to be particularly well-dressed that night, and there was not an article of his apparel, from his carefully tied cravat down to his brightly polished boots, that did not cost him several severe bruises from the jealous mob. At length, with his clothes torn and hanging in ribbons around him, without his hat, and with but one boot, he found himself in a part of the crowd too busy settling their private quarrels, as to the superiority of their respective engines, to concern themselves about him.

Slipping unobservedly through them, while cries of " Stop the nigger! Stop him!" were shouted in vain to combatants engaged in their own disputes, he reached at last the corner of the street. To run hastily round it, and take refuge in an oyster cellar near by, kept by an acquaintance of his, was the work of a moment.

He went in expecting to receive the attention his bruises and other injuries required; but instead of that he soon found himself busy in assisting and comforting others; for lying stretched on a couch hastily prepared in the cellar was its proprietor, in a state of profound insensibility. The blood slowly trickling from some wounds in his face and hands alone showed that he was still alive.

"How did this happen?" asked Americus.

"You know Joshua Mason's people?" asked the wife of the injured man.

"Very well," was the reply.

"Well, you see, they was a goin' to give a dance, and we had been invited, but we couldn't very well go; and they wanted John to send the isters, and John he got them all ready; he cooked them his own self, the very last he'll ever cook, I'm afraid; and then he said, as there wa'n't much business a doin' to-night, he'd take them round himself, and see how they came on, and our little Alfred went with him; and *he* says, that just after they got into Myamensing, a whole gang of Killers and Bouncers, and all them rowdy fellers, ran out from some alley and tried to get the isters away from John; but John he held on, and called for the p'lice as loud as he could; then they all rushed on him, and some had knives in their hands, and Alfred couldn't see 'zactly how it was; but he saw a little feller creep up behin' my husband with a slung-shot in his hand, and give him such a blow with it on the back of his head that he fell down as if he was struck dead; and then they grabbed the isters and ran away."

The poor woman sobbed piteously as she finished her simple story. Her apprehensions proved to be well founded, for her husband never recovered from the injuries he received that night. Yet the perpetrators of that lawless act of violence, though living in the midst of a law and order-loving community, were never discovered nor brought to justice.

It is a true remark of some modern writer, that no barbarians, not even the Goths and Vandals of former times, are so reckless, and fierce, and destructive in their habits as the savages of civilization.

Growing up under the shadow of Christian churches, but unsummoned by their bells; living amid people refined and educated, but who avoid all intercourse with them, as if there were contamination in their approach; thus debarred from their earliest cry from all good influences, and shut up to the teachings of riot and intemperance, and fraud and poverty, that debases where it does not purify, it is but the legitimate working out of the dark problem that such means applied to such natures should produce the results that are read of daily in the purlieus of all large cities.

The Saxon has not the indolent and docile nature of the African, but with strong passions and insatiate desires, he has mighty energies to incite them to activity, and a resolute will that hangs on to its prey with unyielding pertinacity. These qualities, so powerful when directed to any good purpose, are equally so when urging their possessors forward in the downward path, or rather, as one restraint after another drops off, they seem to gain, as they descend, in adroitness in planning and energy in executing their reckless schemes.

If the lazy philanthropists, who give a small share of their income to advance the cause of Christ, and then settle down under the complacent impression that they have done all that is required, and may fairly claim the epithet of benevolent, were but once to wake up and realize how much more good a little activity of the spirit and a little personal influence would do than all their money, they might soon clear the crowded haunts of men from those who, in the hot blood of their youth, waste their energies and degrade their souls by deeds of violence and shame. If the pious and high-minded would but know and employ the almost divine power they possess of uplifting, by their more elevated nature, the lower spirits to a purer sphere, how much might they accomplish!

The state of things which has been described

lasted but a short time. It was only the outburst of a spasmodic phrensy, which seems to seize at intervals upon that class of men who, with vacant minds and undeveloped reason, have yet strong passions with nothing to wreak them upon, and energies that clamor for active exertion.

Americus reached his home safely, and was so kindly nursed that he soon recovered from the injuries he received. Thankful for his escape, he had no desire to punish those who had so wantonly attacked him. His only feeling toward them was a prudent desire to avoid any other encounter with them in any way. When Mr. Patterson told him that some of the rioters were taken up, and that if he went to the magistrate's office he might identify those who had assaulted him, he showed such reluctance to taking the step that Mr. Patterson did not press it upon him.

The lady in whose service he had met this danger called to inquire after him, and sent him a present, which consoled him for his sufferings. Not long afterward, Mr. Patterson deciding to go to Paris to reside for some time, Americus gladly consented to accompany the family there, as he told Clara he had heard that "distinctions of color were unknown in that land."

For two or three years all went smoothly with Ben and Clara, to whose family a little Charley had been added. On Mr. and Mrs. Peyton's annual visits, they always found them happy and comfortable; and although no amount of advice made them less improvident or extravagant, yet their hopefulness and easy tranquillity as to the future at last infected Mrs. Peyton, who declared herself tired of acting the part of the skeleton at their continual banquet, and on her last visit contented herself with praising her husband's namesake, giving Maggie a dress, and commending Clara's housekeeping and Ben's steady conduct.

But the time of trial came at last, as it surely does come in the life of every human being. If the waters of prosperity make the plants grow rank, and full of leaves and blossoms when fruit and seed may be looked for, then is adversity commissioned, with her unsparing fires, to extirpate every root and branch that has left unfulfilled the gracious purpose for which it was appointed.

A few weeks of unusually variable weather in early winter, of warm, spring-like days, alternating with chilling rains and gusts of snow and sleet, during which Ben was more exposed than usual, laid him up with the inflammatory rheumatism in the midst of the season. Mr. Westcott, whose family were among the gayest and most fashionable in the city, was obliged to engage another coachman to supply Ben's place, though he promised to employ him again as soon as he was sufficiently recovered, and continued his wages to him as usual for the first three months of his illness; then, finding that Ben still continued helpless, and that Clara's time was so much occupied in nursing him and attending to the children, that she had but little opportunity for sewing, he advised him to go to the hospital.

But this Ben was unwilling to do, neither would Clara consent that he should leave her. Laying aside all the follies and fripperies on which she had wasted so much time, and thought, and money, she sold her finery, stopped Maggie's music lessons, with a sigh it must be confessed, and set her to taking care of the baby, while in a sixpenny wrapper she seated herself, like the devoted wife she really was, by the bedside of her suffering husband, and sewed day and night, till her dazzled eyes could hardly discern the needle in her wearied fingers.

But there is nothing more dispiriting than to try to make up for wasted time by crowding into one hour the work of three. Each moment brings with it its own duties and its peculiar privileges, and, passing on with no human relentings, leaves behind it a blessing or a curse, as these have been performed and enjoyed, or neglected and unreceived.

Besides, it was a heavy task to fall upon one woman, to support with her unassisted fingers a sick man, two children, and herself. But with the aid of some friends of her own color, and a little assistance from the numerous benevolent societies of that most benevolent of cities, Clara contrived to keep the family in a decent room and in tolerable comfort for a year or two.

But as Ben's disease refused to yield either to time or medical remedies, and the strong man lay helpless as a child day after day, and month after month, their friends grew weary of helping them, and fell away one by one, till even Amanda Fitzwalter, who had proved, by her constant sympathy, that her heart was at least equal to her vanity, said "She didn't know what was to be done. Things was gettin' worse every day, and with three chillun of her own she didn't see her way clar to do much more. It was hard times just now, but if Clara could scrouge along a little while, perhaps they'd mend."

The liberality of the poor to each other would surprise any one unacquainted with the fact. If it had not been for the sympathy and kindness of those hardly one degree better off than herself, Clara could not have borne up so long as she did under the troubles coming upon her.

At length Ben began slowly to recover, and when reduced to their last crust, with not a cent in their possession to buy food for their almost naked children, he managed to brush the coat so long useless to him, and which now hung round his once athletic form in loose wrinkles, and went with the feeble step of a convalescent to his old employer to claim his promise of a re-engagement. But during his long illness, Mr. Westcott had died, the family were separated, and Ben turned away with a great disappointment lying heavy on his heart.

Neither his principles nor his disposition fitted him to meet this emergency, and for the first time in his life he went home reeling with intoxication; having spent in drink a little money some acquaintance had lent him, with which he had intended to buy food for his family.

Their downward course after this was one that has been so often trodden and described, that the particulars need no repetition. With a drunken husband and two children, Clara found herself unable to sustain the unequal conflict with life's burdens, yet she never gave entirely up; her self-respect grew daily weaker, and her principles less able to resist the evil influences around her, yet love for her husband and children preserved her from many temptations that might otherwise have proved too strong.

One bitter day in February, two young ladies were walking with the quick, firm step of those to whom life is an enjoyment as well as a battle, through the crowded thoroughfares of Chestnut Street. The keen wind brought the blood tingling to their cheeks, and even with their muffs and boas, and thickly wadded cloaks wrapped around them, they felt its piercing cold. A little colored girl with bare feet, and apparently nothing but an old blanket shawl wrapped around her shivering frame, stopped them with the entreaty, so pitiful at such seasons, "Please ladies, give me some money to buy a little bread. My mother is sick, and can't work any more."

"Have you no father?" asked they.

"Yes, but he's sick too, and I have a little brother at home; but the baby died yesterday, and we've no money to bury it."

After asking a few more questions, the young ladies decided to follow the child home to see if she told the truth, and if so, to render more effectual assistance than street alms would prove. They were not overly gifted with that virtue which some good old divine prayed to be delivered from, the worldly virtue of prudence, or they would hardly have accompanied the girl through all the alleys, and turnings, and out-of-the-way places into which she led them. At length they came to a narrow alley swarming with negroes. The houses seemed like ant-hills, filled to the top, and the sidewalks were crowded with their overflowings. Fat black faces darkened every window. Stout, lazy-looking men lounged in the doors, and, cold as it was, children of all ages and complexions were tumbling, fighting, and swearing upon the side-walks.

One of the young ladies was alarmed, and wished to turn back; but the other, whose benevolence would have led her unshrinkingly through a battle-field when the contest was at its height, pressed on without giving a glance around her. The child went to the door of a cellar, that seemed rather like a little opening in the pavement, and gliding down, beckoned to the ladies to follow her. Even the more courageous one of the two hesitated to do this, while the other held her back imploringly. During this moment of hesitation, a tall, gaunt mulatto woman, with wild and glaring eyes, approached them.

"Go back, young ladies," she exclaimed, with a theatrical start and gesture; "what are such as you doing here? This is no place for you. Has your senses quite vanished from you, that you come to such a bottomless pit? My daughter! I lost her here; and I come to look for her morning and night. But I never want no other mother to feel what I've felt. Go back this minute, and if any one dares to say a word to you—" and she flourished a broken cane she held in her hand.

Her manner and words so alarmed the more timid one that she could hardly stand, and the other young lady was about to retrace her steps, quite unwillingly though, when she caught sight of a gentleman approaching.

"There is Mr. Lyndsay, the city missionary," said she; "how fortunate!" and beckoning to him, he hurried to her assistance.

He was evidently known in the alley; for the commotion and bustle that had been caused by the entrance of the young ladies was quieted at his approach, and the woman who had accosted them so singularly welcomed him with an approving smile and gesture, and, bidding him take good care of the ladies, left them to him, and disappeared in a house near by.

"That is a half-deranged woman," observed Mr. Lyndsay; "the loss of her only child has affected her intellect; but, notwithstanding that, she has great influence among these demi-brutes. If it had not been for her, I should hardly have met with the tolerance I have here. But how did you happen to come to such a place?"

"We were following a little beggar-girl home, to see if the sad story she told us was really true, and were so intent upon keeping sight of her, that we hardly noticed where she was leading us. She flitted down those steps and disappeared in that dark cellar at our feet, and we are almost afraid to pursue our investigations further; yet she was so miserably clad, and told such a piteous tale, that I do not like to go home without finding out the truth about her."

"If you will trust the matter to me," said Mr. Lyndsay, "I will attend to it, and report to you this afternoon, if you like."

"Thank you," replied the young lady; "that will be the best way, I suppose. But they are probably in immediate want of fire and food, and on so cold a day as this there ought not to be an hour's delay in providing for their necessities. I will leave some money with you that you can spend for them as you think best;" and the young lady drew her purse from her muff.

"Put up your purse, Miss Sumner," exclaimed Mr. Lyndsay, hastily; "wait till we are out of this alley."

But his warning came too late. A slender, sharp-looking colored boy, who wanted but a shade or two of being white, had been hovering unnoticed near them, listening to their conversation. No sooner did his keen eyes catch sight of the purse, weighed down by its burden, than with a sudden dart upon it he clutched it and sprang into the nearest house.

Mr. Lyndsay looked distressed, and Miss Sumner glanced at her empty hand with blank dismay.

"It is my whole quarter's allowance," said she; "papa gave it to me this morning."

"I am afraid you will never recover it," said

Mr. Lyndsay. "There is no one in the whole street but Judith, the crazy woman, who would not, I think, for a little share of the profits, assist the boy in concealing himself. But let me take you away from here as soon as possible," added he, seeing that a new commotion was exciting this hive of drones. "I will return and see what can be done about your loss, and your proteges also."

The young ladies were very glad to accept his offer, for Miss Sumner's companion was trembling with terror, and Miss Sumner herself had lost some of her courage with her purse.

They had but just turned the corner, and were breathing more freely, when their attention was attracted by a loud shout behind them. On looking back, they saw Judith running toward them with the purse in her hand. She had seen the whole affair from a window, and as the boy happened to take refuge in the same house with herself, she flew upon him, and with a celerity and adroitness equal to his own, snatched his prize from his grasp and ran with it after its owner. This had caused the bustle that alarmed Mr. Lyndsay and the young ladies.

Miss Sumner's eye took a hasty survey of the woman's dress. She saw that it was arranged with a certain decency and neatness, which showed that her old habits of order and regard for her personal appearance had not quite deserted her; but it looked old and thin, and on this bitter day she braved the cold air without either bonnet or shawl.

The young lady drew a small gold piece from her purse and offered it to her.

"What do you give me this for?" she burst forth, with increased wildness of look and flightiness of manner; "is it for my honesty? Do you dare to pay me for my honesty? You rich folks think you can buy us poor ones, soul and body; but I'm above you all. I live up in the sky with the Lord and his angels, where you daren't come—where you daren't come, with all your precious gold and silver;" and she glared close into Miss Sumner's eyes with her own, in whose depths of gloom no ray of brightness shone.

"It was for the trouble you had taken for me that I offered you that," said Miss Sumner, quietly and soothingly, "not for your honesty."

"Trouble!" repeated Judith, with a wild laugh; "ha! ha! you call that trouble, do you? Oh! child, child!" with a sudden change to the deepest sadness of tone and look, "if you had a husband and brother in the penitentiary for nine long years for loving money too well, and a daughter in the cold ground because she wanted to live like a lady, and keep her hands soft, and wear silks and velvets like you white ladies, then you would know what trouble was. Take back this money, or I'll fling it in the gutter where it belongs."

Miss Sumner took it, and Judith disappeared round the corner. Mr. Lyndsay accompanied them a little way, and then returned to fulfill his promise of ascertaining the condition of the occupants of the cellar.

He descended the rickety steps, and stood for a few minutes to let his eyes become accustomed to the gloom of the place. He heard a faint voice speaking at intervals from the further corner of the room, and gradually there came out in the dim light the figure of a woman stretched on the ground (for the cellar had no floor); in another corner lay what seemed a bundle of rags, breathing heavily; and a little boy, with hardly an article of clothing upon him, was crouching among the smouldering ashes in the chimney corner. The girl who had led the ladies to this desolate abode stood near the fire-place, with her large eyes, which glittered unnaturally in her thin face, fixed with a painfully eager look on the compassionate visitor.

The least distressing object in the miserable room was the dead body of a babe, whose life was as yet counted only by months and days. The ineffable repose of its softly-rounded features—the perfect serenity and peace stamped on its innocent face—the once restless hands, whose light, uncertain touch had thrilled the mother's heart, now gently laid over in each other with their dimples frozen into them—all that wonderful structure, so perfect and incomprehensible in its minutest details, laid aside by its Maker, while yet the spirit that informed it was unconscious of the glorious gift it had received—in a word, all the halo of blessedness and heaven that lies around the couch of the innocent dead, now seemed to shed its sanctity and silence over that most dreary place and its occupants.

The reader will already have surmised that they who were reduced to this deep degradation were no other than Ben and Clara; and that not poverty alone, but crime, had been at work before they could sink so far. Ben had become a confirmed drunkard, not so much from love of drink as to drown thought and remorse; and Clara, after trying in vain to arouse in him a better spirit, had given up in despair, and allowed matters to take their own course, without attempting to do the little in her power to enable them to retain their old position.

But by how many cords does our heavenly Father draw back the wanderers to his fold! In this, almost the lowest depth to which human nature could sink, there came to Clara this babe, like a dove from the ark of God's mercy; and though, even as the dove found the earth inhospitable and unkind, so the babe lay unwelcomed and uncherished on its mother's breast, yet six months of helpless loveliness and endearing trust could not but soften a heart hardened by despair rather than vice; and when, to complete its mission, the child's soul took its flight for heaven, it went bearing for its olive branch the repentant prayers and tears of its sorrow-stricken mother.

But though prayers that had long been strange to her lips came from her heart, mingled with earnest resolutions of amendment and the bitterest pangs of remorse, yet, situated as she was, sick, cold, and hungry, with a husband who answered every appeal with a drunken growl, and no human aid near, she could not see how she could put her resolves into practice.

It was without her knowledge, while she lay with her head buried in her hands, sighing, moaning, and ejaculating brief and earnest prayers for mercy and deliverance, that Maggie had slipped out on what had been for a long time her daily errand; and now, as if in answer to her cries, there stood before her the man whose business it was to seek out the poor and needy.

Mr. Lindsay, with the promptness of true charity, soon had a fire blazing on the hearth, and an ample dinner provided for them. The pleasant warmth drew Ben from his corner, and he tried to utter a few expressions of gratitude as he hung over the blaze.

The good missionary became interested in Clara's account of their sufferings; who, though she tried to shelter Ben's fault under the plea of illness, related every thing else so artlessly and simply that Mr. Lindsay was convinced of its truth. From the Dorcas Society of a neighboring church he obtained garments for herself and the children, wood from another benevolent society, and with the money Miss Sumner had intrusted to him he hired a better room, to which he had them removed immediately.

Miss Sumner visited them there, and with her assistance Mr. Lindsay discovered some old patrons of Clara, who were very glad to find again the neat seamstress after whom they had made many ineffectual inquiries.

"If you are willing to work hard, Clara," said Mr. Lindsay, "I will promise you enough to do."

"Yes, sir," replied Clara; "I am too glad to get work not to do the best I can—'deed I will; but Ben hain't got no ambition left. I'm afraid for him. May be, sir, if you would talk to him pleasant, he might feel better."

Mr. Lindsay sought an opportunity to speak to him alone, and tried by encouraging words to awaken some of his old spirit in him.

Ben was employed in splitting up a load of wood, a job that had accidentally fallen to him, and, stopping in his work, he said, shaking his head,

"'Taint of the least use to talk to me that way, Mr. Lindsay. I've tried my best, and I ain't any thing but a nigger, and never shall be. I'm just as good and respectable now as when I had twenty dollars a month, and my wife dressed like a lady; and what's the use of doing any thing more. You talk to me about educating my children; but what's the use of it. You see that black man that went by us just now, and held up his head so high when he saw me standing here. Well, I know'd him very well wonst, when I first came to the city. He was a head waiter then at parties, and is now, I believe; and he has been laying up money all his life. He's worth now twenty thousand dollars at least, and what good will it do him or his children? The more they know, the wuss it will be for 'em; for they won't keep company with their own color, and white folks won't associate with them, and thar they are shut up by themselves; and what good do their Brussels carpets and pianny do them, I'd like to know? They may try till they split, and they won't be any thing but just what I am, a nigger that every body despises."

"No person who does their duty," replied Mr. Lyndsay, "is ever despised, no matter what his color may be."

"Perhaps, Mr. Lyndsay, if the world was all made up of good people like you, that might be so. But people for the most part don't stop to ask if I do my duty. They see that I ain't a white man, and push me out of the way. Don't you believe, Mr. Lyndsay, that Clary is a great deal more respectable and well-behaved than some of these poor, miserable white women about here."

"Certainly I do," said Mr. Lyndsay; "Clara is a good wife, and is trying hard now to bring up her children well."

"Clary is a good woman, Mr. Lyndsay; it was all my fault that we were in that hole where you found us. She strived and struggled as hard as any poor woman could, but she couldn't keep me from drinking, and at last she had to give up. But she's never given me a hard word all the time we've been together, and if I leave off drink, as I am going to do, it will be for no other reason but that I don't want to see her and the children suffer. Well, now, good as she is, and nice and handsome as she can make herself look, if I was to take her in the cars, and they was full, the meanest and dirtiest white woman, or man either, would have a seat, and she would have to stand all the way; and if it was the steam-boat, she'd have to sleep on deck, and, like as not, not get any thing to eat—always be shoved a one side, as if she wa'n't made by the same God. Oh, Mr. Lyndsay, it's mighty hard for a man like me, that could be as good as any body, if his skin were a shade or two lighter, to be kept down so all the time, and not get drunk or wicked."

Ben had a great deal more to say, for he had thought more, in his temporary intervals of sobriety during the last two years, than ever before in his life; and this was the first time that his thoughts had found utterance. But, as he was becoming a little excited, Mr. Lyndsay, fearing he might be soon addressing an audience instead of an individual, left him, promising to call and see him soon.

To all religious exhortations Ben turned a deaf ear, and after a time grew restive under them, and sometimes almost rude. To Clara's remonstrances he replied,

"Preaching is very well, I ain't nothin' against it. I wouldn't mind doing a little of it myself. But to keep at a feller from mornin' till night, with 'Do this—it's your duty,' and 'bear that—it's your duty too;' and if you are knocked down, get up and rub the mud off, and say 'Thank you, for that's your duty;' and if you work hard all day, and get nothing but a cuss when you ask for your pay at night, why go home and make a special prayer for the man before you go to sleep, for that's another duty—this is coming it rather too strong. Mr. Lyndsay is a good man himself; but if he'd only keep his preaching for the white people, and let them practice it on us, it would do a great deal more good, I think."

But though Ben grumbled in this way, still the oversight Mr. Lyndsay kept upon him was of great service in keeping him firm in his resolution to be temperate and industrious. A situation was procured for him with some difficulty, where, although the wages were low and the work heavy, and not connected with horses in the most remote degree, yet he performed his duties faithfully, and brought home the money to his wife every Saturday night.

It grieved Clara very much that she could not induce him to renew his old practice of accompanying her to church on Sunday, but he had heard enough pious talk, he said, to last him the rest of his life; and so he passed the day principally in trying to keep asleep.

During all this time, Americus remained in Paris, and Mr. Peyton had been prevented, by affairs connected with his family, from visiting the North, so that their apparent neglect, which weighed heavily on the minds of Ben and Clara, was afterward satisfactorally accounted for. As often happens, when trials are sent upon the weak and dependent, human aid is put far away, that they may learn more readily the hard lesson of faith and trust in the unseen arm of the All-Father.

CHAPTER IV.

LIFE IN CANADA.

Amid all life's quests,
There seems but worthy one—to do men good.
BAILEY.

DURING one of his summer excursions, Mr. Peyton stopped for a few days at Niagara, on his way, with his family, to Montreal and Quebec. While walking about on the Canada side of the Falls, stopping now and then to examine and admire the grand spectacle from some new point of view, Mrs. Peyton's eye was caught by a beautiful flower swaying on its slender stem on a steep slope, high above her head.

The hillside was covered with broken, shingling rocks, and from the midst of these, without even a blade of grass to bear it company, grew up this little delicate flower. Unheeding the overshadowing grandeur of its mighty rival, yet strengthened and refreshed by the few drops of spray now and then flung upon it out of the profusion of its abundance, it went on gathering in some mysterious way every day new strength and beauty from the uncongenial earth around, until at last it lifted its blue eye to the clear sky and soft air of that delicious June day, a perfect flower, speaking its Maker's praise as clearly with its still small voice, as did its glorious rival, whose grand anthem went pealing ceaselessly on day and night, winter and summer.

There was a vein of poetry in Virginia's mind leading her to invest material objects with conscious life and meaning, and the voices of the flower and the cataract spoke as distinctly to her heart as if her ear had heard their uttered words. She was fond too of memorials, and had retained her girlish habit of collecting and preserving flowers and leaves, or some other characteristic memento, from all places of note she visited.

She wished to obtain this flower, which had awakened such a train of pleasant thoughts in her heart; and as Mr. Peyton was a little distance in advance with an elderly lady on his arm, she attempted to climb the slope herself. But the stones slipped under her feet, and, recalling a fatal accident that had occurred near there not long before, she reluctantly gave up the attempt.

"I will get it for you, ma'am," said a voice behind her, and a man sprang up the difficult ascent, and, returning, offered her the little blossom.

She took it, and looking at him to thank him, recognized an old acquaintance.

"Why, Edward," she exclaimed, "is it possible!"

"Yes, Mrs. Peyton," said he; "I knew you as soon as I saw you walking across the bridge, and I ran down to ask you about all the people in Clinton. I was afraid, if I waited, you might get over the other side."

"You wouldn't venture over there, Edward?" asked Mrs. Peyton, with a smile.

"No, indeed, ma'am, I had too hard work to get here to put myself in the least danger again."

Mrs. Peyton gave him all the information she could recall of their mutual acquaintances in Clinton, for they had been born and brought up in the same town; and though the broad gulf that separates the serf from the freeborn, the black from the white race, lay between them, yet integrity and a manliness that commanded respect on the one hand, with a kind and sympathetic nature on the other, spanned the gulf, and made them meet with a degree of pleasure and interest that only those can understand who have been brought up from their infancy to look upon the negro as a member of the same household.

"And now," said Mrs. Peyton, when she had finished telling him of the welfare of his mother and sisters, as well as of all his other friends, "how did you manage to get here?"

"It was a great deal more easy than I thought it would be," replied Edward; "do you remember Miss Lucy's wedding, Miss Virginia?" unconsciously using the most familiar name.

"Yes, it was not long after mine."

"Well, my old master sent me two or three days beforehand with her silver, up in the country whar she was going to live. The other servants had been taking up every thing else to make the house comfortable, and I was to take care of every thing, and have it all in order for her when she came. I had been contriving ways and means for a long time for running away, and had had, I reckon, twenty different plans, but they didn't come to any thing. Still, my mind was made up, that if I had to wait forty year, I would run away at the end of it, if I had a fair chance, for my old master treated me so bad that I never had a happy moment. He didn't beat me so much, but he didn't give me a minute's peace, and he used to call me all the hard names he could lay his tongue to. But, yet, he used to trust me with all his business, and he had made a standing order that whenever he got drunk—and he used to have a frolic every two or three weeks—I should attend to him. I have had as much as three thousand dollars in my care at a time, when he had been selling his crops and got drunk before he put the money in the bank; and yet, though he never lost a cent by me, he'd keep on abusing me till my patience fairly gave out."

"I know he was a hard master," said Virginia; "there was not a person in Clinton who was not glad when they found you were really off."

"I took the silver up to Miss Lucy's place," continued Edward, "and then I thought, as they would all be so busy at home that it would be at least a week before they would find out that I was gone, that I could not have a better time, and so I started. I had ten dollars, that I had earned in different ways, and had saved unbeknown to my master, or he would have taken it away, and that, with the clothes I had on, was all I had in the world. That lasted me till I got to some little town in New York, and then when I was not more than a day's journey from here, I was taken sick, and had to lie there a week. Some of the colored folks about took me in, and took care of me till I was well again, and as soon as I could hold myself up, I set out to finish my journey on foot. That was the hardest part of the way, for I was so weak I could hardly crawl along, and I felt every moment my old master's hand on my shoulder. But I never heard any thing from him, and I was so glad when my feet touched this ground, that it seemed to me I felt well right away. I have been mighty homesick too, since I have been here, and wanted to see all the people in

Clinton but one. I have never heard the first word from my mother or sisters, or any one else there, since I left till now, and 'deed it does me good to hear all about them."

"Have you ever wanted to go back?" asked Mrs. Peyton.

"No, Miss Virginia, I might if I had had a different master, for I had a very hard time the first winter here. I 'most froze to death, and starved too. But I have a good place now, and am doing very well."

"Do the people generally treat you better than they did at home?"

"No, Miss Virginia, nothing like as well. They don't seem as natural to us, nor we to them, maybe, as those we were raised with. Somehow, they don't seem to have the same consideration for us, and I know some here that would be very glad to get back if they were sure they would not be punished. But that's not my feelings. I wouldn't 'vise any one to come here, though, that wa'n't willing to work harder, and rough it as much as they ever did in their lives."

By this time they had overtaken Mr. Peyton, who also knew and recognized Edward. He asked him many questions as to the condition of the colored people in Canada; and Edward's answers, while showing that he had observed and thought a great deal on the subject, gave a faithful, yet sad picture, of the position of his countrymen in a land which needed all the amenities and kindnesses of social life to soften the severities of its climate, so particularly ill suited to the African.

The same exclusion from all places open to the meanest white man, the same disregard of their comfort, and open contempt for their color, made Canada any thing but a pleasant place of refuge. "It is impossible," thought Mr. Peyton, while meditating on this mysterious dispensation of Providence, this placing one race in the midst of another, whose feelings instinctively rebel against all union on the footing of equality; "it is impossible but that some great purpose is to be worked out by these great means."

"When I was a boy, I accompanied my father to Quebec," said Mr. Peyton; "we had a servant with us, a man named Isaac, who left us soon after we reached Canada. He must be an old man now. Have you ever happened to meet him?"

"Yes, sir," replied Edward; "he is living at a little village not far from this place. It is a settlement of colored people, and if you would like to see how most of them live here, you might go there. I know Isaac very well. He often talks about old Virginny to me, and says he was a great fool for leaving it. But he's most always sick, and that keeps him down-hearted. He'd be glad to see you, I know, for he don't talk about any thing else but old times."

"I will stop to see him," said Mr. Peyton, "for he was a good servant."

Accordingly, a few days after, taking Edward as his guide, Mr. Peyton drove over to the little collection of hovels and wretched tenements that was dignified with the name of village. There was not a house in it that seemed able to protect the inmates from the changes of the weather, even during the summer months; and it was hard to imagine how they could make themselves comfortable in the cold weather.

The nucleus of the place was a large frame house, that had been built by some wealthy land-owner in that part of the country. But he had long since deserted it as untenantable, and it had fallen to its present occupants as a matter of course. With its paint washed off, its boards dropping away, and with hardly a pane of glass left unbroken in the windows, it still was by far the best dwelling in the place. The others were mere shantys, or huts, put up hastily when it was found impossible to obtain shelter in the big house, and intended at first only for temporary abodes. But they were never unoccupied, for as fast as one family vacated them another made its appearance ready to take their places.

Mr. Peyton could hardly help smiling as he observed how little change of place or position seemed to affect the strongly-marked yet unobtrusive characteristics of the African. Here in Canada he found the same inertness, the same easy yielding to circumstances and aversion to labor, and the same good-nature that had so tried his patience in Virginia. Every other man and woman had a pipe in their mouths, and, dirty and ragged, they lounged about in the warm sun, basking in its beams, and wearing the placid self-complacent look of those who had voted care an impertinence, and labor an unnecessary degradation.

As he observed them with the eye of a philosopher and philanthropist, they gazed back upon him with the open-eyed curiosity of the vacant mind. Not often had such a presence dignified the path they fondly called a street. Mr. Peyton had the true patrician stamp, and it gave a value to his least word or act far above its intrinsic worth. From the inexplicable charm of this influence, at once innate and adventitious, no one can wholly free themselves, much less the uneducated, who yield to its sweet authority an obedience not the less entire that it springs as much from love as fear.

It was easy for the gazers to discover that he was a Southern planter; many of them knew the little signs and tokens which gave so distinct a character to that class, too well to be mistaken. The carelessly-fitting, yet scrupulously neat dress, with its abundance of spotless linen, the slow and dignified movement, the air at once commanding and benign, told a story easily read by the least observant.

"If I didn't know dat old mas'r had been dead dese many years, I should say dat was him," thought old Isaac, as Mr. Peyton drew near the door in which he was sitting. When the strange gentleman stopped before him, the old man raised his trembling form, and gazed with the anxious, uncertain look of age in his face.

"Don't you remember me, Isaac?" asked Mr. Peyton.

"Oh! it's Mas'r Charles! it's Mas'r Charles!" and Isaac's whole face was convulsed with emotion, while tears streamed down his cheeks. "I never tought to see you or any of de fam'ly dis side de grave again, Mas'r Charles; and you was a little boy when I lef you; but I know'd you as soon as you smiled; and I should ha' know'd you by dat any whar."

"You have had a long life given to you, Isaac," continued Mr. Peyton.

"Yes, Mas'r Charles, I knows dat; but mostly I feels like saying, with ole father Jacob, 'Few and evil have the days of the years of my life been,' for I has had mo' trouble than I know'd how to bar; but de Lord has helped me, and now I's so near to Him that I feels sometimes as if I could look straight into glory."

"You are happy now, then," said Mr. Peyton.

"Yes, Mas'r Charles, my fight is mos' over, and now I'm waitin' with patience for de comin' of de Lord. I feel fo' true that He won't try me much longer."

"Is your wife still living?"

"No, Mas'r Charles; dat was my fust great 'fliction. I had worked hard five years to get money enough to buy her freedom, and den she came here and took sick directly, and only lived seven month. Den I bought my two boys; dey was little boys, and I didn't have much trouble in gettin' 'em here; but one of 'em died two year ago, and I has his two chillun to see to, while dere mother and my other son works for dem and me too. But 'tain't much to work for me now, and dough dey's as willin' as can be, I feels dat I sha'n't trouble dem long."

"Have you lived here ever since you left us?" asked Mr. Peyton.

"Oh, no, Mas'r Charles! dis is a mighty poor place to live in. I used to be a waiter at hotels and gentlemen's families till I was too old, and den I lived in the city, and did mos' any thin' I could get to do. At last, when I couldn't do no more, I went to live in a house jus' at the edge of de town, where a great many colored folks used to come. Dey used to live in de woods, and wander about all summer, and den crowd as many as de could in dat house, and some oders near it, when de col' weather came on. I didn't like it much; but it was better dan dis, for white ladies used to come and talk to us sometimes, and see if we wanted any thin'; and we had a church to go to, which we haven't here—and de Sabber day is just like any oder day; but de people roun' us said that it was a nuisance havin' so many niggers in de houses about; for dar was some on 'em dat didn't do nothin' but beg, and maybe steal a little; and so one cold night, when it was rainin' hard, dey set de houses on fire and burned 'em down to the groun', and I had to take de chillun in my ole arms and hol' em close up to me all night to keep 'em warm, and in de mornin' my son hunted us up and brought us here, and I 'spects to finish my life in dis spot. 'Tain't much matter 'bout me now; but I can't bar to tink dat de chillun will grow up where dey hear so little 'bout de blessed Jesus."

Mr. Peyton remained some time longer talking with this old servant of his house, and left him at last cheered by a visit from one of that family he revered so truly, though a natural instinct had led him to desert their protection. Neither were his bodily wants forgotten, and the money his old master's son left with him provided for his few necessities during the rest of his life, which lasted, indeed, but about six weeks after this interview.

When a person's thoughts are turned steadily in one direction, it is wonderful how much can be seen in a short space of time; and Mr. Peyton's investigations, thorough and patient as they were, only served to convince him more and more that Canada was no pleasant abiding-place for the blacks, and that, held far apart from all intercourse and communion with those who occupied the superior position, regarded as machines rather than as living souls, with little attention paid to their religious training, it was fully as probable that they would deteriorate as improve by a residence in that country. He saw nothing to make him feel that it would be any advantage to the laborers on his plantation to change their residence from Virginia to Canada. On the contrary, he became daily more convinced that his servants held decidedly the most advantageous position, both for their comfort in this world and opportunity for preparation for the next. He felt that he would not be willing to expose those who had been given into his charge—for whose temporal and eternal welfare he had been trained from his childhood to feel responsible—to the temptations, difficulties, and privations that hedged them in on every side in the land whose proud boast it is "that no slave can breathe its air."

With a single, earnest wish to benefit his servants at any self-sacrifice—a wish that time, and thought, and patient endeavor had elevated almost to a holy passion, and made one of the ruling motives of his life—he felt that it would be unjust, both to whites and blacks, to throw upon society those who have as yet proved themselves a burden and a drain, rather than an assistance, whenever the conduct of their life is given in their own hands.

Of course, only the masses are here intended. There have been noble exceptions; and, freed from the crushing superiority of the white man, they have risen up more quickly and in greater numbers than their best friends could have ventured to hope —but not in America.

CHAPTER V.

THE PLANTING OF THE NATION.

I hear the tread of pioneers,
  Of nations yet to be;
The first low wash of waves where soon
  Shall roll a human sea.

WHITTIER.

THE truth of Machiavelli's maxim, that "to make a servile people free, is as difficult as to make a free people slaves," had often occurred to Mr. Peyton's mind, while recalling the results of his experiments, yet without disheartening him; for between difficulty and impossibility is a great difference, and he knew that few objects of any importance can be attained without labor and disappointment.

In the month of December, 1816, he went to Washington on business. He had intended to return by Christmas-day, and his family knew that he had arranged his affairs so that they need not prevent him, yet he wrote that he was detained by business of importance, and that for the first time in his life he could not pass that season, so festive a one in Virginia, with his wife and children.

He reached home for New-year's day, and when the children at last consented to be carried off to bed, and the older members of the family were left to talk in quiet, Mr. Peyton, addressing his sister, said,

"At last, Margaret, I have a plan to propose to you, which I think even you, with all your practical wisdom and cool judgment, must approve. You objected to my making my servants free, for you said that, whether they were nominally bond or free, or whether they lived at the North or the South, the colored people held, in reality, the position of slaves; and that as long as this was the case, they had better have the protection and assistance which the relation of master should, and often does, give to them. We will not discuss that matter now, but what do you say to placing them in an isolated and independent position, where they can develop themselves, free from the presence and overshadowing superiority of the white race."

"If they can govern themselves, which is yet to be proved," replied Margaret, "that would be the best course to take. I would like to see it fairly tried, though I confess I am not sanguine as to its success."

"Several of our wisest statesmen and philanthropists have been engaged in forming such a plan," continued Mr. Peyton; "my delay in Washington was caused by my desire to assist as far as I could in carrying it out; for the more I thought about it, the more did the grandeur and simplicity of the design strike me, and the more did I feel persuaded of its practicability and ultimate success."

"How is the idea to be carried out?" asked Margaret.

"I will read you part of the constitution adopted by a society at which I was present, where Henry Clay presided, and, with John Randolph and Elias B. Caldwell, spoke eloquently and ably in favor of this object.

"*Article I.*—A society shall be formed, and called the American Colonization Society, for colonizing the free people of color of the United States.

"*Article II.*—The object to which its attention shall be exclusively directed is, to promote and execute a plan for colonizing, with their consent, the free people of color residing in our country, in Africa, or such other place as Congress shall see fit. And the society shall act, to effect this object, in co-operation with the general government, and such of the states as may adopt regulations upon the subject. Hon. Bushrod Washington has been chosen the president of the society."

"It is certainly a great idea; I hope it may prove a successful one," said Margaret.

"Many of those who go out to Africa, where I think a suitable location will be found for them, will not only receive a benefit themselves from the change, but act as missionaries to the heathen around them. Even when they do not teach them directly, which perhaps in many cases is hardly to be expected, the silent influence of their regular and Christian mode of life must produce a great effect. If I were to tell the hopes and expectations that fill my heart when I think upon this subject, I should be regarded as an enthusiast."

"Are there any of your own servants that could be induced to try the experiment?" asked Mrs. Fairfax.

"I have been thinking that it would be the very place for Junius," replied Mr. Peyton. "I will speak to him about it to-morrow."

"He needs some encouragement," said Virginia. "Nathan told me a few days ago that Junius was going to give up studying, for it only made him unhappy, and come and help his father on the farm. Nathan seemed a good deal troubled about it, for Junius has always been his pride."

Junius listened with evident pleasure to Mr. Peyton's account of the formation of the Colonization Society and its purposes. Accustomed to reverence his master as a person of superior wisdom and goodness, his sympathies were readily enlisted in favor of any thing that had excited Mr. Peyton's approbation.

He went over to the farm to talk with his father about it. Nathan, naturally averse to change and unenterprising, considerably damped his son's zeal by the discouraging manner with which he made his comments on the untried enterprise. His wife, too, did not at all like the idea of emigrating to an unknown and heathen country with her six children; and Junius, who had come full of warmth and ardor, found himself in a little while quite overpowered by the opposition he met with.

At last he proposed an adjournment to Keziah's cabin, that they might hear her opinion. It was a still, cold, starlight night, and as they approached they heard her voice, reading with great emphasis and feeling.

"Stop a minute," said Sally; "let's yer if dat ain't 'Sinners, turn—why will ye die?'"

They stopped to listen, and found that Sally was right.

"She reads dat yer hymn to Polydore every night," continued Sally; "it was de fust ting dat struck her heart, and she tinks it will 'fect him, if any ting will."

"Ain't uncle Polydore a Christian?" asked Junius.

"Bless you, honey, yes, dese many years; but

Keziah calls him a backslider, and I dun no what else, because he will go to sleep in church, and he takes it all as meek as a lamb; but he is a good man, fo' true, if any body is."

When they opened the cabin door, they found Keziah sitting upright in a rocking-chair, which had been her first purchase for herself, and reading by the light of a blazing fire of pine wood. Polydore was gazing mildly and sleepily upon her, endeavoring, hopelessly, to take in the full meaning of a hymn he had heard till he knew it by heart, with a patient wonder at his own want of feeling in being so little moved by it.

As soon as Keziah comprehended the plan which Junius explained to her, she entered into it with all her heart.

"It is the very place for me," exclaimed she; "I would go there to-morrow if I could."

"Oh, Keziah, don't say so; if you only knew what I know 'bout Africa, you would never want to see it again," said Polydore, wide awake for once. "Don't go, Keziah, please do, don't. I would rather die dan go."

"Nobody said any thin' about your goin'," retorted Keziah; "stay here, if you want to, and be a nigger all your life; but I thinks defferently."

Polydore made no answer to this unkind speech, but sat brooding in silence for some time, while the rest were engaged in an animated discussion. At last he broke forth in a history of his early years. For the first time in his life he was almost eloquent, while relating, in his broken language, all that he had seen and suffered.

He spoke of the devil-man, a frightful figure that came out of a thicket near his native village, and frightened every one by his terrible howlings. The death of some one, by the ordeal of gēdu or sassy-water, a poisonous opiate made from the bark of the sassy-tree, often followed the appearance of this figure, in consequence of having been accused by it of being a witch. Polydore's father fell a victim to this practice. He had been out, in company with many of the other fighting men of his tribe, to procure slaves to carry down to some slave-ships that were waiting for a cargo; they returned with a train of captives; but in the skirmishes, the head man had been slightly wounded. From some cause his wound did not heal, and he died in consequence. A cry of witchcraft was immediately raised, and Polydore's father was pointed out as the suspected person; the trial by sassy-water proving unfavorable, he was compelled to drink more till he died.

Polydore mentioned many other of their cruel customs, and said at last that, not long after his father's death, the whole village was roused one night by a savage yell. As the startled inhabitants gazed out to ascertain the cause of the alarm, they saw that they were now the victims of that fate they had so often brought upon others. Resistance was useless, for they were completely surrounded by their savage enemies. Chained or tied together, Polydore being fastened to a half-grown boy about his own size, they were forced to march for many days until they reached the sea-shore. Meantime, they had been joined by several other bands of captives, nearly all of whom had been obtained in the same way.

Two ships, lying just off the coast, explained the cause of the sudden fury that seemed to have seized the people in that part of Africa; and Polydore was quite relieved when he saw them, for he had been dreading sharing the fate of the many prisoners whom he had seen killed for various purposes.

Of the horrors of the barracoon, where they were pent up together before they embarked on board the ships, or of the still greater horrors of the "middle passage," where, closely packed, and allowed "less room than a man has in his coffin," they suffered from hunger, thirst, and every misery that the most ingenious tormentor could devise, nothing need be said, though Polydore dwelt long upon them. Then he told how he was landed and sold at Cuba. His first purchaser had given a pound of tobacco for him. His second purchaser in Cuba gave twenty dollars, for he was so emaciated that it seemed impossible he should live. After a few months, he was carried to Texas and resold for quite a high price. From there he was smuggled into Louisiana, but, falling into bad hands, Mr. Peyton, the father of the present owner of Cedar Hill, had bought him from motives of compassion; and, three years after leaving Africa, he found himself on a plantation in Virginia, and "better off," said he, "dan I ever was befo'; I is taught 'bout Jesus and my heavenly Mas'r. I no fear de debbil in de bus', no fear de slave-catchers, no fear any body, but has every ting safe and comfable. And now, Keziah, I tink I be mighty fool to leave all dese tings. But if you go, I go too. You's an unprotected single womin, and I can't see you go alone."

"Hush! shut up with yer single womin. I's worth two of you any day," replied Keziah.

"Dese arms is wort' somethin', Keziah," said Polydore, stretching out limbs that might have rivaled Samson's.

"De arms is good enough," replied Keziah, scornfully, yet not without a certain degree of admiration in her look, which strength, either of body or mind, always extorted from her, "but what's de good of strong arms when de heart is a coward's?"

"You are just de hardest womin I ever came

across," said the distressed Polydore; "didn't I tell you I was a goin', and what mo' could I say?"

"But you didn't say it with your whole heart, and de Lord don't 'cept no unwillin' offerin's."

"I wasn't tinking of making an offerin' of myself," said Polydore, resentfully; "only to you, Keziah," he added, in a softer tone.

Keziah pretended to pass over in silent disdain the last few words, but they did not fail to make an impression on her long-besieged heart. Its defenses were fast giving way; yet, showing no outward sign of the weakness within, she replied,

"Dat won't do at all, Polydore; we must make up our minds to be missionaries, and do de Lord's work as well as our own. We has been greatly blessed 'bove our poor heathen brethren, in havin' learned here how to fight de good fight, and gain de heavenly crown. And when we go 'mong de savages, and dey come to visit us, as dey will mos' likely"—Polydore groaned—"we can tell dem 'bout de blessed Savior, and teach 'em to lay down dem wicked habits you's jus' been tellin' us of." Another groan.—"'Fact," continued Keziah, warming up, "I wouldn't be a bit afraid to go and live right among 'em, if I tought I could do dem any good dat way."

"Don't talk so, Keziah, do, don't," said Polydore, beseechingly, "you don't know what dey is."

"Ain't dey our broders and sisters?" asked Keziah.

"If dey is broders, I never want to see no broders while I live," said Polydore; "but don't talk any more 'bout it, please. I's willin' to go. I's willin' to be a offerin', or any ting else to please you, for I has hung about you too long to change now; but I doesn't feel much heart about it, and dat is de truth."

Keziah's warm approbation revived Junius's zeal, and Nathan caught a little of her ardor, and agreed that, if he could look upon the matter in the same light that she did, he would be ready to embark in the first ship.

The idea of living in a land where they would enjoy the blessings of equality as well as freedom, once suggested to them, it soon became their guiding thought and desire. The higher the class of mind to which the proposal was made, the more eagerly was it received and the more warmly cherished. Keziah was a lover of freedom from instinct and nature rather than reflection. While a slave, as long as she was treated like one, she had rebelled almost to death; when brought under kinder influences, and while yielding, from gratitude and affection, the most entire devotion, the Peytons could not help perceiving that the more she was allowed to consider the service one of free will, the more heartily was it performed. She had received with delight the gift of personal liberty ; and now the prospect of a home, where the overshadowing influence of the white man would not be felt, destroying every hope of self-elevation, and almost paralyzing the wish, was welcomed as a gift from Heaven.

Nathan had a slower, calmer mind, and was more inclined to consider the difficulties and objections, "the lions in the way," than Keziah. For that reason, perhaps, his judgment was more to be relied on when he had once come to a decision. But Keziah's warmth and firmness of purpose was of great use in awakening his naturally sluggish feelings, and in preventing his interest from flagging in any subject that occupied them both.

Emigration to Africa was their topic of conversation whenever they met, which was at least once a day. Polydore listened in a meek but troubled silence, which ought to have touched their hearts, but was totally without effect. Sometimes he groaned and shook his head ; occasionally he broke forth into an "I's willin'!" but that came seldomer. However sound asleep he might be, he woke up at the word Africa, as if it were a charm, and his eyes would grow rounder and rounder, and his thoughts more and more confused, as the idea of all the great things they intended to do in that land of terror was held up before him.

Mr. Peyton sent Junius to Richmond to transact a little business for him, and there he met Lott Cary, whose history should be related, not only for its own intrinsic merit, but to show what the African is capable of becoming even now, when weighed down by so many and so great disadvantages. If *he* succeeded in growing to such a perfect stature in mind and heart, what may not be expected from those who are allowed to develop themselves under more favorable auspices.

He was born a slave near Richmond, Virginia, in 1780. His parents endeavored to train up Lott, their only child, in the fear of God; but early hired out as a common laborer in Richmond, he was thrown into companionship with profane and intemperate persons, who led him into vicious habits. While in the midst of his irreligious course, his attention was suddenly arrested by the powerful appeals of a Baptist exhorter. Overwhelmed by a sense of his sinfulness, he resolved to devote himself henceforth to the service of God, and in 1807 he joined the Baptist Church.

Soon after his conversion, hearing a sermon which related to our Savior's interview with Nicodemus, a strong desire to be able to read the passage for himself was awakened in his mind. With no regular instruction and but little assistance, he soon accomplished this, and succeeded also in learning how to write.

His next wish was to become a freeman. He was employed at that time in a large tobacco warehouse, where, by his usefulness and honesty, he had acquired the confidence of the merchants, who frequently rewarded him for his fidelity by giving him small sums of money. In 1813, he found himself the possessor of eight hundred and fifty dollars, with which he ransomed himself and his two children, his wife having died a little while before.

He was afterward employed in the same warehouse at a salary of eight hundred dollars a year. Of the real value of his services there, it has been remarked no one but a dealer in tobacco can form an idea. Notwithstanding the hundreds of hogsheads that were committed to his charge, he could produce any one the instant it was called for; and the shipments were made with promptness and correctness, such as no person, white or black, has equaled in the same situation. While employed in the warehouse, he devoted his leisure time to reading and self-improvement.

He early began to feel a special interest in African missions, and contributed probably more than any other person in giving origin and character to the African Missionary Society, established in Richmond in 1815, and which, for many years, appropriated annually to the cause of Christianity in Africa from one hundred to one hundred and fifty dollars. His benevolence was practical; whenever and wherever good objects were to be effected, he was ready to lend his aid.

For several years he preached on almost every Sunday among the colored people on the plantations around Richmond. Some one has remarked about him that, "in preaching, notwithstanding his grammatical inaccuracies, he was often truly eloquent. He had derived almost nothing from the schools, and his manner was, of course, unpolished; but his ideas would sometimes burst upon you in their native solemnity, and awaken deeper feelings than the more polished but less original and inartificial discourse."

During the latter part of his residence in Richmond, in addition to his weekly duties, he sustained the office of pastor of a Baptist church of colored persons in Richmond, embracing nearly eight hundred members, and received from it a liberal support, and enjoyed its confidence and affection.

Yet so clearly did he see the glorious prospect opened to his race by the colonization movement, that, from the earliest commencement, he watched it with anxious and hopeful earnestness, and declared his willingness to lay down all his present advantages to become a pioneer, and, if necessary, a martyr in the cause. When a clergyman of his own faith asked him how he could determine to leave a station of so much comfort and usefulness, to encounter the dangers of an African climate, and hazard every thing to plant a colony on a distant heathen shore, he replied, "I am an African; and in this country, however meritorious my conduct and respectable my character, I can not receive the credit due to either. I wish to go to a country where I shall be estimated by my merits, not by my complexion; and I feel bound to labor for my suffering race."

A heart thus burning with love toward its brethren, and a desire to do them good, must affect with somewhat of the same zeal all kindred hearts that come within the sphere of its influence. Junius returned from his journey to Richmond fully decided to devote the rest of his life to carrying the Gospel of Christ to the dark regions of Africa. He found Keziah also more and more bent on leaving a country where the sense of her degraded position had always been a heavy burden to her.

But Nathan still shrank from the untried experiment, and it was at last decided that Keziah, Polydore, and Junius should go out among the first emigrants, and if their report were favorable, Nathan, with his wife and the rest of his family, should follow.

The departure of kindred could hardly have caused

greater commotion at Cedar Hill than did the announcement of the determination of the three, who had made up their minds to sail in the first ship for Africa. Philip Fairfax was especially busy, and by his care Polydore's chest was crowded with every thing that the wildest imagination could suggest as possibly useful or necessary in their probable situation. It was well that some one had took it upon himself to attend to Polydore, otherwise he would have fared but badly, as he never seemed to think it even possible that he might need any thing, but sat, when not attending to some errand for Keziah, with his head resting on his hands and his elbows on his knees, absorbed in melancholy thought, or lost in slumber.

On their way to New York, from which city they were to embark, they spent the Sabbath in Richmond, and heard Lott Cary preach his farewell sermon in the First Baptist Meeting-house in Richmond. It was a striking one, and when he concluded by saying, "I am about to leave you, and expect to see your faces no more; I long to preach to the poor Africans the way of life and salvation; I don't know what may befall me, whether I may find a grave in the ocean, or among the savage men, or more savage wild beasts on the coast of Africa; nor am I anxious what may become of me: I feel it my duty to go; and I very much fear that many of those who preach the Gospel in this country will blush when the Savior calls them to give an account of their labors in his cause, and tells them, 'I commanded you to go into all the world, and preach the Gospel to every creature;' the Savior may ask, 'Where have you been? what have you been doing? have you endeavored, to the utmost of your ability, to fulfill the commands I gave you, or have you sought your own gratification and your own ease, regardless of my commands?'" many felt their hearts touched and moved by the solemn appeal.

They left New York in January, 1820, and arrived safely, after a short delay at Sierra Leone, at Sherbro, an island on the western coast of Africa, which the agents sent out by the society—Samuel J. Mills and Ebenezer Burgess—had made arrangements for purchasing from the natives.

The first week or two after the landing of "the pilgrims," for so might the greater part of them be considered, the change from shipboard to the palm groves and genial climate of their fatherland was very pleasant indeed. Polydore, to whom Keziah had held up almost daily, during the voyage, Lot's wife as a warning, an example to be shunned, fell back so readily into the habits of his childhood, that the danger now appeared to be that he would forget all that he had learned of civilization, and become once more an indolent, self-indulgent savage.

All kinds of food—fowls, goats, and fish—were brought in abundance by the curious natives, and could be obtained for a trifle. The most delicious fruits—oranges, lemons, pine-apples, guavas, and many others whose names Polydore did not remember, though in taste and appearance they were perfectly familiar to him—grew in great profusion around their new home.

However, but a short time was given them for rest and enjoyment. The Island of Sherbro was low and unhealthy, and while Mr. Bacon, the government agent, was endeavoring to induce the kings of the neighboring country to make a formal surrender of the land according to their promise to Mr. Mills, he was seized with a burning fever. Almost at the same time, twenty-five of the emigrants were prostrated by the same disease; and soon after, Mr. Bankson, the other agent, the physician, the lieutenant of the ship, and all the crew, were attacked by African fever in its most violent form. Mr. Bacon struggled as long as he was able against his own illness, that he might aid the rest. He was particularly anxious to obtain for those under his care a healthier home. But all his exertions were vain. The chiefs had become cold and suspicious, and the natives, who had at first crowded round them in amicable curiosity, had evidently become jealous and unfriendly.

The colonists could not understand the reason of this change for some time. It arose in a great measure from the representations of the slave-traders, who have been the chief, though often the secret enemy of that settlement, which, with a foresight quickened by their interest, they saw from the first, was to prove a greater obstacle to their nefarious trade than any number of ships or armed men. The kings along that part of the coast derived a great part of their income from the traffic in slaves. Of course, they could be easily influenced by the traders, not only to withhold all encouragement from those who were to cut off their chief source of revenue, but to proceed to open opposition. But while the emigrants were in this state of utter weakness, He, who is pitiful and of tender mercy, withheld the hand of their enemy, that the blow might not fall till they had gathered strength to resist it.

Mr. Bacon's exertions for obtaining a more salubrious location were in vain. Death came upon him while he was "working in the field," and with him Mr. Bankson, Dr. Crozer, Lieutenant Townsend, twenty emigrants, and all the boat's crew, sank beneath the malignancy of the climate, or rather, as experience has since proved, from the want of a knowledge of its peculiarities, and from no proper shelter or comforts having been prepared.

Only sixty-six emigrants remained. Some of these mourned over their situation, thus abandoned, as they thought, to certain death, and were inclined to look back regretfully toward the land they had left. These were the faint-hearted ones, among whom neither Lott Cary nor Keziah could be placed. They both remained firm and full of hope, and their example had no slight effect in encouraging the rest. Polydore was more easily disheartened. Some excess in eating fruit had brought upon him a severe attack of fever a second time, and, although he recovered, greatly to his own surprise, he could not be induced afterward to acknowledge that any thing but evil could spring from so hazardous a movement.

All the leaders thus speedily taken away, the agency and the care of the colony was intrusted to the Rev. Daniel Coker, a colored clergyman of the Episcopal Church. Thrown thus into a situation of such responsibility, with the sick, the dying, and the dead around him, with the charge of the property and interests of the colonists, he found time not only to fulfill faithfully those duties, but also to attend to "his Father's business," and he commenced a course of instruction to the natives. In a letter written in this time of trouble and discouragement, he said,

"We have met with trials; we are but a handful; our provisions are running low; we are in a strange and heathen land; we have not heard from America, and know not whether more provisions or people will be sent out; yet, thank the Lord, my confidence is strong in the veracity of his promises. Tell my brethren to come; fear not—this land is good; it only wants men to possess it. I have opened a little Sabbath-school for native children. O, it would do your hearts good to see the little naked sons of Africa around me. Tell the colored people to come up to the help of the Lord. Let nothing discourage the society or the colored people."

The hope and trust expressed in this simple yet resolute letter were not disappointed. No sooner was it known in America that there were vacant posts waiting to be filled in that country, then regarded as lying under the shadow of death, than devoted men offered themselves as ready for the duty. Four of these were selected, and sent out as agents, one of whom was the brother of the Mr. Bacon who had already fallen a sacrifice.

They were welcomed with great joy by the colonists. Finding that Sherbro was so unsuitable a place for a settlement, they accepted the offer, which the governor of Sierra Leone had kindly made them, of a home at Fourra Bay until they could provide a better one for themselves. The colonists were soon removed there; and although this delay was a great disappointment to Keziah, and troubled her more than all the other trials that had befallen her since she had left Virginia, yet her active and practically useful mind prevented her from being contented to spend the time thus given to her in idle waiting. She busied herself in teaching any native children, who would attend to her, the various little arts of civilized life which they could most readily understand, and soon found herself surrounded by quite a number of pupils, who, although they came and went as they pleased, yet gave in a short time such evident tokens of improvement, that Keziah could not help thinking it was for some good purpose she had thus been forced to cease from active exertion on her own account.

Junius went on missionary excursions into the country around, and sometimes, penetrating far into the interior, returned with wonderful accounts of the beauty and fertility of the country, and the barbaric pomp and power of the chiefs.

Meanwhile the agents were exploring the coast, seeking a better location. Lying about three hundred miles southeast of Sierra Leone was a high point of land called Cape Mesurado. Its position made it healthy, and the good harbor near it rendered it desirable. Another consideration made it still more of an object to obtain possession of it for their own purposes. It belonged to King Peter, a warlike and powerful prince, who was deeply engaged in the slave-trade; and on each side of the cape, above and below, were noted barracoons, or places where the native Africans were kept crowded together, waiting the arrival of some slaver. To make a Christian settlement in the midst of these dark places of the earth would be one great step toward their destruction.

But King Peter refused to receive the agents, and returned their presents. Seeing that there were no hopes of an interview, they prosecuted their search still farther, and had selected a place that they thought favorable, when two of them sank under the effects of exposure to the climate, still too unfamiliar a one for them to judge what course they ought to pursue when first thrown into it.

Mr. Bacon was obliged to return home, and again the colony was left without a leader. But they did not remain long in this condition. The vacant post was soon filled by Dr. Eli Ayres, of Philadelphia.

We extract, with little alteration, from "The New Republic" (an excellent little history of Liberia), the following account of the purchase of Cape Mesurado:

"Soon after the arrival of Dr. Ayres at Sierra Leone, Captain Stockton, of the war-ship Alligator, came on the coast, bearing instructions from the American government to co-operate with the agents of the Colonization Society in securing a suitable territory for the settlement of the emigrants. Dr.

Ayres accompanied Captain Stockton on an exploring agency along the coast. On the eleventh of December they came to anchor in Mesurado Bay.

"'That is the spot we ought to have,' said Captain Stockton, pointing to the high bluff off Cape Mesurado, as they stood together on the quarter-deck; 'that should be the site of our colony—no finer spot on all the coast.'

"'Then we must have it,' answered Dr. Ayres. The resolution was a bold one. England and France had been trying for it for one hundred years without success; the interview with Andrus and Bacon, six months before, was positively refused, and even their gifts scornfully sent back by King Peter. Though well aware of the ill success of every previous attempt at a negotiation, and the uncompromising hostility of the natives to any thing bearing the semblance of a white settlement, these resolute men did not mean to sail tamely or timidly by without making an effort, or at least inquiry; and every new aspect of the coast only strengthened their desires to obtain possession of it. They determined to land. Some headmen met them on the shore, to whom they gave suitable presents; and upon entering into a friendly conversation, it was soon clear that a favorable impression had been made upon their minds. They expressed a desire to see King Peter. Messenger after messenger was sent to beg a palaver with his majesty; but it was not until he had disappointed and deceived them again and again, that he consented to an interview, and then only on the condition that they should *dare* to meet him in his own capital, far into the interior. To accomplish this, they must leave the coast, wade through water and mud, cut through dismal jungles, and in an enemy's country, surrounded on all sides by savages, whose fiercest passions had been nursed by the slave-trade, and who cared not a straw for human life. They must go armed to the teeth, and even then expect at any moment robbery and death.

"Could they dare visit King Peter at such hazards? Could they brave the lion in his den? Yes, they could dare any thing in the prosecution of a great and worthy enterprise.

"'We will go!' was the resolute answer. In order to convince the natives that their object was a peaceful one, they determined to go unarmed, with the exception of a small pair of pocket pistols, which Captain Stockton usually wore in his coat. Wild beasts, and savages armed with muskets, roamed through the forests; but they reached the capital in safety, where groups of naked barbarians came out to meet them, gaping with wonder. Having been conducted to the Palaver Hall, which was spread with mats for their reception, a headman came forward and shook them by the hand, announcing the arrival of his majesty. When the king entered, he took no notice of the strangers, but went to the farthest corner of the hut, where he sat down, with an angry frown upon his brow and a glance of defiance in his eye.

"On being introduced by one of the chiefs, he asked, in a surly tone, what they wanted, and what business they had in his dominions. The plan of the colonists was carefully and minutely explained, all about which he well knew, having been informed of the object of Mr. Andrus's visit several months before, and more recently, through his headmen, of its contemplated renewal by Captain Stockton and Dr. Ayres. Meanwhile large bodies of the natives began to darken around them; but every thing wore a peaceable aspect, until, on the entrance of a fresh band, an unusal excitement began to agitate the crowd. Affairs looked dark and threatening. Captain Stockton arose and took his seat near the king. Presently a mulatto rushed forward, and, doubling up his fist, charged Captain Stockton with capturing slave vessels. 'This is a man trying to ruin the slave-trade!' he cried, in a loud and angry tone.

"'These are the people who are quarreling at Sherbro!' shouted another.

"A horrid war-yell broke from the multitude;

every one sprang upon his feet scowling vengeance upon the agents. Captain Stockton, fully conscious of the extreme peril of their position, instantly arose, and drawing out one of his pistols, pointed it at the head of the king, while, raising his other hand to heaven, he solemnly appealed to the God of heaven for protection in this fearful crisis. King Peter flinched before the calm courage of the white man, and the barbarians fell flat on their faces at the apparent danger of their chief. The captain then withdrew his pistol; their savage rage was hushed; awed and subdued by his fearless energy, some crept away, while their chiefs began to listen with respect to the advances and proposals now made to them.

"Success crowned their efforts. After two or three palavers, the king consented to sell a tract of land to the colonists. A copy of the contract entered into upon this occasion may not be uninteresting.

"Know all men, that this contract, made on the 15th day of December, 1821, between King Peter, King George, King Zoda, King Long Peter, their princes and headmen on the one part, and Captain Robert Stockton and Dr. Eli Ayres on the other, witnesseth: that whereas certain persons, citizens of the United States of America, are desirous of establishing themselves on the western coast of Africa, and have invested Captain Robert Stockton and

Eli Ayres with full powers to treat with and purchase from us (here follows a description of the land), we, being fully convinced of the pacific and just views of said citizens, and being desirous to reciprocate their friendship, do hereby, in consideration of so much paid in hand—namely: 6 muskets, 1 box of beads, 2 hogsheads of tobacco, 1 cask of gunpowder, 6 bars of iron, 10 iron pots, 1 dozen knives and forks, 1 dozen spoons, 6 pieces of blue baft, 4 hats, 3 coats, 3 pairs of shoes, 1 box pipes, 1 keg nails, 3 looking-glasses, 3 pieces of kerchiefs, 3 pieces of calico, 3 canes, 4 umbrellas, 1 box soap, 1 barrel rum; and to be paid the following: 6 bars of iron, 1 box beads, 50 knives, 20 looking-glasses, 10 iron pots, 12 guns, 3 barrels of gunpowder, 1 dozen plates, 1 dozen knives and forks, 20 hats, 5 casks of beef, 5 barrels of pork, 10 barrels of biscuit, 12 decanters, 12 glass tumblers, and 50 shoes—forever cede and relinquish the above-described lands to Robert Stockton and Eli Ayres, to have and to hold said premises for the use of said citizens of America.

"King *Peter*, ⋈ his mark.
"King *George*, ⋈ his mark.
"King *Zoda*, ⋈ his mark.
"King *Long Peter*, ⋈ his mark.
"King *Governor*, ⋈ his mark.
"King *Jimmy*, ⋈ his mark.

"Capt. Robert Stockton.
"Eli Ayres, M.D."

Having now, by the courage and energy of these two commissioners, obtained one of the finest and healthiest parts of the coast for their own, possessing a good harbor and a fertile soil, the emigrants removed from Fourra Bay to it as soon as possible. Keziah's heart was filled with delight when she first landed at her new home; and to all the colonists, the prospect of a safe and pleasant abiding-place, after a season of so much uncertainty and long delay, was delightful. It was with feelings of hope and exultation, which time has already proved to have been true presentiments, that on the twenty-fifth of April, 1822, the American flag was hoisted on Cape Mesurado.

Some time afterward the place received the name of Liberia, as indicating its true character, "the home of the free." Like England, Liberia can boast that "no slave can breathe its air."

CHAPTER VI.

LIFE IN THE NEW SETTLEMENT.

Here the free spirit of mankind at length
  Throws its last fetters off; and who shall place
A limit to the giant's unchained strength,
  Or curb his swiftness in the forward race?

BRYANT.

CAPE MESURADO is a bold promontory, rising at its highest point two hundred and fifty feet above the level of the sea. At the time when the emigrants landed upon it, it was covered with lofty forest trees and thick undergrowth.

Selecting a hill near the Mesurado River, and about two miles from the coast, they began resolutely clearing places here and there, where they might erect temporary cabins until they obtained leisure and means to build dwellings that would better deserve the name of houses. Their little clearing was afterward named Monrovia, in honor of James Monroe, then President of the United States; and this collection of huts, formed in trembling haste by the little band of defenseless colonists, is now a flourishing town, the metropolis of the African republic, with streets regularly laid out and named, with a State House, a prison, and three churches, all substantial stone buildings, with schools, dwelling-houses, stores, and warehouses, many of which are built of stone or brick.

But not without toil, privation, and danger has this state of things been achieved; and though many of those who bore the brunt of the battle are now reaping the fruit of their victory, and they who went "forth weeping bearing precious seed," have returned with rejoicing, bringing their sheaves with them, yet others have been called to receive their reward in another world.

April, the month when the settlers commenced their work, is generally called, in that part of Africa, the tornado month, from the violent gusts of wind and rain that occur during it; and in May the rainy season often commences, continuing for six months, with an interruption of a few weeks in July and August. Though at first this season was dreaded as the most unhealthy one, it was found by long experience to be less trying to a new-comer than the debilitating heat of "the dries," as the other months are generally called.

But to preserve health, shelter from the rain is imperatively demanded, and therefore the colonists labored with little rest until they had erected thirty huts. For the first two or three months after their arrival at Cape Mesurado, the little band were left to their own resources, one of their number, Elijah Johnson, being appointed to take charge of their temporal interests; while Lott Cary, who was every thing by turns as necessity demanded—carpenter, wood-cutter, soldier, a successful physician, and a devoted missionary—officiated as their pastor.

Providentially, while thus defenseless, the natives were withheld from harming, or even threatening them. It was not until after the arrival of the new agent, Mr. Ashmun, who well deserves the name he earned, by his untiring exertions, of "the founder of Liberia," that the savages around them began to show symptoms of hostility.

Dissatisfied with the sale of that valuable tract of land to a people opposed to the trade that was their chief source of income, the natives determined to destroy them utterly—to leave no vestige on that blood-stained, tear-washed coast of the little band of Christians who had brought with them the law of love, against whose silent eloquence their selfish hearts rose in fiendish hatred.

Mr. Ashmun landed, with his young wife and several emigrants, in August. He was then but twenty-eight. He had been a student all his life, and came out to Africa to preach the Gospel of peace and good-will. But hardly had he arrived, before he was called upon to lay aside all his previous habits, and become a soldier, an engineer, and a commander.

Of the one hundred and thirty emigrants who then composed the village of Monrovia, only thirty-five could bear arms, and many of these knew nothing about their management. He spent his days in training this undisciplined company; in directing the building of a stockade around the settlement; in placing in the best position the six cannon, almost their only reliable means of defense, humanly speaking; and in encouraging and strengthening those under his care by his example and prayers. He had the thickets around Monrovia cleared away, that they might afford the enemy no shelter; appointed a night-watch; and his discerning eye and cool judgment foresaw and provided against every emergency.

Yet during this time his wife died, and often his whole nights were passed in the delirium of fever. But when the morning came, laying aside his sorrow and forgetting his weakness, he would wrap himself in his cloak, and go forth to the work that so imperatively demanded his care.

The emigrants played their part manfully. Lott Cary, with his clear mind and undaunted resolution, and Elijah Johnson, who had been a soldier in early life, and afterward distinguished himself by his bravery and skill in the combats that followed their early settlement in Liberia, were strong arms of support to the young missionary.

Meanwhile the savages were gathering in numbers around them, and they nightly lay down to sleep with the dread upon their hearts of awaking to the horror of a midnight attack. But this was spared them. The assault so long threatened came at last, but in the early morning. While hourly expecting it, Mr. Ashmun assembled his little army, and addressed a few words of advice and encouragement to them. He ended by saying,

"War is now inevitable. The safety of our property, our settlement, our families, our lives, depends, under God, upon your courage and firmness. Let every post and every individual be able to confide in the firm support of every other. Let every man act as if the whole defense depended upon his single arm. May no coward disgrace our ranks. The cause is God's and our country's, and we may rely upon the blessing of Almighty God to succeed our efforts. We are weak. He is strong. Trust in Him."

Neither the confidence the leader placed in his soldiers, nor the faith he showed in God's protecting care, proved unwarranted. One Monday morning in November, the savages, who had been hovering like swarms of locusts for several days around the settlement, suddenly rushed upon a post left unguarded for a few minutes. Their sudden onset, their numbers, and their horrid yells, struck a momentary panic into the hearts of the defenders, and they turned to flee. But Mr. Ashmun and Lott Cary met them, and, with unflinching courage, rallied and led them back to the attack. The cannons, instantly brought into action, did great execution. The savages were appalled at the number of wounded and dead that fell around them, and when Elijah Johnson, with a few musketeers, attacked them on their flank, they were filled with consternation. With another yell they fled into the recesses of the forest, and left the settlers to count their losses and bury their dead. But so engrossed were they in preparing against a second attack, which they hourly dreaded, that it was not until the next day they had time to perform this last sad duty.

Not more than seventeen men had been engaged in this defense, while the assailants might be counted by hundreds; yet in half an hour the settlers could look far around them, and see no enemy. Was not the hand of the Lord in this?

A few weeks' rest was given to them; but early in December, that loveliest of months in Liberia, the natives gathered again, and, armed with muskets, again attacked the settlement on each side.

The battle raged for an hour and a half. Four times were the enemy repulsed with great slaughter, and four times they rallied to the attack. At last, seized with terror at the destruction the cannon made in their ranks, and at the courage of the little band who so resolutely defied them, they fled through the forest to their different tribes, carrying with them such accounts of the bravery and strange superiority of the settlers, that it was long before they were again molested. On the contrary, the kings of the tribes around them, of the Veys, the Deys, the Greboes, the Queahs, and many others, sought an alliance with those who had shown themselves so strong in their own defense.

Mr. Ashmun, in speaking of his little army, said that "not the most veteran troops could have behaved with more coolness, nor shown greater firmness than the settlers on this occasion;" and Elijah Johnson earned for himself the title of hero, which he still retains.

While still ignorant that their second contest was to be their last important one for many years, and not knowing how soon or when another attack might be expected, they learned to their dismay that their ammunition was almost exhausted. They had been, of course, unable to till the land or raise the necessary provision, easy as it is to provide for the wants of the body in Africa, and their bread and meat, though sparingly consumed, would last but little longer, and, for want of surgical instruments, the wounded suffered exceedingly.

Yet even in this time of distress their faith did not falter, and the confidence they retained through every thing that the course they had taken was the wisest for them, and would be proved to be so in the end, sustained them.

"There never has been an hour or a minute," said Lott Cary, with great emphasis, "no, not even when the balls were flying around my head, when I could wish myself back in America again."

While in this urgent need, a false alarm during the night led them to fire one of their cannon. When they discovered their mistake, they bitterly regretted that they had thus wasted a part of their small store of ammunition. But they soon found that they could hardly have used it to a better purpose. A British schooner was just rounding the cape as that cannon broke upon the stillness of the night. Thinking it a signal of distress, some of the crew were sent on shore early in the morning, and discovered this "little band of brave men, contending for life amid privations, poverty, sickness, and death, surrounded by barbarous tribes thirsting for their blood."

The officers of the vessel generously gave them all the assistance in their power, and Major Laing, the distinguished African traveler, who was on board, offered to use his influence to propitiate the neighboring chiefs. In this he was successful, the bravery of the colonists having already awed them, and the settlers were afterward left almost undisturbed, with the exception of a short interval, when Mr. Ashmun's health obliged him to leave them.

The best means of restoration for him appeared to be a sea voyage, and reluctantly availing himself of an opportunity for that purpose, he left the colony in the charge of Elijah Johnson, to whom it had been once before intrusted. The natives took advantage of Ashmun's absence to menace them with another attack, and Mr. Johnson applied to a British man-of-war, then in the harbor, for ammunition. This was freely given, and the captain also offered his men to aid in the defense, if Mr. Johnson would grant to England a piece of land large enough to plant her flag-staff upon, as British troops could only be called upon to defend the flag and soil of their country. This Johnson refused. "We do not want," said he, "any flag raised here that will cost us more trouble to pull down than to flog the natives."

He did not regret this refusal, for the natives were soon subdued; and when Mr. Ashmun returned, he found all tranquil.

And, now that peace smiled upon them, they had

time to think of portioning out and cultivating the land. Keziah, with her usual discrimination, selected for herself and Polydore, for their interests were at last united, a fine tract of land, lying a little out of the village. A thatched cottage was soon built upon it, and both she and Polydore worked industriously to clear the land and prepare it for planting. Like many of the other settlers, their first attempts were unsuccessful. Whatever they planted grew as if by magic, and with hardly any trouble on their part; but just as they were promising themselves an abundant harvest, legions of ants, or troops of monkeys, porcupines, or other wild animals, would in one night lay waste whole acres.

Most of the other colonists were disheartened. The unsettled life they had lately been leading rendered them less fitted for steady exertion; and finding that, by trading with the natives, they could obtain what was necessary for their subsistence with much less labor, in the natural desire that all people share for present ease and self-indulgence, they forgot their real and permanent good. The more far-sighted of the emigrants urged in vain upon their companions the advantages of agriculture. It was not for some years that they realized its importance, and only lately has their attention been turned resolutely to it.

Keziah was one of the few who persevered in endeavoring to cultivate the land, and every year it became easier. The little animals that had at first proved so destructive, disappeared as the forests were cleared away. Each failure, instead of discouraging her, was only a new lesson; she learned from them what seasons were most adapted to certain grains and vegetables, and what seeds were best suited to the soil.

All the time she could spare from her own cares she devoted to teaching the native women and children, who frequently visited her. The indefatigable Lott Cary had, with the assistance of another colonist, already established a missionary school for native children, thus carrying out one of the principal objects of the society.

Keziah longed to do the same, but the charge of the farm engrossed her too much; for, although Polydore took the labor upon himself, the direction fell to his wife, who would have been by no means willing to relinquish it.

Becoming dissatisfied, after a short trial, with this desultory mode of teaching the natives only when they chose to attend to her, she determined to adopt two little native girls, that she might train them more effectually in her own way. When Keziah proposed this plan to the savages around her, it was eagerly embraced, and such a number of children were offered, that she found her difficulty lay in selecting and refusing, not in obtaining.

Not long after this addition to her cares, Polydore returned from the village, already become a place of some importance, with the news that a slave-ship had been taken, and that its cargo was about to be landed at Liberia. The settlers, he said, were asked to do all that was in their power for the wretched beings thus thrown upon their charity.

Keziah's heart instantly responded to this appeal, and she offered to provide food and shelter for four if they were sent to her. Fortunately, the cargo was a small one, the ship having been captured before it was fully loaded, and only two were intrusted to Keziah's kindness.

More miserable objects had seldom been seen than were these when they first reached her hospitable door. Emaciated and trembling, they appeared hardly able to stand, much less to walk. Indeed, Polydore had been obliged to carry one of them up the hill leading to the cottage, for he had fallen from weakness while attempting to ascend it. But before the end of a month, Keziah was surprised to observe the great change that had taken place in them. In their tall, muscular forms they almost rivaled Polydore.

For several days this latter personage had seemed very much perplexed. His pipe, which was his great resource in trouble, was in almost constant use. He would sit for hours smoking and gazing into the face of the larger of the savages, without uttering a word. Keziah, meanwhile, was endeavoring to teach them English, in which she succeeded but indifferently; but every word they addressed to each other in their own tongue affected Polydore strangely. At length, one day when he was left alone with them, he approached the one who seemed to interest him so deeply, and addressed a single word to him. The savage looked up astonished. Again Polydore repeated the word, as though he were asking some question. The savage nodded, and quietly replenishing his pipe, Polydore seated himself in the door of the cabin, looking steadfastly in the direction from which he might expect his wife. He knew that she was gone out on some business that would detain her several hours longer; but even watching for her was such a relief to his mind, that he would have preferred to sit there all day to any active occupation.

She came at last, just as the sun was shedding its last faint ray of light. Noticing the wistful glance he cast upon her, she stopped and asked him what he wanted.

"Keziah, dat's my brother."

"What?"

"Dat man yonder is my brother."

"How do you know?"

"I've 'spected it dis long time· since he fust

began to talk. I know'd every word he said, but I couldn't remember the meanin'; and a little while ago I called him by his name, not the name de other nigger calls him, but de name he used to go by when we was chillun, and he said yes."

"Does he know who you are?"

"I don't know; I hain't said nothin' to him since."

Keziah found, on entering her cottage, that the savage had relapsed into his usual state of apathy. It was some time before she could induce him even to try to understand the news she labored to impart to him. When he did fairly comprehend it, it seemed to produce but little effect upon him. But both Polydore and Keziah being unwearying in their endeavors to instruct him, they soon had the pleasure of being able to understand his broken English. From that time his improvement was more rapid. He consented to take the land usually allotted to every settler, and they helped him to build a cottage for himself near them. Whether Keziah's earnest exhortations, or the silent influence of Polydore's example had the most effect, can not be known now, but before three years had passed by they had the unspeakable delight of welcoming him as a member of the same fold, and under the same shepherd with themselves.

"Is not this worth all we have endured since we came to Africa?" asked Keziah.

And Polydore answered yes with his whole heart.

Meantime, Mr. Ashmun's health had become so seriously affected, that he was obliged to return to his native country. The day on which he took his departure was one of the saddest that has ever darkened over Liberia. Yet while all crowded around him, to take a mournful leave of one who had been their great support through so many trials, they hardly thought they were bidding him adieu forever in this world. He only lived to greet once more his country, and died at New Haven a few days after he landed. His last prayers were for Africa, for "the poor people among whom he had labored."

Mr. Ashmun had left the colony under the care of Lott Cary, who continued to manage it with the same liberal spirit as his predecessor. His main object was to elevate the moral and intellectual standard of the African. For this purpose he exerted himself to establish schools, and labored both as a pastor over his own church and a missionary to the heathen around him. He was also energetic and prudent in his management of the business affairs of the colony, and it had never been more prosperous than when it was under his charge.

His horror of the slave-trade, and his resolute determination to oppose it whenever an opportunity offered, was the worthy cause of the death of this truly heroic man. A king of a neighboring tribe had obtained possession of a factory belonging to Liberia, and situated a few miles north of Monrovia, which he had given to a slave-trader. After attempting uselessly to obtain restitution by pacific means, Mr. Cary determined to compel the king to grant his just demand. While engaged in preparing cartridges to be used for this purpose, one of the men overturned a candle, which, falling into some gunpowder, caused it to explode, and several persons were instantly killed. Lott Cary was one of the number.

It would seem as though the loss of two persons of such importance to Liberia as Mr. Ashmun and Mr. Cary would have been almost irreparable. Yet, though they were mourned with exceeding sorrow, and each colonist felt as though some member of their family had been taken, able men came forward to supply their place, and the temporal interests of Liberia seemed unaffected by the change in the human instruments that controlled them. It went on increasing steadily, though slowly, in numbers and in size. Every year added something to its importance, and saw it elevated a degree higher in the scale of nations.

Though the ardor of some spirits, that were overzealous at first, has been dampened by the slowness of its growth, yet, to its more discerning friends, this very circumstance has been a cause of gratulation. For, if the colored people had been poured into Africa as emigrants have swarmed to our coasts, received, as they would have been, among savages and heathen, themselves, many of them, not yet fixed in their opinions and habits, there would have been great danger that they would have reverted to the customs of their fathers, and thus lost all the benefit of their early training. Now this danger is past. A Christian nation calls for its wandering children to come under its protecting care, and the entreaty can hardly be too readily obeyed.

The light in which the settlers themselves regarded their enterprise can not be better shown than by a few extracts from an address they drew up at a meeting of the citizens of Monrovia, in 1827, five years after they first landed on the cape. This was sent to America, to correct some false impressions that were prevalent there with respect to them. They say,

" The first thing which caused our voluntary removal to this country, and which we still regard with the deepest concern, is *liberty*—liberty in the sober, simple, but complete sense of the word ; that liberty of speech, action, and conscience, which distinguishes the free, enfranchised citizens of a free state, and that liberty which was denied to us in America ; and now we truly declare to you that our hopes and expectations in this respect have been realized.

"Forming a community of our own, in the land of our forefathers, having the commerce, soil, and resources of the country at our disposal, we know nothing of that debasing inferiority with which our very color stamped us in America. There is nothing here to create the feeling on our part—nothing to cherish the feelings of superiority in the minds of foreigners who visit us. It is this *moral* emancipation, this liberation of the mind from *worse* than iron fetters, that repays us ten thousand times over for all that it has cost us, and makes us grateful to God and our American patrons for the happy change which has taken place in our situation.

"The true character of the African climate is not well understood in other countries. Its inhabitants are as robust, as healthy, as long-lived, to say the least, as those in any other country. Nothing like an epidemic has ever appeared in this colony; nor can we learn from the natives that a sweeping sickness has ever yet visited this part of the Continent. But the change from a temperate to a tropical climate is a great one—too great not to affect the health more or less, and, in cases of old people and very young children, often causes death. In the early years of the colony, want of good houses, the great fatigues and dangers of the settlers, their irregular mode of living, and the hardships and discouragements they met with, greatly helped the other causes of sickness, and were attended with great mortality. But we look back to those times as to a season of trial, long past and nearly forgotten.

"People now arriving have comfortable houses to receive them; will enjoy the regular attendance of a physician; will be surrounded and attended by a healthy, happy people, who have borne the effects of the climate, who will encourage and fortify them against that despondency, which alone has carried off several in the first years of the colony. A more fertile soil and productive country, so far as it is cultivated, there is not, we believe, on the face of the earth. Its hills and plains are covered with a verdure which never fades.

"Cattle, swine, fowls, ducks, goats, and sheep thrive without feeding, and require no other care than to keep them from straying. Cotton, coffee, indigo, and sugar may be cultivated at pleasure, to any extent. The same may be said of rice, Indian corn, millet, and fruits, and vegetables too numerous to be mentioned.

"Our trade is already valuable, and fast increasing. It is carried on in the productions of the country—consisting of rice, palm oil, ivory, tortoise-shell, dye-woods, gold, hides, wax—and brings us, in return, the products and manufactures of the four quarters of the world. Seldom, indeed, is our harbor free from European and American shipping.

"Not a child or youth but is provided with an appropriate school. We have a large public library, court-house, meeting-houses, school-houses, and fortifications.

"Our houses are built of the same materials, and furnished in the same style, as in the towns of America. We have an abundance of good building-stone, shells for lime, and clay for brick.

"The cheerful abodes of civilization and happiness which are scattered over this verdant mountain; the flourishing settlements which are spreading around it; the sounds of Christian instruction and scenes of Christian worship which are heard and seen in this scene of pagan darkness; a thousand contented freemen united in founding a new Christian empire, happy themselves, and the instruments of happiness to others—conclusively testifies to the wisdom and goodness of the plan of colonization."

This was the grateful and confident language of the colonists, while yet in the infancy of their existence, while savages were lurking around their outskirts, ready to take advantage of any weak or unguarded point, and while they were still obliged to look up to and lean upon the Colonization Society as their protector and guide.

When, twenty years after, they stood up in the self-reliance of vigorous youth, and with the consent of their early guardian, declared themselves an independent nation, how many more mercies had they to acknowledge?

CHAPTER VII.

A LIBERIAN VISITS AMERICA.

He that bears himself like a gentleman, is worth to have been born a gentleman.—CHAPMAN.

AFTER the first few years of trial, the accounts from Liberia were so encouraging, that Nathan yielded to the earnest entreaties of Junius, and emigrated to Africa with his family. At Mr. Peyton's request, Junius continued to write to him frequently, and keep him informed of all that happened of interest in the community, and more especially in the two households that had once been members of Mr. Peyton's family. Hardly a letter came without bringing some confirmation of the increasing stability and prosperity of the colonists. Every step they took was a step upward and onward. He became convinced that the great problem which had occupied so much of his thoughts was at last solved, and that in Africa the African might be allowed to grow to his full stature—to become a man.

When, in 1847, Liberia proclaimed itself a free and independent nation, no one welcomed it more warmly into its new rank as a republic than did Mr. Peyton. Not long after this important event, he passed a few weeks in Philadelphia. He had heard nothing of Ben or Clara for two or three years, and had supposed them prosperously employed all that time.

He was troubled at the condition in which he found them, though it was so superior to the one from which Mr. Lyndsay had rescued them. Wishing to excite in them a desire to share the privileges which Nathan was enjoying, he sent them the letters he had received from Junius, most of which were filled with accounts of the happiness and comfort in which his father's family were living.

He succeeded so far as to awaken an interest in them as to all the concerns of Liberia, but he could not arouse in Ben enough energy to induce him to leave even the poor home which was all he could hope to call his own in America.

The influence of Americus was a great obstacle to Mr. Peyton's wishes. He had returned from France quite a finished gentleman in manners and appearance, and with his ideas of his own consequence greatly exalted, and he scouted at the thought of leaving "the comforts of civilized life," to use his own words, "to live in cabins and fight with savages. The United States was his native land; he had as much right to all the advantages he could derive from living in it as any other of its citizens; and he was not going basely to give up his rights, but rather to nail his flag to the mast and demand them. There was a better time coming; the hour would surely arrive, however long delayed it might be, when the distinctions of white and black would be unknown, and man would be estimated by his own intrinsic worth."

Speeches like these had a great effect on Ben. Clara, like most women, looking to the immediate and practical, rather than far into the dim future, asked what good that time would do to them, if, as Americus observed, "generations must pass away before that state of things could be looked for."

"While you are talking about it, and waiting for it here," said she, "Nathan and Polydore are helping it forward in Africa; for in Liberia whites and blacks do meet in terms of equality, or, rather, the colored people are the most important persons there, and that is the only Christian place I ever heard of where that is the case."

Americus had heard of several others, but he seemed willing to make a trial of none of them. "He was determined," he said, "to live and die in America, and no colonizationist should force him to leave it."

"I am sure you are welcome to stay here if you like," said Clara; "the white folks are too glad to have somebody they can order about and make do their hard work, to compel us to leave; but for my part, I would like to go where I can be as good as any body else. I know Nathan and Keziah very well. They have too much sense not to know whether it is better for them to be there than here, and they wouldn't speak so well of it if they did not like it."

"Have you never heard of the fox that lost his tail in the trap, and tried to persuade his companions to cut off theirs too?" asked Americus.

"Yes," said Clara; "but I've knowed Nathan more than thirty years, and I never knowed him to tell a lie in all my life, and it isn't likely that he would begin now."

Ben confirmed Clara's assertion, and Americus himself was too well aware of its truth to deny it.

While this conversation was going on in Clara's room, Mr. Peyton was sitting with his wife in a private parlor of one of the principal hotels in Philadelphia, reading partly to himself, and occasionally aloud to her, such passages from different periodicals that were lying on the table around him as particularly struck him. From one of the foreign reviews he read the following:

"What a wonderful continent is this rounded, smooth-shored Africa, known from the earliest dawn of time, yet so unknown; the granary of nations, yet sterile and fruitless as the sea; swarming with life, yet dazzling the eyes with its vast tract of glittering sand! North America, first seen but the other day, has been probed from end to end; its Philips, Tecumsehs, and Montezumas have been bridled and broken by the white man; but Africa has seen no Cortez, or even a De Soto or La Salle, "wringing favor from fate." Some solitary Mungo Park, or faithful Lander, or persevering Burckhardt, alone has tried to read the secret of the mother of civilization—the gray-haired Africa.

"If we seek a land of romance and mystery, what quarter of the globe compares with that which holds the Pyramids; the giant Theban temples, under one roof of which clusters a modern village; the solemn, hewn mountain cliff of a Sphinx; the ruins of Carthage; the Nile, with its hidden sources; the Niger, with its unknown outlet; the heaven-bearing Atlas; the dimly-seen Mountains of the Moon!

"There the slave rose, romantically, to be the ruler of millions; there Moses, floating in his cradle, is saved by the king's daughter, and like the hero of some earlier chivalry, breaks the bonds of his people and founds a new and mighty nation. There was the home of Dido, of Hannibal, the scene of Scipio's triumphs, and Jugurtha's crimes; there lived Tertullian, Athanasius, and Augustine: the last breath of Louis of France was drawn there.

"Africa is the home of the leviathan, the behemoth, the unicorn, the giraffe, the antelope, the elephant, the lion, the buffalo. It is the home, too, of the mysterious negro races yet lying dormant in the germ, destined, perhaps, to rule this earth when our proud Anglo-Saxon blood is as corrupt as that of the descendants of Homer or Pericles.

"The past, present, and future of Africa are alike wrapt in mystery. Who can tell us of the childhood of dark-browed Egypt, square-shouldered and energetic? Carthage, the England of the old world's rulers, has not even a romancing Livy, still less an unwearied Niebuhr, to explain her rise and untangle the mysteries of her constitution. Of all the vast interior, what do we know more than the Punic merchants, who, like us, dealt there, taking slaves, ivory, and gold?

"And what can we hope hereafter to see in those immense, unknown lands? God has enabled the European to drive out the North American, and given a great continent the full development and trial of whatever permanent power the Caucasian race possesses; but Africa he has preserved—for what? For future contest? For an imported foreign civilization, to be entered through Liberia and the Cape Colonies? France and Britain are watching each other now along those burning sands, as they once watched by the icy rocks of Canada and

Acadia: is it to end in the same subjection of the aboriginal owners to one or both of these? Or does the dark race, in all its varieties, possess a capacity for understanding and living out the deep laws of the world's ruler, Christianity, as the offspring of the followers of Odin never did, and never can, understand and act it?

"If the old Egyptian Sesostris had paused to contemplate the illiterate wanderers of Greece, to whom Cadmus was just striving to make known the letters of Phœnicia, would not Plato and Aristotle have seemed as impossible to him as the existence in Africa of a higher Christianity than has yet been seen seems to us? Would not the present position of the Teutonic race have appeared equally incredible to the founder of the Parthenon, the loungers in the gardens of the Academy?"

Here he was interrupted by the entrance of a lady who came to call upon his wife. She was a Mrs. Vaughan, who belonged to the Society of Friends, as was easy to see by the grave simplicity of her dress, which accorded so well with the calm, unworldly expression of her face, that the impression of its oddity was lost in its suitability.

"I have called to see thee," said she, after the usual words of greeting had passed, "to tell thee of a very interesting visit I have been making this morning. Thee knows that Joseph Roberts, the

President of Liberia, is here on business connected with his adopted country. I heard a little while ago that his wife was with him, and I have been to see her. She is a pretty, intelligent young woman. I was very much pleased with her indeed. I knew that thee was interested in all that concerns that country, and as I had an opportunity to ask a great deal about it, I thought that thee might like to hear what she said."

"Is Mr. Johnson a white man?" asked Virginia.

"Oh no, my dear," replied Mr. Peyton; "he is the President of the Republic of Liberia, and no white person is allowed to hold any political office whatever there. He was once a slave in Virginia, but was emancipated and sent to Liberia when he was quite a lad. He has raised himself by his own exertions to the station he now occupies, after having filled with credit and honor the important position of general of the forces of Liberia, at a time when they were engaged in a serious contest with one of the most powerful of the neighboring tribes. The quarrel was occasioned by a demand for slaves, and this tribe, which had long carried on their commerce with the Europeans almost exclusively by means of the slaves they obtained in their forays, attacked Millsberg and Hedington within a short time, in order to get possession of several of the natives who had taken refuge under the protection of

Liberia. Do you not remember, my dear, the account I read to you from one of the letters I received from Junius, of the attack on the latter place by three or four hundred savages, and of the brave defense the inhabitants made, though so taken by surprise. At last, Zion Harris, a citizen of Liberia, who emigrated from Tennessee, put the whole band to rout by a fortunate shot, which struck down their head man. They rallied, and by another shot he killed the second chief. This made them hesitate for a moment, and, taking advantage of the pause, Harris blew a large bugle. Supposing this to be the signal of a re-enforcement approaching, the savages fled in all directions."

"Yes," replied Virginia, "I do remember it. It was on that occasion, I believe, that the barbarians brought a kettle to cook the missionary in."

"They were sure of victory," said Mr. Peyton, "and were amazed at being defeated by such a handful. They thought the settlers had greegrees or charms to protect them. Fortunately, Buchanan was then Governor of Liberia, a man of great ability and energy; and he determined 'to settle the matter at once and forever,' as he said. Therefore he, with General Roberts, the same man who is now President of Liberia, went with three hundred men twenty-five miles into the interior, to attack the tribe in their own fortress. He gained so complete a victory, that the settlers have not since been disturbed by the natives. On the contrary, most of the kings around them, and some who live far in the interior, have sent to beg an alliance with the Liberians. I have been glad to see that one stipulation which has always been made before receiving them as allies is, that they should never be in any way engaged in the slave-trade."

"Does it not seem a pity to thee," asked Mrs. Vaughan, "that this bloodshed could not have been avoided—that the Liberians did not make a treaty with the natives, as Penn did with the Indians?"

"Under the circumstances, that was impossible," replied Mr. Peyton. "There were no slave-traders in Pennsylvania to excite the natives to war by telling them that their commerce was about to be destroyed by the unwelcome intruders. If the selfish passions of the Indians had been awakened by interested and designing men, there might have been a very different account to give of Penn's colony."

"I would like to have seen it fairly tried," said Mrs. Vaughan.

"It was tried more than ten years ago," replied Mr. Peyton. "Quite a large number of emigrants went out under the auspices of the Pennsylvania Young Men's Colonization Society, and established themselves at Bassa Cove, a beautiful and fertile spot on the St. John's River. They named the settlement Port Cresson, in honor of Mr. Elliott Cresson, who, you know, has been such an efficient and liberal patron of this enterprise. In fact, he was the founder of the society which sent out these emigrants. They bound themselves before they left to refrain from ardent spirits and the arts of war, and to act as missionaries as far as they could. A letter I received from Liberia, a few months after they landed, was filled with accounts of the satisfaction of the settlers with their new home. One of the pleasantest and finest portions of Liberia had been selected for them, and they were improving it very fast. There were but two guns in the whole colony, but yet, trusting in the influence of their Christian principles, they did not feel the least alarm, although they were surrounded by savages. They were told several times of what might be the consequence of their defenseless situation; but they paid no heed to the warnings, and therefore were taken completely by surprise when one evening the savages rushed upon them from the thickets around, killed several, and compelled the rest to take refuge in the swamps and woods. Only two houses were left unmolested, and they belonged to the two settlers who had provided themselves with fire-arms."

"Perhaps the colonists had not treated the natives kindly," suggested Mrs. Vaughan.

"No; the savages had no cause of complaint against the settlers, except that they had established themselves on land which had been bought for that purpose. It seems that there was a barracoon much used by the slave-traders quite near Port Cresson, and when they discovered that there was to be a Liberian settlement at the Cove, they told the king of that part of the country that they could not think of buying slaves so near to the Americans, and should remove their factory immediately. This aroused the king's cupidity, and he promised to drive the emigrants away."

"Did he succeed?" asked Mrs. Vaughan.

"He did, at first; and was so pleased with his good fortune, that he refused to listen to the messengers the Liberians sent to him, and was preparing for an attack on some of the other towns, when they marched a force against him, which completely destroyed his towns and defenses, and returned without the loss of a single man. After that, finding that the Liberians were not the weak, defenseless people he thought them, he became their firm friend and ally, and entreated the settlers to return to Port Cresson, offering to repay them as far as he could for all the injury he had done them, and promising them any part of his country to settle in, if they would only give him 'God's book and 'Merica trade' again."

"I hope the settlers accepted his offer," said Mrs. Vaughan.

"Yes, they did. But their new settlement was made about two miles above its former location, and is now called Bassa Cove. There are, however, a few houses still at Port Cresson, and I have no doubt but that it will be a flourishing town before many years. You see I am well informed concerning Liberian affairs," continued Mr. Peyton, smiling. "There are few subjects in which I take so great an interest."

A note was just then handed to him. After reading it, he turned to Mrs. Vaughan, saying, "This is from your brother-in-law, Mr. Elias Vaughan. He says that several gentlemen are to spend the evening with him to meet Governor Roberts, and to learn from him more particularly the condition of Liberia. He is kind enough to ask me to join them, and I shall be very glad to have an opportunity to talk with a responsible person from that country. We can learn a great deal more about the real state of affairs in that way than in any other."

Mr. Peyton was detained by some visitors, and it was quite late in the evening before he reached Mr. Vaughan's. When he entered the room, the guests were conversing in little groups around it, while Mr. Roberts was standing by himself. As each person entered, the host had introduced them to the President of Liberia; but after speaking a few words to him, so intolerable a feeling of awkwardness and constraint stole over them at the unusual position in which they found themselves thus placed toward a colored man, that each, unwilling to make himself conspicuous by any long conversation with him, turned to those with whom they felt themselves on common ground. Mr. Vaughan did all that he could to prevent Mr. Roberts from perceiving any want of courtesy, but he was too much occupied by receiving his guests to allow him to devote much of his time to him.

Mr. Peyton perceived the state of things at a glance, and could hardly repress a smile at the inconsistency between the principles and conduct of the assembly. There was not a gentleman present who did not profess to be an ardent friend to the colored race. Many of them supported vehemently the most liberal and ultra views with regard to their rights and capabilities. Yet here was one whose appearance and manners showed him to be a gentleman—a man of tried bravery, fidelity, and uprightness—intelligent, unassuming, and self-possessed—whom they had assembled for the purpose of meeting; and each one of them was trying to appear unconscious of his presence. Yet uneasy glances were cast toward him from time to time, that showed that it was not the desire to be courteous that was wanting, but a "decent respect for the opinions" of others. There is something in the human race that has a striking similarity to the docility of the sheep. Any lead taken with confidence will be sure to find followers. And the innate dignity, the lofty presence, and perfect good-breeding of Mr. Peyton well fitted him for a leader. People felt instinctively that, following him, they could not go wrong.

He had come for the express purpose of meeting and talking with Mr. Roberts, and was soon engaged in an animated conversation with him. This could not fail to be an interesting one, both from the nature of the subject discussed, and from the clear, straight-forward, and satisfactory manner in which Mr. Roberts gave this account. Soon, one by one the guests drew near to listen, until at last Mr. Peyton and his companion found themselves the centre of an audience composed of all the persons in the room; while Mr. Roberts, apparently as unconscious of the marked attention now paid him as of the neglect he had experienced a short time before, went on quietly but earnestly explaining the condition, the wishes, and the claims of Liberia.

His inaugural address, when he entered upon his duties as the first president of the little republic, had impressed Mr. Peyton very favorably, and this interview elevated him still higher in his opinion. The clear good sense, the calm judgment, and the piety that appeared in all that he said, could not fail to inspire confidence in his listeners.

Mr. Peyton returned to his wife with renewed zeal in favor of colonization.

"Besides the advantages it offers to the colored race," said he, "and if Mr. Roberts is a fair specimen of a Liberian, they are well worth all that has been done for it, its efficiency in suppressing the slave-trade ought alone to induce us to support it. We have spent millions of dollars in maintaining fleets there, yet they have done but little for us in comparison with Liberia. Nearly five hundred miles on the western coast are now entirely free from that curse; and I hope and confidently expect that the time will come when from that little spot the laws and principles will go forth that will control all Africa."

"I wish we could induce Ben to go," said Mrs. Peyton. "Americus is so well adapted to his position, that it would be a pity to persuade him to leave it; but I think if Ben could only get his ambition aroused once more, he would make a valuable citizen of that new country."

"I have spoken to Mr. Lyndsay about it," replied Mr. Peyton, "and he has promised me that he will not lose sight of them, and will do all that he can to excite in Ben a desire to emigrate. I think he will succeed. I am sure if Ben had seen Mr. Roberts last night, he would have been convinced that he could become something more than 'a nigger,' as he calls himself."

Mr. Peyton was disappointed that President Roberts was obliged to leave the United States without having obtained a formal recognition of the independence of his adopted country. Great Britain and France were more ready to welcome the nation that had thus sprung into existence than its own foster-mother; and in both these countries the president was received with the honor befitting his rank.

The following extracts from a letter from him will show, more forcibly than any account can do, how little effect the color has, when the position and character is such as to inspire respect. Mr. Lyndsay sent it to Americus, asking him how many generations he supposed must pass away before a colored man from the United States would be so received by the governments of Europe.

"London, October 25, 1852.

"MY DEAR SIR,—A week or two since I wrote you, giving a somewhat detailed statement of my proceedings here and in Paris up to that time; and now I have nothing very special to communicate, except that there is a decidedly increasing interest in England and France in favor of Liberia. By the government and people of both these countries I have been received in the most kind and flattering manner. I mentioned to you that, in consequence of the departure of the prince president for a tour in the south of France just about the time I reached Paris, I had promised to make another visit in the course of a month. Accordingly, I returned on the 15th instant, to be present and witness the entiy of the president on the 16th.

" The minister for foreign affairs, M. Druyn de Lhuys, had heard of my arrival, and Sunday morning, the 17th, I received an invitation from him and madame to dine with them the following day; and, as you may suppose, I did not fail to avail myself of the occasion to state fully my wishes, and to press upon his excellency the importance of dispatch in my case. The party at the table consisted of ten or a dozen, and all, except one, spoke English pretty well, and in compliment evidently to me, the conversation of the evening was carried on in my own language, notwithstanding the subject of discussion. All appeared deeply interested in favor of Liberia.

" About nine o'clock the minister was sent for to meet the president at Saint Cloud. Before leaving, however, he said to me that he had spoken with the prince the morning before respecting Liberia, and had informed his highness that I was in Paris, and that my stay would be very short. The prince had therefore, notwithstanding the fatigue of his journey, consented to give me an audience the next day, Tuesday, at twelve o'clock. The next day at ten, I received a note from the minister, to say he would call for me at eleven to accompany me to Saint Cloud. He was punctual, and appeared in full court dress, and off we posted in his carriage. I, indeed, had a very pleasant interview, and found the president quite as well informed in regard to Liberian matters as I expected. He said he felt greatly interested in the effort that was being made in Liberia to test the capacity of the African race for self-government, and that he was well pleased at the progress that had been made; and that Liberia would be supported by the French government, not only to that view, but also as the best means for suppressing the slave-trade, and introducing civilization and Christianity into Western Africa. In proof of his good wishes—upon my application for a few hundred stand of arms, uniforms, &c., for our militia, and a small ten-gun brig—the prince readily consented to supply the uniforms, &c., and said he would speak with the minister of marine respecting the vessel. On returning to Paris, the minister for foreign affairs remarked to me, I might feel assured that all I asked for would be granted. The minister of marine was absent, to return in a few days, and as soon as he can be consulted, I shall know definitely through the French embassy here.

"With respect to my visit to London, I have continued to receive every attention from her majesty's government. I have had frequent conversations with Lord Malmsbury and Mr. Addington; and have had a long and tedious correspondence with them respecting Liberian affairs, and I think I have succeeded in convincing them thoroughly of the justice of the course pursued by the Liberian government toward British merchants trading upon that coast, and that the complaints which have been made from time to time by said traders are without just cause.

"Liberia stands to day upon a better footing than ever before in regard to her foreign relations. I have accomplished much, and shall not regret my visit to Europe. The government have kindly placed at my disposal a vessel to take me to Liberia, and I shall probably leave about the 1st proximo.

"October 20th. I have just received a communication from the foreign office, in which all my matters have been arranged quite to my satisfaction, and upon the basis as stated above. Her majesty's government recognize the sovereignty of Liberia over the points of coast which have been disputed by

British traders, and thereby relieve us from future difficulty on that score, and the greatest source of annoyance we have had to contend against for years past.

"Very truly your obedient servant,

"J. J. ROBERTS."

Some months before the date of this letter, Ben had decided, to Clara's great joy, on seeking the land where so many advantages awaited him. A letter he received from Junius, written at Mr. Peyton's request, and giving a plain statement of his father's situation, his own feelings and opinions about Liberia, and ending with a cordial invitation from both Nathan and Polydore, for Ben and Clara to make them a visit, and decide, after seeing the country, whether to return or remain, was the circumstance that had the greatest effect in bringing about this decision. Americus exerted all his influence against it; but when he found that it was unavailing, he generously offered to supply them with the means of returning whenever they wished to come.

"I care more just now," said Ben, "about getting the money to take me there. I have not ten dollars in the world."

"The Colonization Society will send us at its own expense," said Clara.

" But what shall we do after we arrive ? I suppose we must expect to go through the acclimating fever, and of course we can be earning nothing then."

" The society will provide a house for us, and food, and medical attendance for the first six months, if we need help so long," replied Clara.

" I would rather have something of my own to depend upon," said Ben; " how long do you suppose it will take us to save two hundred dollars. I would not like to start with less."

" If you had as good a place," said Clara, " as you had when we first came here, we could do it without much trouble, but as it is, I don't see how we can lay by any thing."

" Let us try," said Ben, " we may find it easier than it seems."

Mr. Lyndsay knew the motive that had awakened Ben's long dormant energy, and encouraged him in his new course. After nearly a year had passed in constant efforts toward the attainment of his purpose, Ben confessed to Mr. Lyndsay that he was almost discouraged. Several things had been very much against him. One of his children had been ill, and his wife had been out of work part of the time. " He was afraid," he said, " he must be contented to live here all his life, making only enough to keep his family from suffering."

"When Mr. Peyton returned to Virginia," said Mr. Lyndsay, "he told me that whenever you wished to go to Liberia, I might obtain the needful funds from him. But, in accordance with his wishes, I did not tell you of this until I had seen that you were so far in earnest in your intention that you were willing to practice exertion and self-denial in order to obtain it."

This was cheering news to Ben, and he with his wife and children were soon prepared to take advantage of Mr. Peyton's liberality.

"Mr. Peyton has sent through me three hundred dollars;" said Mr. Lyndsay to them the day before they sailed, "sixty dollars is considered a fair average by the society for the expenses of the voyage, and of the first six months in Liberia; so, as there are but four of you, there is more than you really need; but take good care of it, you will find it useful."

Ben promised to act with the greatest prudence, and, with hearts full of hope, the family embarked for their new home.

CHAPTER VIII.

LIBERIA AS IT IS.

I wave a torch that floods the lessening gloom
With everlasting fire!
Crowned with my constellated stars, I stand
Beside the foaming sea,
And from the future, with a victor's hand,
Claim empire for the Free!

J. Bayard Taylor.

After a pleasant voyage of thirty-five days, Ben saw the high promontory of Cape Mesurado rising in bold relief against the clear sky. It was a bright, sunshiny day in July when the emigrants landed at the cove near the base of the cape. Polydore and Nathan were on the beach to greet them on their arrival, and make them feel less like strangers in a strange land, and they were struck with the improvement manifest in Polydore's language and bearing.

The pretty town of Monrovia also excited their surprise and admiration. Its substantial, well-built houses, its churches, and its warehouses were superior to any thing that they had imagined. The streets were shaded with the singular and beautiful trees of the tropics, and by many of the houses were gardens filled with flowers and vegetables.

"Our farm was very near Monrovia," said Polydore; "but we found out that the land was better a little farther from the sea-shore, and so, when Nathan came, we moved to a place near Caldwell, on the St. John's River. There's some of the best land there that I've seen any wheres. It's 'bout nine mile from here; but I have a wagon, with some little African ponies, that will soon take us there."

"Are these houses well furnished?" asked Clara.

"I reckon they are," replied Polydore; "some of them are most equal to ol' mast'r's house at home. Here's one of our newspapers," continued he, handing "The Liberia Herald" to Ben; "we've another one besides that."

"Is this written by colored men?" asked Ben.

"Yes, po'try and all. Don't you 'member Colin Teage, that came over here the same time Keziah and I came? His son, the Reverend Hilary Teage, is the editor."

"Yes, I remember it," said Ben; "he freed himself and his two children."

On their ride to Caldwell, their road lay for a little while along Stockton Creek, the southern fork of the St. John's. They passed the little village of New Georgia.

"The people there seem to be paying a good deal of attention to their land," said Ben.

"Yes," replied Nathan, "most all the vegetables used in Monrovia are raised here. The persons about here are mostly native Africans, and have been slaves. If you could only have seen what poor, mis'able wretches they were when they first came, you would not have thought they would ever have had such comfortable homes."

"Are they considered Liberians?" asked Ben.

"To be sure they are—one of them was sent to the Legislature a few years ago."

"This is the St. Paul's," said Polydore, after a while.

"What a beautiful river!" exclaimed Clara. "It is so wide and full of islands. What are all those strange-looking trees?"

"That tree with the leaves growing out of the top is the palm. It is the most useful tree in the world, I think. I can't tell you what the natives don't do with it. They thatch their houses with its leaves, and make cloth and ropes out of its bark, and wine from its sap, and a great many other things, besides the oil from the nut, which is the most valuable part of it, and is one of their principal articles of trade."

"How do they make it?" asked Ben.

"The natives have a very rough way of managing it. They dig a square pit in the earth, and fill it with the palm-nuts, pounded shell and all together; then the women trample the oil out with their feet. When they think they have pressed it all out, they pour water into the pit, and skim off the oil as it rises with their hands. But in this way, of course, a great deal of oil is wasted; yet it is wonderful how much they make. They sell it to the traders for about thirty-three cents a gallon. You know a great deal of fine soap is made with palm-oil, and so it is always in demand. We have presses to use; and one of our settlers, Mr. Henning, of Bassa, has invented a machine for extracting the oil from the kernel. This is much finer than that which is made from the whole nut. It is as pure as water, and can be made quite hard. Many persons use it instead of lard or butter. The common oil makes very good candles, and can also be burned in lamps."

"Does Mr. Henning make any money by his oil?"

"It sells for one dollar a gallon, and he can make ten gallons a day. You can judge for yourself whether it is profitable or not. The palm is one of our most common trees, so that nuts can always be obtained. Do you see that weed growing through the woods?"

"Yes."

"Well," continued Nathan, "that is indigo. It is a great trouble to the farmers here. We have the hardest work to get rid of it. It grows every where, even in the streets. Once Keziah said she meant to make some use of it, to pay her for all the labor it had cost her, and she made some very nice indigo, that my wife dyed these stockings with; but it was a good deal of trouble, and she has not tried to make any more. The natives make a fine blue with it, and at Monrovia they manufacture it a little. People say a fine living might be made out of it by those who are willing to take a little pains."

"Does cotton grow here?" asked Ben.

"Yes; there are several kinds of native cotton. It grows much higher than ours, and is a tree rather than a plant. Junius, who has been traveling about a great deal in the interior, says that he has stood under a cotton-tree whose branches were so heavy with their bolls that they had to be supported by sticks. He says that the cotton was as good as any he ever saw. The natives manufacture it for themselves. We have never tried cultivating it enough to know whether it will be profitable to us or not. Keziah has one small tree on her place, and she gets cotton enough from that to knit all the stockings her family need during the year, and she has quite a large one."

"There is one thing in its favor here," said Ben; "there are no frosts to ruin the crop."

"Yes," replied Nathan, "the plants will live and

yield a good crop for six or seven years, with but little trouble besides what is necessary in picking it."

"I thought this was the rainy season," said Clara; "but the sun has been shining all day."

"This is what we call 'the middle dries.' It is the pleasantest time of the year, and one of the most healthy. I am glad you came during this season. We shall not have much more rain now till September."

"Is it never any warmer than it is now?" asked Clara; for the cool breeze that blew so refreshingly over her face was very unlike the scorching heat she had expected to find.

"Yes; our warmest weather is in January and February. That seemed mighty strange to me when I first came over here, and I have hardly got used to it yet. In January we have a very dry spell, and if it were not for the sea-breeze, we should suffer from the heat. But yet our thermometer has never risen above ninety degrees, and it is often much warmer than that in Virginia."

"I see a great many rice fields along here," said Ben; "I suppose you have a plenty of that."

"Yes; but the natives raise the most of it. They take very little trouble with it. They just scratch the ground and throw the seed in, some time in April generally, and by August the rice can be harvested. The crops are very abundant, and, though the Africans will not work on their farms more than three or four months in the year, they raise much more than they need. Many of these little dwellings and farms along this river belong to the natives; and we find we can get our rice from them cheaper than if we sowed it ourselves. Some of the farmers are beginning to cultivate it a little."

It was night—one of those beautiful moonlight nights of the tropics when every thing seems bathed in a flood of silver light—before the travelers reached Polydore's farm, where they were to remain until they had decided where they would make their future home.

They had only time to observe that the house, a low building of one story, but covering quite a large space of ground, had a pleasant, well-shaded look of coolness and comfort, when they were surrounded by so eager a group of welcomers, that they had no opportunity to notice any thing farther. Sally and all her children had come over from Nathan's place, and Polydore's brother had joined them, with his family, evidently looking upon the new-comers as old acquaintances. Keziah's adopted children were also there. One of them was married, and settled on an adjoining place; the other was still a member of Keziah's family.

Ben and Clara were too much occupied in asking and answering questions of personal interest to gain many new ideas on the subject of Liberian affairs; but the next morning Keziah took them over her farm, and showed them her arrangements with no little pride. Nathan had warned Ben beforehand not to think that every place in Liberia was as well attended to as Keziah's.

"They might be, easily," said he, "for every settler has the same chance; but some folks are lazy, and won't take the least trouble. They seem to think they oughtn't to be expected to do any thing but open their mouths, and the food will drop into them, ready cooked."

"You know," said Keziah, "that every single man receives five acres of good land when he comes here. He can have a town lot, if he prefers it. If he is married, and has a family, more land is given to him; but never more than ten acres. If he would like a larger farm, there is plenty of land to be bought for a dollar or two an acre. We only have ten acres, though, and find we can raise a great deal more than we want from them. Nathan has more. He has a little coffee plantation that he is very proud of."

"What is this?" asked Ben.

"That is our sugar-mill. Polydore made it himself. We make all our own sugar and molasses, and generally have some to sell, though we only plant one acre in sugar-cane. It grows very high.

Some people who came from Louisiana say it is a great deal larger here than they ever saw it there.

"Here are a few cotton trees," continued Keziah. "I suppose, one of these days, we shall raise a great deal of cotton, for it grows very easily; but we have hardly tried it fairly yet. And here is my arrow-root. Did you notice the biscuits we had this morning, and the bread and cake that were on the table last night?"

"Yes," replied Clara; "they were very white and nice."

"Well, they were all made of arrow-root. You see, it can be raised without any trouble hardly, and when it is ripe, we take the roots and pound them, and throw them into some water, stirring them about for some time; then we strain the water into another tub, and let it stand until the arrow-root is settled at the bottom of the vessel, and we keep on washing and straining it until it is perfectly pure and white. Then we dry it in the sun, and it is ready for use. It is so easily made, and so very wholesome, that we use a great deal of it."

"Do you ever make any to sell?" asked Ben.

"Yes, we sell all we do not want. We have never planted more than an acre with it, and last year I made from it fifteen hundred pounds of the best arrow-root I ever saw. I sold eight hundred pounds for fifteen cents a pound, and made one hundred and twenty dollars.

"This is my orchard," continued Keziah, as they stood in a little grove of fruit trees. "I am not going to let you taste much of the fruit now, for that is the way so many of the emigrants get sick. Polydore almost died from eating too many bananas and pine-apples."

The children found the denial a very hard one. The orange-trees, laden with their golden fruit hanging just above their reach, was a strong temptation, and Keziah could not resist their entreaties. There were a number of lemon and lime trees, and many others which the new-comers had never seen before.

"That is the guava-tree," said Keziah, pointing to one about as large as a peach-tree; "and that other is the mango plum. Those two make the best preserves I ever tasted. I sent some to Mast'r Charles, made with my own sugar, and he sent me back word that they were as nice as any West India preserve. We have a great many other fruits. Pine-apples grow wild all through the woods. There are tamarind-trees all about here, and African cherry and peach trees; and I have two or three cocoa-nut and bread-fruit trees growing near my house. In fact, I can't tell you all the kinds of fruits we have, for I hardly know them myself yet.

"Here is my vegetable garden," continued she. "These are plantains; they are very nice when they are well cooked, and we are never without them through the whole year. Those are bananas; here are my Lima beans. I planted them four years ago, and there has not been a month since when I could not gather the greatest abundance of beans from them. These are sweet potatoes. They can be raised, like every thing else here, with but little trouble, and are very fine. We get enough from this little patch to supply our table nearly the whole year round."

"And there are some black-eyed peas," said Ben.

"Oh yes, we have plenty of them, and Indian corn too, though some of our folks think it is not quite as good as what we had in Virginia; but I don't see much difference in it."

"What is this tall plant?" asked Ben.

"That is the cassada. The root of it is the part we use; we generally roast or boil it, and I like it better than sweet potatoes. The natives almost live upon it. You see them walking about every where with a roasted cassada in one hand and a bunch of bird-pepper in the other, that they use for seasoning."

"That must be what I saw the children eating in New Georgia as we rode through," said Clara. "Every one we met seemed to have a long potato in one hand and something else in the other. What is bird-pepper?"

"Some people call it African cayenne," said Keziah. "It is a kind of pepper that grows all around here. You can find quantities of it through the woods about, and good judges say that it is better than any kind that is raised in other countries. It would be worth while, they say, to gather it for exportation. All that any one would have to do would be to pick the pods when they are ripe, and spread them out to dry."

"There seems to be no end to the valuable plants that are growing wild about Liberia," said Ben.

"Oh, you have not heard half of them yet," said Keziah; "there are ground-nuts that can be gathered by the barrelful, and very fine ginger growing in the greatest abundance. We raise a great deal of it, and make two or three hundred dollars a year by it. But coffee is, I think, what we shall find the most profitable. You can find coffee-trees growing wild through the whole of Liberia. At Bassa many of the woods are full of coffee thickets; and by transplanting scions from them, and taking a little trouble with them, we can make quite a good income in a few years. Nathan planted five acres in coffee about six years ago, and last year he made six hundred dollars by them. Our coffee is said to be as good as that from Mocha."

"I wonder more people don't go into the business," said Ben.

"They are just beginning to understand it," said Keziah. "Judge Benson, of Bassa, has twenty acres of coffee. There are seven thousand trees on them, and from many of these he can get six pounds of berries a year."

"That does not seem much to get from a tree," observed Clara.

"It is a very fair quantity," said Keziah; "they often do not yield as much as that; though I have one tree that I gathered twenty pounds from last year."

"How long do they continue to bear?"

"From ten to twenty years; and I will promise you that, if you will devote three of your ten acres to coffee, you will be able to support yourselves entirely, clothe yourselves, and put your children to school with the produce of the seven acres, and be able to lay by all the money you get from your coffee-trees."

"How much ought that to be?"

"Why, at first it will not be much; but after they begin to bear well, which will be in six years, you ought to make at the very least three hundred dollars a year.

"Besides all these," continued Keziah, "the bean that castor-oil is made from grows wild here, and the Croton oil is made from the seeds of one of our bushes. We have a great many valuable trees, too, that a settler might make a good deal of money by cutting, besides doing the country a good service; for the more it is cleared the healthier it grows."

"What are the trees?" asked Ben.

"Besides the palm, the most valuable of all—and, by-the-way, did you observe our candles last night?"

"Yes, they were quite good."

"They were made of palm-oil. Well, besides the palm, there is the Cam wood. That does not grow much near the coast; the natives generally cut it, and bring it down here to exchange it for what they want. It is used for dyeing, and is very valuable. The gum-elastic-tree, and the trees that gum Arabic, and the copaiva balsam, and frankincense are obtained from, all grow around here; and there are many kinds of timber that are useful for building."

"You seem to have a great deal of poultry," said Clara.

"Yes, we have more chickens, and ducks, and geese than we care about, and lately we have begun to raise turkeys. We have a good many sheep and goats too."

"Have you any cows?"

"Oh yes; but they do not give as much milk as those in America. We have some small native oxen that we use for plowing, and find that they do very well. The people in the interior bring us down plenty of beef, so that we seldom take the trouble to raise any ourselves. We could easily do it if we wished. We have plenty of pigs, and all the care we have to take of them is to keep them from straying."

"I am almost afraid to walk through this long grass," said Clara; "for I heard, before I came here, that Liberia was full of poisonous snakes. Have you ever seen any?"

"I used to see one occasionally when I first came up here from Monrovia, but I haven't found one for a long time; and there never have been half so many as there were in Virginia. Don't you remember how many rattlesnakes Polydore killed in one year there? and the copperheads and moccasins we used to see?"

"But you have a great many insects?" said Clara.

"Yes, we have, to be sure, and they give us some trouble; and the woods are full of monkeys, that do a good deal of mischief sometimes; but the more settled the country gets, the less we are annoyed by any thing of that kind."

"What pretty bushes these are," said Clara.

"That is my fence," replied Keziah; "you see I have only a small place, and I wanted to keep it as nice as possible; so Polydore found those bushes in the woods, and we made a hedge all around our farm with them. It looks very pretty, and, besides, it never needs any repairs."

"Do you and Polydore keep the farm in order yourselves?" asked Ben.

"Oh no. I never do any thing but give my opinion now and then. There are plenty of natives that are glad to help us, and think a shilling a day a great deal."

"By the time they had examined Keziah's place in all its details, the sun was so warm that she thought it unsafe for them to expose themselves to its influence longer. After dinner, in which a nicely cured ham, and plump turkey, and sweet potatoes showed their familiar faces amid a variety of strange vegetables, Keziah left her guests to attend to her school.

This consisted of about a dozen native children, and a few women whom she had collected, and was teaching to read and sew. The African girl whom she had brought up taught them in the morning, and Keziah usually devoted an hour or two in the afternoon to them, being regarded by these ignorant and docile children of the forest as a wonder in learning and skill.

Late in the afternoon she walked over with Ben and Clara to Nathan's place. On their way they passed a farm, where every thing seemed to be growing in wild luxuriance, certainly, but very much at its own will and pleasure.

"That belongs to Polydore's brother," said Keziah; "we can't make him believe that it is at all worth while to take the least trouble to keep things in order. He thinks if he makes as much as he and his family want off his place, he does all that is necessary. But he is very much improved since he came here. At first he wouldn't work at all, but said it was the women's place to do all the planting and raising the vegetables."

They reached at last a substantial farm-house, standing in the midst of a well-cleared and cultivated plantation of about forty acres, which Keziah informed them, belonged to Nathan. The order and neatness in which the whole place was kept, and its flourishing condition, filled Ben with admiration.

"It looks just like him," said he; "I always knew if Nathan had a fair chance he would be a rich man."

Keziah informed them that, besides attending to his farm, he preached every Sunday to the natives, and had collected from among them quite a large Sunday-school.

"The Africans are mighty curious to know how to read," said she; "they think that it is the book learning that makes us so much ahead of them in every thing. One of their kings, Joe Harris, said that 'God made first white man, den black man; den God held out both his hands—book in one, rice and palm oil in other. White man choose book, black man choose rice and palm-oil. Book tell white man how to get every thing else; black man never get nothin' but rice and palm-oil.'"

"Have you good schools here?" asked Clara.

"Yes, we have very good schools, and they are all free. They are supported by the different churches and societies in America. There is one at Monrovia that people say is equal to any common school the white folks have at home. We have three high schools, perhaps more, for I remember, when I was last at Monrovia, they said there were to be two more established; and we are trying to get up a college."

In talking with Nathan, Ben asked him if he had ever wished to go back to America.

"Never for one minute," said Nathan, with energy; "the first moment I stepped my foot on Liberia, I felt like a different man; and if I had known that I should have died in the first six months, I would not have regretted my coming. It is a blessed thing to be able to bring up a family of children where they need not be ashamed of their color, and where their feelings as well as their rights are respected.

Besides, they have such a good opportunity to make something of themselves here. I intend this little fellow," said Nathan, putting his hand on the head of a bright-looking boy about ten years old, "to be a senator or a judge, if not a president. He is a native Liberian, and I mean him to show the world what stuff they are made of."

"You seem to be quite proud of Liberia," said Ben, smiling.

"To be sure I am," replied Nathan. "When I think how little while it is since we have been any thing at all, I am surprised at the improvement we have made. I do not believe there ever was a nation before that has grown so rapidly. And the natives look up to us as something wonderful. Soon after I first came here, one of the kings, Long Peter they call him, said to Junius,

"'Here am I and my tribe, always afraid lest the bigger kings get mad, or get poor, or want goods; then they come pounce on us, steal us, handcuff us, whip us, sells us slaves over the seas. Now settlers no such fear. Here I, my tribe, Devil King make us drink sassy-water—we die—we don't want to die—we die—settlers don't drink sassy-water—I'll be settlers—I'll be.' And he was almost beside himself with joy when we consented to receive him and his people under our protection."

"Don't these natives give you any trouble?" asked Ben.

"Very seldom. Last November Cresson, or, as the natives call it, Fishtown, was attacked for the second time by Grando, the chief of the tribe of Fishmen, and afterward they made an attempt on Bassa Cove; but President Roberts went to the assistance of the people with some men, and the natives fled directly. Such things are very uncommon though, and the Africans are generally urged on by the traders. In this part of the country there is not the slightest danger, and in fact nowhere but in the extreme outskirts."

The next day was Sunday, and the new-comers were taken to a plain but comfortably-thatched church, where they heard a very good sermon from a missionary in the morning, and one in the afternoon from a colored clergyman. The Sunday-schools were well attended by the natives as well as the Liberians, and among the congregation Nathan pointed out to Ben several, who, he said, were converted Africans. One of them was a teacher in the Sunday-school, and also officiated occasionally as a missionary.

"The Baptist mission among the Bassa tribe has been for two or three years conducted by a native African and four native assistants, who were all educated in Liberia," said Nathan.

One morning, a few days after Ben's arrival, he was awakened by the firing of a cannon, and numerous guns and pistols, at short intervals. He had been dreaming of America, and sprang up in great haste, thinking that it was the Fourth of July. He soon recollected himself, and said with a smile to Polydore, whom he found out enjoying the cool morning breeze,

"What does that noise mean? I thought, when I first woke up, that it was Independence day."

"So it is," said Polydore; "it's our Independence day. The twenty-sixth of July is the day we keep here. I was in Monrovia last year at this time, and we had a procession there, and an oration, and some very good music too. I wish we could have taken you there to spend the day; but we was afraid you might be made sick."

"I do not feel very well this morning," said Ben; "my head aches, and I have a little fever."

"I s'pose you is going to have the 'climating fever; people generally has it when they fust come over; but it won't last long if you keep your spirits up—not more than a week or two. Keziah is a fust-rate doctor; she has nussed I don't know how many people through it, and knows jest what to do."

"But is there no regular doctor about here?" asked Ben.

"Oh yes; we has a white doctor and a colored one. I don't know which is the best, for I's thankful to say I never needs one; but some folks likes one best, and some the other."

Ben's illness lasted only four or five days. At first it was rather severe, and he was somewhat alarmed; but Keziah, knowing by experience that the most effectual cure in such cases was to prevent the patient from desponding, and to keep his mind as calm as possible, assured him that he was in no real danger.

"Just think you are going to get well," said she, "and you will sure. I never knew it fail. But give up, and expect to die, and I don't know nothing that will do you any good. I know 'zackly how this fever works, and I tell you if you only keep up good courage, you will be well in a week."

Thus encouraged, and with every thing around him calculated to cheer and animate him, Ben soon threw off his temporary illness. Clara was even more fortunate than he; for, being naturally of a more tranquil temperament, she was less affected by the change of climate than he had been. Their children also suffered very little; and within a month after their landing, Ben and Clara acknowledged with thankfulness that they had never felt better in their lives.

"People don't always get off clear with one fit

of sickness," said Keziah; "sometimes they have several attacks in the first few months. But, if you take proper care of yourselves, you won't be likely to be sick again. People that's imprudent must suffer for it."

Ben selected his ten acres as near Polydore's and Nathan's as he could. A little cottage was put up for him for fifty dollars, that was amply large enough for his family.

"The first house I had built," said Nathan, "cost only twenty-five dollars, and it lasted me five years. I thought it was mighty nice then; but we get proud after we have lived in Liberia a little while. Don't you notice the difference, Ben, between the colored people here and in Virginia. I can tell a man that's been raised in Liberia from an American as soon as I see him."

"How?" asked Ben.

"Why, they seem more like men. You know Ben, you never felt like a man in America."

"No," said Ben, with some reluctance; "I used to try mighty hard, but I never could feel like any thing but a nigger."

"Well, here you forget all about your color in a little while, and every body else that comes here, white or black, seems to do so too. See if it isn't so."

Ben did notice, and by his observations he received the same impressions so clearly stated by the Rev. Mr. Gurley, in his report concerning Liberia to the Senate of the United States, where he says:

"From personal observation, I may speak with confidence of the mighty effects wrought upon the intellect, hopes, and purposes of the authorities and people of Liberia, by the freedom which has ever been theirs upon that shore, and by the high position which they have now taken of national independence. Some of the most distinguished men in the republic are among those who went thither in childhood, have received their entire education in its schools; and bear in their manners, their whole deportment, and upon their very aspect, the signs of a just self-respect, of subdued passions, of virtuous resolution, and of a mature and well-disciplined judgment."

The opinion of Dr. Durbin, well known as one of the most prominent divines of the Methodist Episcopal Church, also founded on facts coming under his own knowledge, should not be without its effect. In an address to the House of Representatives in the capital of Pennsylvania, he observed:

"I am a native of, and was reared in a slave state. I have seen the colored man under all conditions in this country, from the rice plantations in Georgia and South Carolina, to the cold regions of

Maine and Canada. I know his position and capabilities in America; I know he never can obtain freedom and equality before the law of the Legislature, and still more imperious law of society; he can not obtain such freedom and equality as his heart naturally and justly yearns after. The differences between his race and ours are such, that political and social equality is impracticable. What changes, moral, political, and physical, agents acting through centuries to come may work out tending to assimilate the white and colored races, no man can foresee. We are called on to act under the present conditions of the case; and to act for the good of the colored man, and for the honor, safety, and peace of our country. I say, then, knowing as I do the positions and capabilities of the colored man in America, he can not attain to the functions and enjoyments of a man among us. He is not, and can not be free in the proper sense of the word; the pressure that keeps him down is irresistible; he can not rise to a manly hope or ambition; he can not develop his powers here, and show what he could do if circumstances were favorable. If by industry and good fortune he make money, and rear a family of sons and daughters in a respectable manner, where will he find suitable alliances for them? I need not pursue this subject. I have talked with such, and found them faint and discouraged with the prospects before their children.

"But transport these people to Africa, with our religion, our civilization, though in a low degree, and our political institutions, and experience has shown that there they become men, and show themselves to be men. After large opportunities, and long and patient observation, I am persuaded that nowhere else but in Africa is the African *a man.* I have reason to know that there he is a man. Shortly after I went to New York, to take charge of the missionary affairs of our whole Church, I received large dispatches from our African mission. Among them were the minutes of our mission conference in Liberia, composed wholly of some twenty colored men; also the annual report of the superintendent of the mission; together with reports on education, on Church property, and the extension of the mission, and on various subjects. Upon opening the papers, I was struck with the clear, bold hand in which they were generally written; and, upon reading a portion of the annual report and minutes, I was astonished at the perspicuous arrangement of the matter, and the clear and forcible language in which it was expressed. I turned to the clerk, who had been accustomed to see dispatches from Africa, and asked him if colored men wrote these papers. He smiled, and replied there is no white person in the colony, except one lone woman, Mrs. Wilkins, a martyr to the education of the children of the colonists. The position, the circumstances of the African colonist in Liberia make him a man and give him action. Transplant him there, and he becomes a man, and takes place among men. His descendants, in a few generations, may stand forward grandly in the affairs of this world."

Ben experienced in his own spirit the invigorating effects of the moral atmosphere of Liberia. His ambition once more aroused, and his energy called into exercise by objects worthy of it, he soon laid aside the habits of indolence into which he had fallen during the latter part of his life in Philadelphia, and set himself so vigorously to work clearing and cultivating his farm, that eight months after he landed at Monrovia, he sent word to Mr. Peyton, through Junius, that "he was living of his own, enjoying vegetables of his own raising, and that he and his family had never been in better health or spirits, and that he was already beginning to feel proud of being called a Liberian."

And well might he cherish the title. But thirty years had passed since the colonists first landed, a little band of weak men on the coast, and but four since they became a nation, and already their influence was felt by nearly a million of people. Wherever their power extended, the slave-trade died away;

abolished by their firm, though gentle control more surely and effectually than by all the armaments of England or America. More than six hundred miles of a coast once dotted by barracoons, and given up to that abominable traffic, were now freed from its accursed influence.

The independence of Liberia had been acknowledged by Great Britain, France, Belgium, and Prussia. Its reputation and commerce was rapidly increasing, and its influence over the natives was astonishing. Though there were not, in 1852, eight thousand emigrants in Liberia and the Maryland colony together, yet they had nearly two hundred thousand Africans living in their republic and submitting to their laws. More than three times as many had given up the slave-trade as the first step toward becoming their allies. And without being reproached as an enthusiast, the calmest mind might regard it as a moral certainty that the time would come when all Central Africa would look to Liberia for protection, for instruction, and for laws, as well as for Christianity.

CHAPTER IX.

AFRICA.

The voice of my departed Lord,
" Go teach all nations," from the Eastern world,
Comes on the night air, and awakes my ear,
And I will go.

ANON.

THE fifth article of the fifteenth section of the Constitution of Liberia has the following provision:

" The improvement of the native tribes, and their advancement in the arts of agriculture and husbandry, being a cherished object of this government, it shall be the duty of the president to appoint in each county some discreet person, whose duty it shall be to make regular and periodical tours through the country, for the purpose of calling the attention of the natives to these wholesome branches of industry, and of instructing them in the same; and the Legislature shall, as soon as can conveniently be done, make provision for these purposes by the appropriation of money."

Although the Liberians have not yet been able in their short existence to carry out this purpose to any extent, yet, through Mr. Peyton's liberality, Junius had, almost from his landing at Sherbro, been at liberty to devote himself to this cause. While the other emigrants waited at Fourra Bay until a home could be found for them, he, unfettered by any ties, resolved to comply with Mr. Peyton's wish, and act as a missionary among the heathen tribes around him. Freely he had received, and freely he was willing to give.

He found the people sunk in the deepest ignorance and superstition. They, indeed, acknowledged a God as the creator of the world, but worshiped the devil as the ruler of human affairs; and their mode of worship, their actions and feelings, were such as the spirit of evil might be supposed to have inspired. At the entrance of almost every village which he visited, Junius found a pole set up, with a rag or a few fibres of the bark of some tree dyed black fluttering at the top. This the people considered sacred, and called their gree-gree pole; and the mysterious motions of the gree-gree, as it waved in the wind, was supposed to prevent the entrance of the devil or conciliate his favor.

Besides this general gree-gree or charm, each house and individual had their private gree-grees or fetiches, which they regarded as endowed with intelligence, and possessing power to do them evil or good, according to their deserts. By means of these, they thought that their priests were made acquainted with the most secret thoughts and intentions of their owner. The gods to which this benighted people attribute this power, and to which they pay awful reverence, are pieces of yams, broken pots, feathers of fowls, horns of animals, broken bows and arrows, knives and spears. To these they erect altars, and place before them dishes of rice, maize, and fruit. Those who can afford it, sacrifice weekly to them a cock or sheep.

In the centre of some dense forest, a portion is selected, and called the gree-gree, or devil-bush. Into this no woman or boy is allowed to intrude, under heavy penalties ; but once a month the headmen meet there, and sacrifice to the power of evil a goat or some other animal; and the control of the oracles that proceed from the devil-bush is absolute over the ignorant African.

The belief in witchcraft was and is universal, where the spirit of Christianity has not shed its blessed light. This gives the priests immense power over the inhabitants.

Dark and magical rites, incantations, and barbarous customs are continually practiced, accompanied by all the terrors that the dread of a malignant being and the fear of unknown evil can invest them. Upon the death of any one, excepting infants and aged persons, the cry of witchcraft is immediately raised, and the friends invariably institute an investigation to discover who "made witch" for the deceased.

The power of determining the question rests with the priests, and is one of the chief sources of their influence over the people. They have several ordeals, to which all who are objects of suspicion are forced to submit. Sometimes they are obliged to grasp heated iron, or to plunge their hands into boiling oil; if innocent, it is alleged that they suffer no pain; if they are burned, they are punished as guilty. The most common and severest test is the ordeal of sassy-wood. This is regarded as infallible. The suspected person is forced to drink a strong decoction of the bark of the sassy-tree. This is sometimes soon thrown off the stomach, when the individual is regarded as innocent; but this seldom happens, and when it does not, the sufferer is invariably condemned to death. At one time Junius arrived at a village a few miles from the coast just after the death of the headman. A secret investigation was going on to discover the witch. Anxious to see the result, he remained. For a long time the search was fruitless. At length a gree-gree man, by continued incantations and daring diabolical communications, succeeded, and the hapless murderer was brought to light. He protested his innocence in vain. The result of the ordeal was unfavorable, and he was condemned to die. Junius exerted all his influence against the sentence; but in vain. He remained with the tribe two weeks, and during that time three persons fell victims to this practice. The other two were women, who were accused of causing the death of a man who died from a wound he had received in battle.

This ordeal is so powerful an engine of state policy, that the kings are unwilling to abandon it. It is the right arm of an African monarch. By keeping on terms with the gree-gree men, they can rid themselves at any time of a dangerous or aspiring subject. And the priests can so arrange these tests as to make them produce any result they wish. By weakening or strengthening the decoction of sassy-wood, they can make it innocent or fatal, as interest or inclination may lead. If the trial is to be made by heated oil or iron, they can, by previous application of some preparation to the part to be operated upon, enable it to resist the effect of heat, and the accused escapes uninjured. Thus this system puts the life of the whole community in the hands of the priests, who, of course, would use every effort to perpetuate a custom so favorable to their power. But wherever the power of Liberia extends, whether over the native tribes who have become their fellow-citizens, or over those who are only their allies, these mock trials have been abolished. If that had been all that this settlement had effected for our common humanity, it would be enough to repay those who established it for all their efforts.

Junius also found slavery prevailing among all the tribes he visited. And the condition of the slaves was indescribably worse than any thing that he had ever seen, or heard, or imagined before. By far the greater number of the people were in a state of the most abject servitude to masters, who, without the slightest compunction, would inflict on them the severest punishment, and would even kill and eat them, or throw them alive on the funeral pile at pleasure.

He had heard a great deal of the power of the King of Dahomey, a country lying in the interior of Africa, nearly two hundred miles from Liberia, and he resolved to venture upon a visit to that place. On his way there, he narrowly escaped twice from the hands of the slave-hunters. Once he was obliged to conceal himself in the forest for several days, and at last crept out to take refuge in a large village that he had passed through a few days before.

He found it dismantled and in ruins. A few old people sat in despairing apathy amid the desolation, and the wail of some neglected infant arose occasionally on the air. Junius asked the cause of the change, so great and sudden, and learned that the slave-hunters' had made a sudden descent on the village the night before, and left not a single strong man, or woman, or child in it. A few years after, he passed over the same spot, and it was so overgrown with rank grass and bushes, that he could hardly realize that it had not long before been the abiding-place of so many people, happy and contented in their few wants, and the abundant provision nature had made for them. Nor was this a single instance, but as years rolled on, many other similar cases came under his observation.

As he went farther into the interior, he found a great improvement in the country as well as the people. The land gradually became higher and more hilly. There were no burning sands or unwholesome swamps as along the coast, but an undulating surface of hill and valley, covered with trees larger and loftier than any that he had ever seen before. Beautiful streams of cool and pure water crossed his path at short intervals; and the soil was evidently of exceeding fertility.

But though rich in all natural resources, the large country through which Junius had to pass was very thinly peopled, owing to the devastating wars and slave hunts of which for more than a century it had been the theatre. The region lying near Dahomey was subject to the inroads of this terrible people, whose king derived all his revenue from the sale of his slaves.

At last he reached Dahomey, and found his way to its capital unharmed. Taking his stand under a palm-tree that grew near the houses, he began to tell the idle throng that soon gathered around him some of the more important truths revealed in the Bible. They discovered that he was from Liberia, of which place they had heard wonderful accounts. Without heeding the precepts he was enforcing, they began to ask him all kinds of questions, some idle and childish, and others showing a great degree of acuteness. At last rumors of an American having come to his dominions, reached the ears of King Gezo, who commanded him to be brought to his presence. A troop of Amazons, the king's female guard, and his bravest and most trustworthy soldiers, were drawn up to receive the stranger, and impress him with a feeling of awe. All around the king's residence the ground was paved with human skulls, and Junius was obliged to push them away as he walked if he did not wish to stumble over them.

He found the king, a commanding, intellectual-looking man, proud, stern, and haughty, simply dressed, and sitting amid his wives and ministers. He asked Junius many pertinent and comprehensive questions about the objects and state of the settlement at Liberia. Junius answered them satisfactorily, and went on to tell him about many of the strange things to be seen in America, about the condition of the civilized portion of the world, and their wonderful inventions.

While they were conversing, word was brought that a town, that had long held out against the Dahomans, was at last reduced to submission.

"That would please my father," said King Gezo; "I must let him know it. Send a slave here."

A slave entered calmly. The king gave him the message to be delivered to his father, and when he had finished, at a nod his prime minister arose, and, taking a rude ax, in one moment the slave's head rolled in the dust.

"I have forgotten something," said the king; "send me another."

Another entered, and, the message being finished, the same scene occurred.

Junius looked on in horror.

"Why is this?" asked he.

"My father is in the land of spirits," said the king; "is there any other way to communicate with him?"

Junius had heretofore used all his eloquence to excite a feeling against the slave-trade; but now he thought that even to live a slave would be preferable to so uncertain a tenure upon existence as the subjects of King Gezo possessed. He suggested to that monarch the pecuniary advantage he might derive from selling those whom he sacrificed so wantonly. The king proudly answered,

"I have killed many thousands without thinking of the slave-market, and shall kill many thousands more. Some heads I place at my door, others I throw into the market-place, that people may stumble over them. This gives a grandeur to my customs; this makes my enemies fear me; and this pleases my ancestors, to whom I send them."

Junius found it impossible to convince him of the enormity of this practice, or to induce him to set the least value upon the life or comfort of a slave; but he listened to him with a degree of forbearance and respect that could only be accounted for by his clear perception of the superiority of the civilized man over the savage, and he seemed to desire the friendship of the Americans, as he called the Liberians, rather than their enmity.

The missionary did not remain long there, for he saw that the time had not yet come when the Gospel might be proclaimed with any prospect of success in that bloody land. He went where he could employ himself more usefully than in gratifying the idle curiosity of the vacant-minded savages, who crowded around him daily to question him.

There were many kings who received Junius with great kindness, and listened to him with the utmost respect. One of them went so far as to wish that "his son had been a slave in America, that he might have learnt 'Merican fash." He asked Junius to take two of his children to Monrovia, that they might learn what they could there, saying, that he wished them to be wiser than their father.

As the principles and character of the settlers of Liberia became better known, a missionary from among them was welcomed with increasing warmth, till at last their eagerness for teachers, or men with the "book," as they called it, became so great that it was almost painful.

A few months before Ben's arrival in Liberia, Junius had been on one of his usual tours through the interior, visiting, as far as he could, every native village within twenty miles of Liberia. He found that a great change had taken place among the people since he first journeyed through their towns. The desolating wars that each petty tribe had felt obliged to keep up with their neighbors in self-defense had ceased. The quiet of a universal peace prevailed throughout that once-troubled land. Never had they been so willing to listen to God's messenger, or so anxious to learn His will. In whatever place he stopped, he had only to say, "I wish to talk God palaver to you," and in a few minutes a crowd would be assembled to listen to what he had to say. Neither was it necessary to use flattering words, nor to speak with respect of their superstitious observances. With the utmost boldness he was accustomed to denounce their ordeals, their gree-grees, and their fetiches, as delusions of the devil, and to tell them that to God alone they must look for salvation; and kings as well as people would listen in meek submission to the words of one, who swept away as cumbering rubbish the whole system of worship on which they had been accustomed to rely for temporal and eternal safety. They seldom argued against or opposed his teachings, but would say, "We never prayed to God; we don't know how to come to him. How must we seek God? What must we do to find him? How can we forsake our sins?" And not withheld by the pride that often prevents the civilized man from openly acknowledging his dependence on his Maker, when the missionary revealed to them the only way of approach to Him, they might often be seen the same hour kneeling, king and people together, imploring the mercy of God.

Of course there were difficulties to be overcome and privations to be endured on these journeys. After toiling all day over hills and through the thick undergrowth, Junius was often obliged to throw himself upon the bare earth at night, without food, and sleep with no protection but a fire from the leopards and other wild animals that infested the forest. But he forgot all his sufferings when he entered one of their villages, and met the warm reception of the people, and saw how anxious they were to hear and learn the truth. Often they pressed him with such urgent entreaties to remain, that it was with difficulty he could force himself away from them. There was hardly a town through which he passed where a teacher might not have found full employment—and what employment yields so rich a harvest as this of teaching the inquiring heathen?—but there were no laborers ready for the work. The Macedonian cry, uttered with an earnestness that almost amounted to agony, was heard on all sides; but there were few who seemed willing to emulate the self-devotion of St. Paul.

Junius had a favorite project to which he had directed his thoughts and exertions during this last tour. It was to select some spot that would be eligible for the location of an inland colony. He found it easy to do this. After traveling a few miles from the low lands lying along the coast, the country became at once beautiful and healthy. No longer level and marshy, but hilly and undulating, with clear streams flowing through it, and shaded by dense forests, there was no malaria to dread or guard against.

The great difficulty was not to find a suitable place for a settlement, but to obtain settlers who would be fitted for their work. If he could but see established in these dark places of the earth a Christian colony, "with their houses, barns, and mills, wagons, roads, fences, farms, and waving fields," with their schools, their churches, and the influence of their regular and Christian life, he felt that one great step would be taken toward the conversion of the whole surrounding country.

Pent up within their coasts as the Africans are, with no large gulfs or rivers, as in Europe and America, giving free access from the ocean to their farthest centre, almost the only way of reaching the inland tribes to do them any permanent good, is by planting Christian colonies among them, from which an influence may radiate that will transform the whole continent.

Much has been done for Africa in the last thirty years. The first step, in all enterprises the most difficult, has been taken and proved successful. Liberia has outlived the doubts of the weak-hearted, the sneers of the disbelieving, the open opposition of its foes, and is now a great and triumphant reality. But much yet remains to be done. The promise so assuredly given, that "Ethiopia shall stretch out her hands unto God," is on the verge of fulfillment. Let not the heavy blame of delaying that blessed event one day or hour rest on the head of those to whom Providence has intrusted so many of its exiled and homeless children.

APPENDIX.

APPENDIX.

We have subjoined in this Appendix documents for the most part written by colored persons from and about Liberia, showing the estimation in which that country is held by those who have the best opportunity of judging concerning it. Only a few letters are inserted, not for any want of materials, for enough could be obtained to fill a volume, but because the main object was to show that the statements in the preceding work have not been exaggerated. Most of the writers are well-known inhabitants of Liberia, whose names are sufficient guarantees for the fidelity of their assertions.

The American Colonization Society, commenced amid distressing discouragements, now occupies a commanding position, having branches or co-operating societies in nearly every state and territory in the Union. A few years will see the national government engaged in this great work of colonizing the free colored people in Liberia.

BEVERLY R. WILSON.

Mr. Wilson is an emigrant from Norfolk, Virginia. He was a freeman, and exercised the office of a clergyman, while he supported himself by his trade as a carpenter. In 1837, he went to Liberia for the purpose of examining the colony. On his return, he made an Address to the Free People of Color in the United States. In it he says:

"After more than a year's residence in Liberia, I have returned to the United States. I went to satisfy myself; I sought every opportunity of informing my mind. Some of the things already said about the colony are a fair and candid exposé of things as they exist; other persons are too favorable in their estimates; while a third class, with hearts bleeding for the loss of friends, or angry at the loss of property, have wielded their pens to bring the whole scheme into disrepute. I hope to correct these statements. The facilities held out by Liberia are rarely equaled. Industry and economy meet with a sure reward. For proof, look at a Williams, a Roberts, a Barbour, and others, who, a few years ago, possessed limited means, but who now can live like the wealthy merchants of Virginia.

"The morals of Liberia I regard as superior. A drunkard is a rare spectacle. To the praise of Liberia be it spoken, I did not hear, during my residence in it, a solitary oath uttered by a settler. The Sabbath is rigidly observed and respected.

"If the colored man desires liberty, Liberia holds out great and distinguished inducements. Here you can never be free."

To prove by his actions as well as his words his high appreciation of the advantages enjoyed by his race in Liberia, Mr. Wilson soon sought a permanent home there. After his arrival, he writes:

"I am more in favor of the colony of Liberia than when I left it on my return home. No, there is no place like this for the colored race to be found in their reach, where they can enjoy the same privileges as here. To fly to the North or South is all folly; to go to Canada or Hayti is nonsense; for in either there are obstacles as high as mountains. Here is our home."

In 1840, during the contest with Gatumba, which terminated so fatally for him, Mr. Wilson's eldest son was killed while bearing a flag of truce to the savage tribe. But this, instead of disheartening, seems rather to have strengthened his love for his adopted land. In a letter written shortly after this event, he says:

"Since I have been in Africa, up to the first of December last, I can truly say I have enjoyed almost uninterrupted pleasure; but O, since that time, I have had sorrow. My eldest son was sent by the governor to a hostile native prince with the terms of peace; and this fellow would have nothing to do with the embassadors, but drove them from his town, and they were followed by a merciless mob; and my son, with Mr. Peale, a very worthy man, was slain on the second day of December last. I would give you a detail of the whole affair, but it will be seen in the 'Luminary.' This has caused much grief, but I hope the Lord will give us grace. Pray for us.

"Here, at White Plains, we are doing well. We have been greatly blessed in our own labors. Our native boys and girls make rapid improvement. They read and write. Many of them promise great usefulness, and to be future blessings to their generation, for many of them have already embraced the religion of Jesus Christ. We have a considerable farm under cultivation, and we intend to connect a sugar plantation and a saw-mill to this institution. Our work-shops are doing well. We are making wheels, bedsteads, tables, and other articles, such as are useful in the colony. The native boys are remarkably ingenious. Indeed, sir, there is a glorious reformation going on in this vicinity; and as we believe the present wars are very near at an end, we must look forward to a more glorious day. But I must say that a great deal depends upon the advancement of the colony; for we plainly see, as she grows and strengthens, in the same proportion do the heathen superstitions yield to her influence, and thus the way is open for the Gospel. This we have sufficiently proved. Our first object was to extend our labors as far as possible into the interior, even beyond the general influence of the colony; but we soon found that our labor was lost. Then we changed our labors to the natives under the influence of the colony, and we find that every thing goes on well. My opinion is, that the only thing now wanting is men and means, and the barren land will soon become a fruitful field."

The colony in which Mr. Wilson's heart was so bound up became, in the course of a few years, a nation; and he, with ten others, was chosen to draw up the Declaration of Independence and Constitution. Both documents are such as would do honor to any class of men in any country.

AARON P. DAVIS.

The Rev. Aaron P. Davis was born a slave in Virginia. In 1834, when he was about forty years old, he, with one hundred and nine others, was emancipated by the will of Dr. Aylett Hawes. On the twenty-fourth of October of the same year he sailed with his freed fellow-servants for Liberia, under the auspices of the Colonization Society. Soon after his arrival at Liberia, he turned his attention to the improvement of his mind. He taught himself to read and write. His business as a blacksmith demanded all his time during the day, but he devoted his evening hours to study, and his progress was rapid and remarkable. He is now independent and comfortable in his worldly circumstances, and the successful pastor of the largest Baptist church in Liberia.

Letters from Rev. A. P. Davis

Bassa Cove, October 11, 1849.

A brief statement of things passing under my observation, at the request of Rev. R. R. Gurley.

I came to Africa in the year 1834, in December, had a very severe attack of fever, lost a wife and child. Before I recovered from the fever, in 1835, the 10th of June, the massacre occurred, but I sustained no bodily hurt. The main part of the survivors removed to Monrovia. I remained at Edina. In 1835, November 29, the principal part of them returned to the Cove, and I with them, and the expedition from Savannah joined us. In January, 1836, Governor Buchanan arrived with supplies, and gave employment to all who would work, and encouraged the hearts, and strengthened the hands of every one possessing the spirit and independence of a man. In that year I drew the lot on which I now reside, and built a blacksmith's shop, and followed that business, principally, from 1836 to 1847, when I accepted an appointment as a missionary, in the service of the Southern Baptist Board. I was in low circumstances when I came to the colony, but by industry and economy purchased my tools, built all necessary houses, supplied them with furniture, and paid all debts in less than six years, after making such improvements as made us both comfortable and independent, by laying out town lots, planting fruit trees, &c., cultivating farms, &c. I then accepted an appointment as a missionary, which was not until about the time last written. My time as a missionary is employed in various ways. 1. In the dry seasons, I preach through an interpreter in as many of the adjoining native towns as possible. My circuit embraces eight native towns. The women and children sit on a mat of hides of animals, flat on the ground. I have preached to large and attentive congregations. I think the preaching of the Gospel among them has not been without effect, though not many among the vast number make any profession of religion. All inquire after the day (Sabbath), and many observe it. All seem to be ashamed of their superstitious trust in gree-grees, while others have entirely renounced them. Their views as to a future state are like those of the heathen of other lands. They believe that a man dies and passes into a snake, fish, a monkey, or leopard. They also believe that a person, while living, can transform himself into a bird or animal, &c.

2 I supply destitute churches with the Word of Life, and perform other needful services.

3. In the rainy season I teach a day-school at Bassa Cove. I was present at the organization of the first Baptist Church in the county of Grand Bassa, and took part in the services. I was pastor of the first Baptist Church in the county of Grand Bassa. I assisted Governor Buchanan to organize the first Sabbath-school in Bassa Cove, on the spot where *he now silently sleeps* under those large trees. The first Bible-class in Bassa Cove was taught by Governoı Buchanan in my house. I still have the honor to be pastor of that Church at Bassa Cove. I have not less than 75 members of the congregation, a prosperous Sabbath-school, at least 25 Congoes and other natives besides.

Bassa Cove, October 4, 1851.

VERY DEAR SIR,—Your favor of July 18th came safe to hand; also the file of the " Colonization Herald," and the religious newspapers, by Judge Benson's hand. I sincerely thank you for all. I am happy, indeed, that the coffee I sent as a token of my good wishes for you, and the good cause, reached you, and found acceptance. I hope soon to be able to send some for your market, but at present it brings us a better price on the coast; however, you did not say what price might be relied upon. I also received the letter and books from Dr. Malcom, and can say that they will prove a blessing to my Sabbath-school, particularly the class on whose account I wrote for them. In it are many men and women of families, some native youths. His books prove to be the very thing. I introduced them last Sabbath, to take up the morning lesson only; read Testaments in the evening. Our new settlement (Cresson) is going ahead; I still think it destined to be the greatest sea-port town on the coast.

More natives are to be seen in our town than ever before known. Confidence being fully established, they now acknowledge our power as a government. As a proof of this, the fishermen, who considered themselves so formidable a few months ago, were indicted for giving some of their fellows sassy wood, by which they put each on the trial for matters of great importance, and not unfrequently put each other to death that way. It has a stupefying effect, and operates differently on persons differently constituted. It possesses medical properties, rendering one insensible to pain, on others causing violent vomiting. Some of the fishermen were arraigned, and punished for committing offenses against the peace and dignity of the laws of the republic. Thus I trust light after light will shine, and influence after influence spread, till the vast tribes of Africa be raised to the level of men and women. Education is to do this, to take away their present views and give them better. I rejoice to say, I have lived to see that which I once thought could not be accomplished—the settlement of Fishtown and Grando; the great annoyance to our settlements is now as harmless as a lamb. Why? Because a spirit of bravery, under God, went against him.

Yours truly, A. P. Davis.

ZION HARRIS.

The hero of Hedington is an emigrant from Tennessee. He is a carpenter by trade, and at the time of the attack upon Hedington he was engaged there in building a church and schoolhouse for the Mission. The reader will remember that by his presence of mind and courage the enemy were driven back, under circumstances of such great disparity of numbers, that his success seemed miraculous to the simple-minded natives. Some came from great distances to see him, begging for his "greegree" or charm, and exclaiming "'Merica man's God is God for true."

He is as famous for his skill in hunting as for his bravery in battle. During one year Mr. Harris supplied the Liberia market with more than two hundred dollars' worth of venison, the product of his own rifle; and his promise of taking a boa constrictor is no idle boast.

A few years ago he visited the United States, in fulfillment of a promise made to his father-in-law, the Rev. Mr. Erskine, on his death-bed, to assist his remaining children and grand-children to emigrate to Liberia. He returned with thirteen of Mr. Erskine's descendants.

Letter from Zion Harris.

Caldwell, May 26, 1851.

Rev. R. R. Gurley:

Dear Sir,—I write to inform you that we are all well, hoping you and family are the same. I never will forget you for the great good in telling me and my father about the land of Liberia. I have got a good home. I would not change it for any under heaven I have tried it twenty-one years. I have borne the heat and burden of the day, and it gets better and better. I was eighteen years old when I came here. I have grown to be a man; in America I never could have been a man—never would get large enough. Would my colored brethren believe this? They keep writing to me to tell them all about the country. Let me tell them a little: Liberia has raised up her bowed-down head, and has taken a stand with some of the greatest nations of the earth. She has struck off the stone that bowed us down in America. I have grown so large that I have had the honor and the pleasure of being a member of the Legislature five or six years. Did you ever hear of such a thing in America? No, no—nor never will. I was in America a few years ago; it was all the time, boy, where are you going? old man, which way? I was really tired; I wanted to be a man again; but never found it until I hit the coast of Africa. I even saw the change in the captain; he talked so familiar to you: "What is the matter, Harris? Harris is going to be a man again." Sweet Liberia! the love of liberty keeps me here.

All of you that feel like it, my friends, come on home—the bush is cleared away—you can hear no one say there is nothing to eat here. Why, one man, Gabriel Moore, brought better than two hundred cattle from the interior this year; another a hundred; some sixty, some fifty, &c. There are no hogs there, they say; no turkeys; why, I saw fifty or sixty in the street at Millsburg the other day. No horses; I have got four in my stable now. I have a mare and two colts, and I have a horse that I have been offered a hundred dollars for here; if you had him, he would bring five hundred. If you don't believe it, let some gentleman send me a buggy or a single gig; you shall see how myself and wife will take pleasure, going from town to town; throw the harness in too—any gentleman that feels like it—white or colored, and I will try to send him a boa constrictor to take his comfort. I know how to take the gentleman without any danger. My oxen, I was working them yesterday; and as for goats and sheep, we have a plenty. We have a plenty to eat, every man that will half work. I give you this; you are all writing to me to tell you about Liberia, what we eat, and all the news—I mean my colored friends.

Yours truly, ZION HARRIS.

REV. MR. WILLIAMS.

The subjoined letter from Rev. Mr. Williams will show how he estimates Liberia. Mr. Williams went out in the packet in July, and therefore had been but a short time in Liberia when he wrote. He went from Columbia, Pennsylvania, and is also well known and respected in this city and Baltimore.

Bassa Cove, Liberia, October 5, 1851.

Dear Sir,—I write you a few lines by the packet, to let you know that I have not forgotten the kindness I received from you and the Colonization Society in preparing me for this land of liberty. I never shall forget the heartfelt thankfulness due to the society for helping me and my family here. We had one of the finest passages any one could have. Plenty to eat; a good captain, and one that was kind to all in sickness and health. All hands were good to us. I have not wanted to return once since I left the United States. I was twelve days at Monrovia. It is a fine town; the people are kind, and doing well. I think this is a much better place for new beginners. I had the African fever; myself and wife both took it on the same day. We had it about fourteen days. The doctor says we are over it, though we are weak; but it is not so bad as I expected. Mr. Benson is preparing a house at Cresson for me. It is a fine location for a town —the best one I have seen. I shall be the first one there. I look for more by the September vessel. I shall feel lonely for some time until more arrive.

There is, and can be plenty of every thing raised here. The climate is fine and the land productive. Sweet potatoes of the finest quality, and as good as produced in New Jersey; rice, sugar, coffee. I will send you some as soon as I can get about. I wish you would come out in the packet; you need not fear the fever. I want you to see the finest country you ever saw. Cows, sheep, goats, chickens, and hogs are plenty. I helped to kill a hog since I came here, and saw it salted and smoked nearly as good as in Pennsylvania. It is cool here. I can and do wear two cloth coats. I have not felt a warm day since I left Baltimore. I think all the colored people that can take care of themselves in America had better come here, for this is the place where they will do well. All they need is a small start; and, above all, he is a freeman from the highest to the lowest. If I were seventy years of age, and knew as much as I now know, I would come to Liberia and be a man, and no longer a nigger. I shall write more when I see more; I only write what I see and feel

I am truly yours, LEONARD A. WILLIAMS.

JASPER BOUSH.

Jasper Boush is one of the company who went from Norfolk, Virginia, to Liberia, in July, 1850. And as he was extensively known to be an honest, upright Christian—one of the most intelligent of his class — industrious, economical, and prosperous; standing high in the regards and confidence of the free colored people, he was selected as a fit person to inquire of concerning certain evil reports that have been industriously circulated, viz., that the emigrants from this country can enjoy no health in Liberia; that the soil is sterile, refusing a support to the industrious; that the laws are oppressive, and the government badly administered; and that the few who yet remain are a miserable set of wretches, always sick and sighing to get back again.

His letter is a matter-of-fact refutation of those false and injurious rumors.

Clay—Ashland, Liberia, May 10, 1852.

Truly I am better and better pleased with Liberia each morning when I awake and find myself in it. I could not be prevailed on by any earthly consideration to leave Liberia, or exchange it for any other country. Here I am in the land of my forefathers; here I can enjoy all those rights which a benevolent God hath so liberally vouchsafed to man; here I can exercise and improve my gifts and graces in enlightening, instructing, and exhorting the benighted sons of the forest in the truths of the Christian religion; here I can bow down in the sanctuary of the Most High, or at home, and unmolestedly worship the God of my fathers under my own vine and fig-tree, while none dareth to molest or make me afraid, here my children to their latest generation can enjoy the privileges of freemen in storing their minds with education and useful knowledge, and participating in the duties, &c., of civil government; and here I have as many political, social, and religious rights as *any man any where* beneath Heaven's wide-spread canopy. And should not these considerations endear this my *own* country to me? I say, from the bottom of my soul, with gratitude to my good God for what I enjoy—yes.

In addition to these blessings of situation, I am thrice blessed in the blessings of condition. I live in my own house, on my own farm of eighty acres, and eat every day of my life provisions and breadstuffs of my own raising. I have now growing, as my 1852 crop, a large quantity of cassadas and potatoes, several acres of sugar-cane, several acres of rice, and several also of ginger. I have now to be transported from my nursery several thousand coffee scions, nearly one hundred cocoa scions (not cocoa-nut, mind you, but the chocolate), and about the same quantity of mango plums. My present crop, when it matures, will be worth about $600 or $700. My sugar crop alone will be worth over $200. I will have about one hundred and fifty croos of rice, which is worth from 75 cents to $1 per croo.

I shall labor to benefit mutually myself and my country. I intend to be well represented in the commerce of Liberia, which is now increasing, and commanding the respect of the commercial world. I am convinced fully that agriculture is to be the great dependence of Liberia; *that* will furnish an extensive commerce, produce manufactories, and in every way benefit the country. In America the free colored man can never be "a man." I believe it true that the free colored women are the great hinderance to the full tide of emigration which would have, and, indeed, ought to have poured long since into Liberia. Let them alone, however, if they do not come now, they will *come soon;* if they are so stupidly blind that they can not have an intelligent sight at their own and only interests, I am sure the inevitable force of circumstances by which they are surrounded, the organization of the social elements, both as to the circle in which they move and that in which the whites belong, and the genius of legislation, will soon, very soon convince them of their situation and condition.

Sir, the free colored people can not go any where else but to Liberia, and they are beginning now to know that. They must come, and would to God that they would do it, not compulsively, but willingly and cordially, like rational beings.

I and my family are well; we enjoy as good health here as in America. I eat my allowance every day, setting down at each meal with a good appetite, made so by my industry, and rising satisfied. I tell you that the enjoyment of one's self in Liberia, by him or them who appreciate Liberia, is much like religion—it can well be felt, but illy expressed. Please oblige me by representing this letter, and my special exhortation to brothers Lemuel Bell, John Williams and families, and all my acquaintances, to come at once—*come now* to Liberia, without unnecessary delay. Believe me truly to be yours in Christian love,

Jasper Boush.

The following letter was written by an intelligent and respectable colored man, who left the city of New York for Liberia in October, 1851. It was addressed to a colored friend of his in the city:

Monrovia, Wednesday, April 7, 1852.

With respect to this country, my expectations are more than realized. I have found that the opinion I formed of Liberia while in America was very nearly correct. This country is certainly a most beautiful one, and the climate delightful. I have often thought, since my arrival here, how the better class of colored people, or at least a portion of them, would flock to Liberia if they knew the real condition of the country and people. I always thought that it was their ignorance of the country that caused their opposition to it, but now I am convinced of that fact.

With regard to the United States having claims on Liberia, I would ask if England, France, Prussia, and Brazil would acknowledge her independence if the United States had any rights to or claim on the country? England has made this government a present of an armed schooner, and has a consul residing here. Brazil has also a minister residing here, but of a higher grade than consul; he is chargé d'affaires. The facts are, I think, sufficient to convince any reasonable person that Liberia is really an independent republic, and that the United States has no claim to this country. There is a kind of blind prejudice which keeps most colored people from coming to this country, and for the life of me it is difficult to conceive why this prejudice exists; for in the United States we are exposed to all kinds of insults from the whites, which, in nearly every case, we dare not resent; whereas, in this country we are all equal, and can enjoy the shade of our own vine and fig-tree, without even the fear of molestation. In the United States we are considered the lowest of the low, for the most contemptible white man is better in the eyes of the law, and in the opinion of the majority of the whites, than the best colored man; whereas, on the other hand, in this country there are no distinctions of color; no man's complexion is ever mentioned as a reproach to him; and furthermore, every one has an equal chance and right of filling any office in the government that they may be qualified to fill. Liberia ought to be the most interesting country (to the colored people of the United States) in the world, from the fact that it is the only republic entirely composed of and governed by the colored people, and it is the only country where a colored man can enjoy liberty, equality, and fraternity, without having to encounter the prejudice of the whites, which exists more or less, in some degree, in every country in which the whites predominate. If this prejudice ever dies away, I believe that many generations yet unborn will have passed away before it. Although this country offers many inducements to colored people, yet it is not a paradise; it has a few unpleasant features, owing principally to its being a new country. The most unpleasant feature that I know is the acclimating fever, and that is far from being as bad as most people in the United States think it is. On account of the improvements made, such as clearing, &c., it is much more healthy here than formerly; and also, the kind of treatment best adapted to the acclimating fever is better known. The acclimating fever is nothing more than a simple chill and fever, and persons are affected with it according to the degree of care they take of themselves, and also much depends on the constitution of the person. Some persons have told me that they were sick only one day, and that slightly; while others (I speak of old settlers) had it one week, and some have had it from six months to a year or more. A person is seldom sick more than from one day to three weeks at one time. I have been in the country a little more than three months, and have had several attacks of the fever. The longest time I was confined to bed was one day and a half. The symptoms in my case were a slight chill, followed by a very high fever. I felt no pain whatever during the continuance of the fever, but always after it I would have a slight pain in the back, which soon wore off. I would sometimes be sick in the morning and well in the afternoon. I once had the fever in the forenoon, and was well enough by night to attend a tea party. I am told that all children born here, even the natives not excepted, have the fever while very young. This I have been told by mothers, and I have seen children with the fever who were born here. The general health of the place seems to be very good. A person coming here will not find large cities with splendid buildings, and large bustling populations; but we have only small villages with corresponding populations; you will not hear the sound of numerous carts, drays, &c., but all the carrying is done by native laborers, for the people have not yet begun to use horses and oxen for such purposes. Both may be had from the interior. Bullocks are brought down from the interior, but only to kill. There are at present only three horses in Monrovia; they are used only for riding. I have ridden several times myself. The buildings are generally quite plain, built of wood, stone, or brick. There are, however, some very neat brick buildings in Monrovia, and along the banks of the St. Paul's River. I made an excursion up this river a few weeks ago, and never did I enjoy a trip more than I did this one. The waters of the St. Paul's are delicious to the taste. The river is about half a mile wide; its banks are from about ten to about fifteen feet high, and lined with fine large trees with a thick undergrowth. Among the other trees may be seen the bamboo, and that most graceful of all trees, the palm. This is the most useful tree in Liberia. I have drank the wine made from this tree, and have swung on hammocks manufactured from it, and I have seen very good fishing-lines made from it; besides, numerous other uses are made of this tree. There are four villages on this river: Virginia, Caldwell, Kentucky, and Millsburgh. I saw in many places people making bricks, and busily engaged on their farms of coffee, sugar-cane, &c. I must now come to a close, as I have but little more space to write. I will remark that I advise no man to come here unless he has a little money to begin with. A single man should have at least one or two hundred dollars; although many come here without a cent, and yet do well; but it is generally difficult to get a start in this country without a little means. For my own part, you may infer from what I have said that I like my new home.

ABRAHAM BLACKLEDGE.

We learn that the writer of the following letter, addressed to the Rev. Mr. Pinney, has been appointed consul to Liberia by the British government, in place of Hanson, removed. Mr. Blackledge seems to be a sensible man, and will, no doubt, prove an efficient officer and a valuable citizen to his adopted country:

Upper Caldwell, Liberia, May 8, 1852.

DEAR SIR,—I embrace this opportunity to address you a line. I am still doing what I can to demonstrate that Liberia is a rich and productive country. My crops of cane in 1850 produced 8000 lbs. of good sugar, and 500 gallons of sirup. My crop last year (1851) was not so large—only about 3500 lbs. of sugar, and 250 gallons of sirup. This falling off was in consequence of having to neglect my sugar-cane farm to give attention to J. R. Straw's cotton farm. I sell my sugar at 8 and 10 cents a pounds, which is quite a saving to the people of Liberia. This year I am giving my whole attention to cane-raising, and I have a crop now in the ground which will produce a much larger quantity of sugar and sirup, and beat, possibly, both my preceding crops together. A few days ago, I, with one or two others, noticed, in many hills of cane on my farm, from *forty-nine to sixty stalks.* This can not easily be surpassed, I am persuaded, in any country. I am certainly fully convinced that by industry a man may have all the necessaries of life, and a surfeit of the luxuries, in this very prolific and God-blessed country. I have the privilege, doubtless, of saying what no other person can say in Liberia—certainly before any other could say it, if there is any other who can say it now—that is, I use at my table coffee, sugar, sirup, and molasses of my own raising. I have now about twenty-five hundred coffee-trees, which will very soon enable me to export a small quantity to America.

In connection with my sugar-raising, I would just say, that I have to regret that I have not a proper sugar-mill. In consequence of our very poor facilities, in both materials and manufacturing mills (being compelled to do with wooden fixtures entirely), not more than two thirds of the juice can be expressed from the cane; hence, had I an iron mill from the United States, I, and others who make sugar, could, by even less labor than we now perform in grinding, have at least one third more of sugar, &c., from the same quantity of cane, than we now get. This, you perceive, is a clear loss. You see, therefore, we need some help, both in means and advice, to the development of our enterprise and industry.

These remarks are not confined to sugar-growing, but are in every way applicable to the subject of agriculture in general in this country. I have been here now between nine and ten years, and am able to say something respecting Liberia's resources and the means necessary to their development. By the aid of capital (and where are we to expect it from rather than from the United States?), arrow-root, ginger, cocoa, coffee, sugar, and other products of superior quality can be successfully raised here in large quantities, and exported to the United States, so as to create a competition in the market. Who, then, is sufficiently enterprising among your acquaintances to embark in so noble a scheme, that of developing in Liberia her agricultural resources?

The want of means, together with the holding out no inducement whatever for industrial enterprise, are what have kept me so long in the background. Let us, therefore, have the means, have the *tin*, and let a door be thrown open in your country to invite Liberia's productions especially; let an interest be thus awakened there in our behalf, and an impetus will be given to Liberia, which will force her forward in advance of the age. Be you sure, sir, that agriculture is the dependence, and will become the future glory and greatness of our youthful country. I speak here for myself; others are capable of speaking for themselves. I believe, sir, that all the farmers in Liberia need help in the way I have alluded to.

I am, most respectfully, sir, yours, &c.,

ABRAHAM BLACKLEDGE.

JOHN MUSU NEAPO.

We could not give a more touching evidence of the blessings conferred on heathen Africa, through the instrumentality of Christian education, than in the subjoined letter of Musu. It is but a few years since this consistent Christian was an ignorant Pagan. After acquiring a partial knowledge of the English language, he was admitted into the missionary school of Cape Palmas. This letter is a fine specimen of the happy change he has experienced —his walk and conversation being in beautiful conformity with his Christian profession, and rendering him a most useful auxiliary to the devoted men whose lives are dedicated to the regeneration of that dark Continent.

All spiritual blessings be on my dear friend—whatever the tender heart or the almighty arm of the loving Jesus has to bestow, may it be all yours! What glad news you wrote to me about Mrs. ——. Did you see her? Yes, glad and joy speak to my heart, and laugh come to my mouth. I believe that you have seen her; you told me that you saw her, and that she wants very much to return to Africa as a missionary. I have got a letter from her, and my believing and wishes are one, my gladness and happiness follow after. Oh my happiness is very great; and a good, happy Christian, who is fixed to a point, go where he will, one object is his all. The crucified Savior is his happiness; and this heaven he carries about with him. No time, no place, no circumstances, make any change. He has one Lord, one faith, the same yesterday, to-day, and forever. Come pain, sickness, death, the Savior's love and power bears him up. Come temptations of all kinds, I will be with thee in the hour of temptation, says Lord God. Where he is, nothing need be feared, because nothing can hurt. Oh, my dear friend, the true knowledge of Jesus Christ is certainly a cure for all the miseries which come upon the world by sin. There is no evil of mind or body, temporal or eternal, but our precious, dear Lord is by office engaged to remove. And shall not you, and I, and our friends value and love him? What we set our hearts upon, what can bid so high for them as this adorable Savior?

Dear Mr. Rambo, I wish very much to see you. How glad and happy I should be when I meet you, and Doctor May, and Mr. Hoffman; and then—then my heart will talk to my mouth, and my tongue will speak all what I have done or seen.

I am your affectionate friend,

John Musu Neapo.

JACOB VONBRUM.

The writer of the following letter is a native of Grand Bassa. One of the Swiss missionaries (the Rev. Mr. Sessing), who were invited to Liberia by Mr. Ashmun, took him, when a child, under his charge, and subsequently he pursued his studies in the schools of Sierra Leone. He is employed by the Northern Baptist Board, and has a very good reputation as a Christian and teacher.

Bexley, July 5, 1850.

Reverend and Dear Sir,—In the following lines, which I have taken on myself to address you, I hope to find you in the enjoyment of good health, the same as we are at present. Our mission still continues, with its different operations, in which we are severally engaged, endeavoring daily to instruct the poor, benighted heathen. Not long ago we received a letter of instruction from our Board, that the lead of the mission affairs is now considered to be under the superintendence of my native brother and cousin, Lewis K. Crocker, at Little Bassa, and myself; which serious charge to keep we humbly depend on God to help us. Our schools are still kept daily, this, and that of Little Bassa, where brother Crocker resides. Our children are improving well in their acquisitions of the different branches of knowledge, such as spelling hard words, reading, writing, arithmetic, grammar, natural philosophy, &c. I am glad to state that the grown people of this country, though they have not the privilege of improving themselves by daily instruction, like the children, yet many of them are getting civilized, getting acquainted with the law, political economy, and secular improvement; forgetting their old habits, and adopting those of their civilized fellow-creatures.

I am, dear sir, respectfully yours, Jacob Vonbrum.

ABRAHAM CAULDWELL.

Mr. Abraham Cauldwell was sent out to Liberia by an association of colored persons in New York, to examine the country and prepare the way for emigrants to go there.

New York, November 24, 1852.

Brethren and Fellow-countrymen,—You are aware that I was appointed traveling agent to Africa on the 23d of last December, 1851, by the New York and Liberia Agricultural Association. I returned to New York on the 12th November, 1852, and it now becomes my duty to give you some account of Africa, and of the benefits to be obtained by emigration to that country, and whether there are any benefits to be obtained by so doing, or not. I will endeavor to give you as true a statement as my humble ability will admit. In truth and soberness, it would be needless for me to tell you that Africa flows with milk and honey, or that corn grows without planting. Liberia truly is a garden-spot; her lands are beautiful, her soil is most fertile, her prairies and her forests are blooming and gay, her rivers and streams abound with fish, and her forests with game. Her Constitution is a republican government, and a most excellent code of laws are strictly observed. There are several churches and schools in Monrovia, and they are well filled with people and scholars. The Monrovians are the most strictly moral, if not the most strictly religious people, I ever saw.

I shall now speak of emigration, which I have some knowledge of. In 1823 I emigrated to Hayti, and in 1839 I emigrated to the island of Trinidad, West Indies, and lastly to Africa, where I find a peaceful home, where storms of prejudice never come on account of my complexion. I have been noticing for several years the movements of the Abolition Society, and once thought they were right, and still believe they are sincere and really desire to elevate the colored man. Some of them have shown it too plainly for me to be mistaken. For instance, Mr. Gerritt Smith, who gave away part of his fortune. Many others have also sacrificed their good names and their money. But, alas! how many good men have been deceived. I, for one, have been blind to my best interest. I hesitate not to say that colonization is the only thing to elevate the colored man. It is vain for many of us to talk of settling on Mr. Smith's land, or of emigrating to Canada and settling on land without money, which, comparatively speaking, few have. Africa holds forth inducements whereby the colored man may be elevated, without money and without price. There are many noble-hearted philanthropists, who stand ready, with willing hearts and open purses, to aid in the cause, if called upon. Awake, brethren, to your best interests!

.... The government grants ten acres to each family, and if they want more they can get it for about 50 cents per acre. ...

.... Liberia calls for you. Emancipated slaves are not the men to enlighten a heathen nation, for they are not enlightened themselves. Liberia calls for men of understanding, energy, and capital. Come, brethren, let us leave our beloved country; there is an asylum for you in Africa. You can there raise every thing to make you happy. There is a wide field open for the farmer. If a man plants ten acres of coffee, in four or five years he will realize a handsome income. Coffee requires very little labor, and it would be of more value than what you could make in America in twenty years by labor. Every thing grows abundantly, with very little labor. It is a fine country for cotton, corn, and rice, though cotton is not much planted as yet. .... You can salt down beef, pork, and fish. I would, in particular, recommend farmers to emigrate to that country. Monrovia is decidedly the best market, in my opinion. If you go there to labor by the day, month, or year, you will not make much, for laborers' wages are very low.

I would advise emigrants to take as much house furniture as they need—for every thing they want here they want there—besides a little money, if they can. Mechanics may find work, though wages are low. Men of capital, as mechanics, can do well, and are much wanted. Young men of energy, now is your time. Freemen of the North, Africa calls for you. There you can enjoy the luxuries of life and the freedom God intended for man. To all those who may feel friendly to the cause of emigration to Liberia, and wish to aid the same by giving, I say that donations will be thankfully received and forwarded to Liberia by the Association. ABRAHAM CAULDWELL.

The following letters were for the most part sent to the Secretary of the Colonization Society, Rev. J. Morris Pease:

From William H. Taylor.

Edina, June 6, 1852.

Dear Sir,—I am well, and hope you are the same. I arrived safe after a passage of thirty-seven days from the Capes. I am happy to inform you that instead of being received in Baltimore in chains, as I was told I would be, I was received very hospitably. I am certainly grateful to the society for sending me to Africa. I am perfectly satisfied with the change, only that I had not started in 1842 instead of 1852. Here I stand erect and free, upon the soil of my ancestors, and can truly say to all of my race, you that would be free, Africa is your home, and the only home where he that is tinctured with African blood can enjoy liberty. This alone of him that loves liberty, for it is liberty alone that makes life dear. He does not live at all who lives to fear. Please say to any that may come to your office, that I say, come to Africa and assist us in raising a light that may never go out. Enterprise is what we want to make this country and people equal with any on the face of the globe. Should any of the people of Camden county, New Jersey, come to you for information, show them this letter—tell them that I say there is land enough and provision enough, by industry, for every enterprising colored man in the United States. I find in Edina a fine soil, that will raise any thing that a tropical country will produce. A fine, healthy-looking people, that are kind and benevolent—who receive the emigrants with the greatest kindness, and welcome them to the land of liberty.

Should Charles S. Miller or Benjamin Griffin come to your office, please encourage them all you can, and show them this letter, and tell them to come over and help to fight the battles of the Lord against the mighty. I stop writing to eat my palm-nuts, which are very delicious when roasted; the stone of the nut tastes just like the cocoa-nut. I add no more at present, but when I see more I will add more. I remain,

Yours respectfully, Wm. H. Taylor.

From D. A. Madison.

Buchanan, July 2, 1852.

Most respected Sir,—Liberia is destined to be the glory, the home, and the resting-place for all the dark race. Then let them come home, and rove abroad no longer, and that the chains of all who will or could come and will not may be made tenfold faster, because here they can come and be free. I mean my brethren of color. There has been no disturbance with the republic by the natives.

I believe the American Colonization Society is doing more now to alleviate the condition of the colored race than ever; for I do not know when I have seen as good-looking a set of people as came out in the Ralph Cross and by the Morgan Dix.

I sent you a small box of coffee of my own raising, which I hope you may have got before this time. Our Sunday-school is doing tolerably well, and wishes to be remembered to you and their friends in America.

Excuse my blunders. I think I said to you before that I have not had a day's schooling in my life.

Yours in truth, D. A. Madison.

From Charles Deputie.

Mr. Deputie was born free—a native of Pennsylvania.

Monrovia, January 10, 1853.

Dear Friend,—Through a kind Providence we landed here on the 6th instant, in forty days from Baltimore. All well. I went ashore and met for the first time in my life on the same platform with all men, and the finest people in the world. I never met with more kindness in my life, and every attention is paid to visitors. On Sabbath day there were seven flags flying in the harbor. I attended the Methodist Sabbath-school, and found it interesting; was invited to address it, and made some remarks. There were seventy-five scholars in the school. I have been up the St. Paul's River. It is the finest country in the world. Mr. Blackledge's sugar farm is splendid. Dined with Mr. Russel,

Senator of New Virginia, and think his land somewhat better than some of the rest. The river is sixty feet deep. Every thing is getting along well, and all that is wanted are industrious men and good mechanics. I would say to my friends, that every thing that I have seen surpasses my expectations. Should I be spared to return, you shall see some articles that I intend bringing with me. I wish you would try to make some arrangement with the society to let me off with a free passage home, as I want to labor for the cause, and my means will be far run by the time I get to Philadelphia. Brother Williams intends doing all he can for the cause. We intend to go into the coffee business. Our object is to get five hundred acres of land in one plot, and have it settled by none but respectable people from Pennsylvania; and I think that if you could send some from Philadelphia it would have a good effect.

Respectfully yours, in the cause of liberty,

CHARLES DEPUTIE.

P.S.—The immigrants by the bark Linda Stewart are all well, and almost all have settled at Millsburgh.

From Henry M. West.

A native of Philadelphia—born free.

Buchanan, January 17, 1853.

DEAR SIR,—I avail myself of the present opportunity to address you a line or two, hoping they may find you as well as they leave me. I had laid off to write to you before this, but I have not done so; however, I hope you will take the will for the deed. I have now been a resident of Liberia for upward of two years, and I think I can now safely express my opinion as regards the advantages to be gained by locating here. Unquestionably this is *the* place, and *these* are the shores which are to contain the multitudes which have for ages been laboring under the greatest disadvantages, and who have been allured into the belief that they will not be placed under the inconvenience of removing; but the time has come which proves to a demonstration, more and more, that this is a forlorn hope. Doubtless there are many who a few years ago spurned the thought of leaving, who now turn their eyes in solicitude to various parts for relief, but there is no quarter which presents equal attractions with that presented by Liberia, and they know it; and although they may be men of penetration, who foresee that something must be done, and these may be men of influence, who will exert this influence in a contrary direction, yet I believe the masses will speak for themselves, and such a mighty flood will be poured upon these shores as has not been witnessed since the world began. I have not written any on this subject, but I watched with increasing interest the "signs of the times," as exhibited in the United States, and I am convinced that my impressions are not erroneous. There are many false representations made to deter persons who are anywise inclined to emigrate to this country, but I feel confident that those who use this means to oppose us had better begin to think of some other method, for they will ultimately be exposed in the midst of their base attempts. Truth will eventually triumph over falsehood.

All that Liberia was ever represented to me to be I have found it, with the exception of a few base misrepresentations, to avoid which I spoke to but few of my intentions. I am here, and I am right glad of it. "The flesh-pots of Egypt" present no attractions to me. But to be deprived of my present privileges and advantages would be to me a sore calamity. But I have said more than I intended, and I fear lest I should tire your patience. But when I consider that so many of my brethren suffer themselves to be deprived of rights and privileges which they are constantly attempting in vain to gain; and when I know from experimental knowledge that it needs no such crouching, that the very things they want are within their reach, if they would only make the effort; and when I see that they will obstinately refuse a blessing, in hopes of obtaining what I consider a curse, I can not refrain from speaking. But I am thankful that I discern a ray of light through the heavy darkness—that men, laying aside old prejudices, are beginning to examine the subject in a different light—and hope the day is not far distant when my brethren will cease to contend against their own interests, and when Liberia will have as many friends as now she has opponents.

Pardon me for my lengthy remarks. For the last twelve months we have been blessed with tranquillity, a few rumors of war, but no outbreak. I hope to hear from you shortly. No more at present, but I remain

Yours respectfully, H. M. West.

P.S.—You will doubtless remember me as being one of that company that sailed from New York by the bark Edgar, October 2, 1850. I was originally from Philadelphia, Pa. H. M. W.

From John D. Johnson.

Mr. Johnson for some years kept a shaving and hair-dressing saloon, and also a refreshment saloon, in the Equestrian Institute of Williamsburgh, N. Y. He was well known and esteemed by the community.

Monrovia, January 23, 1853.

Messrs. Bennett & Smith:

Gentlemen,—I promised to let you hear from me when in Liberia, Africa, but although I have been here two months, I can not at this time give you much account of the place. This little republic is so far ahead of what I expected to find it, that your good people of the United States would scarcely think I were narrating truth were I to describe all that I have seen. Liberia is a fine, fertile country. Things of every kind grow here. The people are more comfortable in every respect, and enjoy themselves much better than I have ever known them to do elsewhere. The houses are very large, and are built mostly of brick and stone; they are two stories and two stories and a half high; from 30 to 50 feet front, and from 25 to 40 feet deep. The steps to these houses are composed of iron ore—a substance on which the city is built. Iron ore is as plentiful in Monrovia as common stone is in Williamsburgh.

Most of those who farm it are located on the banks of the St. Paul's River, about five miles from the city, and some are doing well. Allen Hooper, of New York, has been here a little over two years. He had but small means to commence with, but now has one of the best coffee plantations on the river. He has seven thousand trees growing, two thousand of which are loaded with coffee; and he is of opinion that next year all will bear. Next I will mention A. Blackledge, who is making about twelve thousand pounds of sugar a year, and some hundreds of gallons of molasses and sirup—all of which will favorably compare with the best imported articles of the kind.

Sweet potatoes, Lima beans, Indian corn, cassada, plantains, and other table vegetables are raised up this river, which is 25 or 30 miles long. A fine town is situated at the source of this stream; it is called Millsburgh, and contains a population of 800 or 1000 persons—the most of whom employ themselves in making brick and in hewing timber of all kinds for market.

I have not ability to describe the advantages to be reaped in this country, nor have I the time. My business is so much better than it ever was before, that I am constantly occupied in attending to it.

One word as to the fever. My children have all had it; so have all the emigrants who came out with us, except my wife, myself, and two others. None of them kept their beds more than two or three days. The fever is not as bad as it is represented to be. I have seen persons who have lived here for from two to twenty years, and who never had it at all.

This is a great country for men and women who love liberty, and who love themselves, for money can be made here.

Please to give my thanks to the gentlemen in your city whose philanthropy was the cause of my success. I trust you will publish this letter for the information of those who may wish to know something of this country. My next letter shall be longer, and will contain much more information respecting this colony of Liberia—a day-star of hope for the colored race.

JOHN D. JOHNSON.

From Stephen A. Benson.

Mr. Benson was taken to Liberia when a child.

Buchanan, February 1, 1853.

VERY DEAR SIR,—Fishtown was reoccupied on the 11th of October, and the settlement is progressing rapidly—far in advance of what it was before the massacre. The immigrants by the Zeno, Morgan Dix, Liberia Packet, and Ralph Cross, enjoy much better health down there than they did up at this place, and even the old settlers moving there have derived much benefit. It has already commenced attracting settlers from other settlements in this county, and I am sanguine that in one or two years it will be in advance of the other settlements of this county. Physicians pronounce it a good place for emigrants to pass through their acclimation, and I know it to be an excellent place for them to to do well after acclimation. Sharp, Till, and Taylor, by the Ralph Cross, from New Jersey, are doing pretty well for beginners. They seem to be fine, industrious people, especially the two former. They occupy three of the houses I built on the banks of the St. John's River, opposite Factory Island, by direction of your Board, and their produce is growing around them finely. They would have settled at Fishtown had it been occupied sooner.

It affords me much pleasure to communicate, as it no doubt does you to hear, that our saw-mill has been in successful operation nearly three months. It is certainly a great acquisition to Liberia in general, and to this county in particular. The aborigines in our vicinity find abundant employment in cutting logs (timber), and floating them in rafts down to the mill. I assure you they are not idle in this respect; they seem to take an interest in the matter in common with Liberians (proper).

Though gradually, yet how certainly is civilization spreading over this Continent. Please say to the worthy gentlemen constituting your Board, that the pecuniary aid tendered the company (loan) in 1851 may be classed among the most prudent and beneficial acts in the annals of colonization.

I had the pleasure of being handed your letter of introduction, to and by Captain Lynch, United States Navy. I accompanied him up to Bexley on the 8th instant, and found it quite a treat to spend a day in his very agreeable and enlightened company. I am preparing some specimens of coffee from my farm, which he has kindly promised and offered to exhibit at the World's Fair, next June, in New York. I must close by subscribing myself, respectfully,

Your obedient servant, STEPHEN A. BENSON.

From Thomas Mason.

Mr. Mason was born free, in Pennsylvania—went to Liberia a year or two ago.

Cape Palmas, February 3, 1853.

MY DEAR SIR,—In your letter you expressed a desire to know my first impressions of Liberia and Liberian society. On my arrival at Monrovia, Mr. James very kindly invited us to spend the day at his house, which invitation we accepted. While on shore, I became acquainted with quite a number of intelligent ladies and gentlemen. The society at Monrovia I think similar to that of Philadelphia, while that at Bassa Cove and Edina I think less favorably of. I am now living at Mount Vaughan, about two and a half miles from Cape Palmas, at which place I am employed as an assistant teacher in the high school belonging to the Protestant Episcopal Mission, for which I receive three hundred dollars. The society at Palmas, when we compare the number, is equal to that of Monrovia in point of intelligence. This colony is in quite a flourishing condition. There are in Palmas seven yoke of oxen, well broken, and work quite steadily. We get the bullocks from the natives, at eight dollars a piece. I have drawn my farm land, and planted five hundred coffee-trees, twelve pounds of ginger, and a thousand cassada sticks, besides arrowroot, pea-nuts, and fruit trees. We have an abundance of fresh vegetables, egg-plants, tomatoes, and fine large cabbage. Plenty of venison, fresh fish, and oysters. We are on the eve of declaring our independence. The spirit with which the people take hold of the subject would do credit to 1776. There will be a Convention held next week, to prepare a Constitution for our new state.

Yours most respectfully THOMAS MASON.

From Samuel H. G. Sharp.

Born free, in Camden, N. J.

Grand Bassa, February, 1853.

Dear Sir,—I received your letter in answer to mine, and was very glad to hear from you; also to receive those papers you sent me. My health and that of my family is tolerable. At present we are perfectly satisfied, and glad we came here. The society did a good part by us. I have a house and ten acres of good land; all but three acres in cultivation. I do not find it so warm here as I had been told or as I expected. I have tried both seasons. Tell the colored people they need not be afraid to come, but they must be industrious, or they had better stay where they are. I would not change homes now if they would give me five hundred dollars and free toleration. Every man can vote. I visited the courts, where I saw colored men judges, grand and petit jurymen, squires, constables, &c. Business is carried on as correctly as in the United States.

I remain yours truly, Samuel H. G. Sharp.

From Henry B. Steuart.

Mr. Steuart is from the South—born a slave—was freed, and went to Liberia about four years ago.

Greenville, Liberia, February, 1853.

Dear Sir,—You wish that I would give some statement of things in general, and in particular of the growth of cotton, rice, &c. Our answer is this: this is emphatically a tropical region, as all geographers will tell you. You have only to put your seed into the ground, and with half the labor you have to perform in the states you here may make a comfortable living. Cotton and rice grow here as well as in your Southern States. It is true, a fair trial was never made for the culture of that valuable staple (cotton), enough to prove that it can be raised in great quantity. Rice is indigenous to this country: it will grow almost any where you may plant it, on high or low land. We have coffee, potatoes, ginger, arrow-root, and pepper. There has not been much pains taken with the planting of corn; enough has been done, however, to satisfy one that it can be made, for I have eaten as much as I wanted in proof of it.

As respects coffee and other products, for a recent comer and a young man, I need only refer to Mr. Joseph Bacon, one among many others who bid fair to become independent farmers, to say nothing of those who are living at ease on their farms. Come and see for yourselves. Born and raised for the first part of my life among the very best farmers of Liberty county, Georgia, I know that these things can be raised in great quantities.

You wish to know what is my occupation. I answer, a little of any and every thing, from a house carpenter to a boat-maker. I have not yet seen the day that I have regretted my coming to this country. All my objects have been realized, while I have contributed my humble aid in laying the foundation of a civil and religious government.

From J. M. Richardson.

Monrovia, February 13, 1853.

To the N. Y. Emigration and Agricultural Association:

Gentlemen,—Since I have been here I have done very well, better than I expected. I have bought five hundred dollars worth of goods and paid for them. I have bought ten bullocks. I have on hand one hundred bushels of rice. I paid in trade about forty cents. If I keep which I shall do three months longer, I can get $1 50 per bushel for it. I also have on hand six tons of cam-wood. I want to increase it to ten tons by next month, and shall ship it to England by the steamer on the 7th, and remit the money to New York by a bill of exchange, so as to have more funds here in the vessel which I understood will sail from New York with our emigrants in the spring. I had only eight hundred dollars worth of goods when I started from New York. I have on my shelves one thousand dollars worth now. Notwithstanding, I shall send one thousand dollars to New York after more goods. I also have fifty pounds of ivory, worth here one dollar per pound. I write this to show you what can be done here with a very little money. If a man has half what I had he would soon get rich, if he conducted himself aright; if a man has nothing, and came out under our Association, having a house and lands cleared, he would soon rise, if he has any spirit; therefore, come one, come all to the sunny climes of Africa.

Our expedition are all getting along finely; most of them have the fever now, but they are now all able to be about, with a prospect of soon recovering. I was attacked with the fever on Christmas-day, and am now considered entirely well. I, at all events, feel as well as ever I did in America.

I am now in Monrovia, where I have been one week trying to buy coffee scions, but there is such a great demand for them that I fear I shall not be able to get more than a thousand. I want seven thousand to plant in April.

I have had several interviews with the president—I had not this pleasure in the States. He is very affable and gentlemanly; he received me with great cordiality. I should have told you beforehand that he and his lady called at my store, up the river, and invited me to call and see them; they also bought quite largely of my wares. He offered to assist me in any way he could, if I wished any assistance.

As the steamer is about to sail, I must close. Give my respects to all the boys; tell them that I am in good health and spirits; tell them, if they want to feel like men, to come to Liberia.

Please write to me via England; the steamer stops here once a month. Your most obedient servant,

J. M. Richardson.

From William W. Findlay.

Upper Caldwell, Liberia, March 8, 1853.

To Governor Wright, of Indiana:

Sir,—As I look upon you as being an old friend of mine, I take pleasure in addressing you a few lines to let you know something about how we are getting along in Liberia, believing you to be a true friend to Liberia, and to the colored race.

I am much pleased with this country, and I do believe that

every colored man that respects himself as a man would do well to come here, for truly I do think that it is a good country; but, like all other new countries, a man has privations to undergo, and a reasonable man can not expect that he can get every thing here as handy as he can in old, settled countries. But if he has money, he need not lack for luxuries here, and some that he can not get in America.

To be sure, there is some sickness here in going through the acclimation process; but when we come to look at the people who come here, we must expect it. But in the last three or four expeditions that have come out, there have been but few deaths.

Now I shall say something about agriculture and the prospects. This country is, I suppose, as good a coffee and sugar country as there is in any place in the world; at least, it is pronounced so by those that pretend to judge of these things. We may plant coffee, and on the same land raise arrow-root, bird-pepper, or ginger at the same time, and, by so doing, keep the coffee clean after it is planted—raise a crop of arrow-root, ginger, or bird-pepper, which I believe will pay all the other expenses, and will pay the interest until the coffee commences to bear, which will be about the third year.

And now in the States there are several gentlemen that have offered to find men to go into the coffee speculation, which they can not help making money at. If there should be a friend of mine, or a friend to Liberia, who will go into that business, I should be happy in hearing from him. The pepper, ginger, and such things as I should raise, I should expect those who went in with me to attend to in America, to sell these things, and send me in return such things as I should need to carry on business with. If there should be any that would be willing to risk money in that way, I should be glad to hear from them.

I have been appointed a justice of the peace in Caldwell county. Nothing more than I remain your humble servant,

W. W. Findlay.

From Samuel Williams.

Mr. Williams, a free colored man of Pennsylvania, intelligent, respectable, and rich for one of his class, was sent about a year since to Liberia, by an association of his people in this state, who desired to learn the prospects that country held out for the emigrants. The following is an extract from his report:

"Here I must end my advice and my report of what I have seen. Much that is to me deeply interesting I must omit. It only remains for me to return my sincere thanks to those whose friendship has cheered me, in undertaking a voyage fraught with anxiety and peril, but which has richly repaid me. I see in Liberia the elements of a great state. From her borders I behold an influence issuing which shall yet elevate my race in the future to that proud position which it once held in the past. Although they are my birth-place, and the birth-land of my fathers, and endeared to me as holding the bones of a now sainted parent, it is my wish only to remain in the United States until a company can be organized which shall go out together, taking with them a saw-mill and an apparatus for making iron—ore yielding, in Liberia, 90 per cent. In a few months longer, I trust, I shall go to the home of my fathers, there to aid in upbuilding a new republic, and in founding a mighty empire. Would to God I could persuade my brethren every where to go with me, so that after being aliens and exiles, like Israel in Egypt, for so many long years, we might at least die in the land of our fathers.

"SAMUEL WILLIAMS."

The following documents, addresses, &c., all written by colored men, will show the character of the government established in Liberia, and also the character and talents of the people who have formed, adopted, and now uphold just, wise, and righteous institutions.

Declaration of Independence.

We, the representatives of the people of the Commonwealth of Liberia, in Convention assembled, invested with authority to form a new government, relying upon the aid and protection of the Great Arbiter of human events, do hereby, in the name and on behalf of the people of this Commonwealth, publish and declare the said Commonwealth a *Free, Sovereign, and Independent State*, by the name and title of the *Republic of Liberia.*

We, the people of the Republic of Liberia, were originally the inhabitants of the United States of North America.

In some parts of that country, we were debarred by law from all the rights and privileges of men—in other parts, public sentiment, more powerful than law, frowned us down.

We were every where shut out from all civil office.

We were excluded from all participation in the government.

We were taxed without our consent.

We were compelled to contribute to the resources of a country which gave us no protection.

We were made a separate and distinct class, and against us every avenue of improvement was effectually closed. Strangers from all lands, of a color different from ours, were preferred before us.

We uttered our complaints; but they were unattended to, or only met by alleging the peculiar institutions of the country.

All hope of a favorable change in our country was thus wholly extinguished in our bosoms, and we looked with anxiety abroad for some asylum from the deep degradation.

The western coast of Africa was the place selected by American benevolence and philanthropy for our future home. Removed beyond those influences which depressed us in our native land, it was hoped we would be enabled to enjoy those rights and privileges, and exercise and improve those faculties which the God of nature has given us in common with the rest of mankind.

Under the auspices of the American Colonization Society, we

established ourselves here, on land acquired by purchase from the lords of the soil.

In an original compact with this society, we, for important reasons, delegated to it certain political powers; while this institution stipulated that whenever the people should become capable of conducting the government, or whenever the people should desire it, this institution would resign the delegated power, peaceably withdraw its supervision, and leave the people to the government of themselves.

Under the auspices and guidance of this institution, which has nobly and in perfect faith redeemed its pledges to the people, we have grown and prospered.

* * * * * * * * * *

Among the strongest motives to leave our native land—to abandon forever the scenes of our childhood, and to sever the most endeared connections—was the desire for a retreat where, free from the agitations of fear and molestation, we could in composure and security approach in worship the God of our fathers.

Thus far our highest hopes have been realized.

Liberia is already the happy home of thousands who were once the doomed victims of oppression, and if left unmolested to go on with her natural and spontaneous growth; if her movements be left free from the paralyzing intrigues of jealous, ambitious, and unscrupulous avarice, she will throw open a wider and yet a wider door for thousands who are now looking with an anxious eye for some land of rest.

Our courts of justice are open equally to the stranger and the citizen for the redress of grievances, for the remedy of injuries, and for the punishment of crime.

Our numerous and well attended schools attest our efforts, and our desire for the improvement of our children.

Our churches for the worship of our Creator, every where to be seen, bear testimony to our piety, and to our acknowledgment of His Providence.

The native African, bowing down with us before the altar of

the living God, declare that from us, feeble as we are, the light of Christianity has gone forth, while upon that curse of curses, the slave-trade, a deadly blight has fallen, as far as our influence extends.

Therefore, in the name of humanity, and virtue, and religion—in the name of the Great God, our common Creator and our common Judge, we appeal to the nations of Christendom, and earnestly and respectfully ask of them that they will regard us with the sympathy and friendly consideration to which the peculiarities of our condition entitle us, and extend to us that comity which marks the friendly intercourse of civilized and independent communities.

Constitution.

We give Article I. entire, as it is the exponent and guaranty of true republican principles—harmonizing with the Gospel precepts of "loving our neighbor as ourselves," and doing to others as we would be done by—which, we trust, are, by the blessing of God, to be extended throughout Africa.

Article I. *Declaration of Rights.*

The end of the institution, maintenance, and administration of government, is to secure the existence of the body politic, to protect it, and to furnish the individuals who compose it with the power of enjoying, in safety and tranquillity, their natural rights, and the blessings of life; and whenever these great objects are not obtained, the people have a right to alter the government, and to take measures necessary for their safety, prosperity, and happiness.

Therefore, we the people of the Commonwealth of Liberia, in Africa, acknowledging with devout gratitude the goodness of God in granting to us the blessings of the Christian religion, and political, religious, and civil liberty, do, in order to secure these blessings for ourselves and our posterity, and to establish justice, insure domestic peace, and promote the general welfare, hereby solemnly associate and constitute ourselves a free, sovereign, and independent state, by the name of the Republic of Liberia, and do ordain and establish this Constitution, for the government of the same.

Sec. 1. All men are born equally free and independent, and have certain natural, inherent, and inalienable rights; among which are the rights of enjoying and defending life and liberty, of acquiring, possessing, and protecting property, and of pursuing and obtaining safety and happiness.

Sec. 2. All power is inherent in the people; all free governments are instituted by their authority and for their benefit, and they have a right to alter and reform the same when their safety and happiness require it.

Sec. 3. All men have a natural and inalienable right to worship God according to the dictates of their own consciences, without obstruction or molestation from others; all persons demeaning themselves peaceably, and not obstructing others in their religious worship, are entitled to the protection of law in the free exercise of their own religion, and no sect of Christians shall have exclusive privileges or preference over any other sect, but all shall be alike tolerated; and no religious test whatever shall be required as a qualification for civil office, or the exercise of any civil right.

Sec. 4. There shall be no slavery within this republic; nor shall any citizen of this republic, or any person resident therein, deal in slaves, either within or without this republic, directly or indirectly.

Sec. 5. The people have a right at all times, in an orderly and peaceable manner, to assemble and consult upon the common good, to instruct their representatives, and to petition the government or any public functionaries for the redress of grievances.

Sec. 6. Every person injured shall have remedy therefor by due course of law; justice shall be done without denial or delay; and in all cases not arising under martial law or upon impeachment, the parties shall have a right to a trial by jury, and to be heard in person, or by counsel, or both.

Sec. 7. No person shall be held to answer for a capital or infamous crime, except in cases of impeachment. Cases arising in the army and navy, and petty offenses, unless upon presentment by a grand jury; and every person criminally charged shall have a right to be seasonably furnished with a copy of the charge, to be confronted with the witnesses against him, to have compulsory process for obtaining witnesses in his favor; and to have a speedy, public, and impartial trial by a jury of the vicinity. He shall not be compelled to furnish or give evidence against himself, and no person shall for the same offense be twice put in jeopardy of life or limb.

Sec. 8. No person shall be deprived of life, liberty, property, or privilege, but by the judgment of his peers, or the law of the land.

Sec. 9. No place shall be searched nor person seized, on a criminal charge or suspicion, unless upon warrant lawfully issued, upon probable cause supported by oath or solemn affirmation, specially designating the place or person, and the object of the search.

Sec. 10. Excessive bail shall not be required, nor excessive fines imposed, nor excessive punishments inflicted; nor shall the Legislature make any law impairing the obligation of contracts; nor any law rendering any act punishable, in any manner in which it was not punishable when it was committed.

Sec. 11. All elections shall be by ballot, and every male citizen, of twenty-one years of age, possessing real estate, shall have the right of suffrage.

Sec. 12. The people have a right to keep and to bear arms for the common defense. As in time of peace armies are dangerous to liberty, they ought not to be maintained without the consent of the Legislature, and the military power shall always be held in exact subordination to the civil authority, and be governed by it.

Sec. 13. Private property shall not be taken for public use without just compensation.

Sec. 14. The powers of this government shall be divided into three distinct departments, the Legislative, Executive, and Judicial, and no person belonging to one of these departments shall exercise any of the powers belonging to either of the others. This section is not to be construed to include justices of the peace.

Sec. 15. The liberty of the press is essential to the security of freedom in a state; it ought not, therefore, to be restrained in this republic.

The press shall be free to every person who undertakes to examine the proceedings of the Legislature or any branch of government; and no law shall ever be made to restrain the rights thereof. The free communication of thoughts and opinions is one of the invaluable rights of man, and every citizen may freely speak, write, and print on any subject, being responsible for the abuse of that liberty. * * * And in all indictments for libels, the jury shall have a right to determine the law and the facts, under the direction of the court, as in other cases.

Sec. 16. No subsidy, charge, impost, or duties ought to be established, fixed, laid, or levied, under any pretext whatsoever, without the consent of the people, or their representatives in the Legislature.

Sec. 17. Suits may be brought against the republic in such manner and in such cases as the Legislature may by law direct.

Sec. 18. No person can, in any case, be subjected to the law martial, or to any penalties or pains by virtue of that law (except those employed in the army or navy, and except the militia in actual service), but by the authority of the Legislature.

Sec. 19. In order to prevent those who are vested with authority from becoming oppressors, the people have a right, at such periods, and in such manner as they shall establish by their frame of government, to cause their public officers to return to private life, and to fill up vacant places by certain and regular elections and appointments.

Sec. 20. That all prisoners shall be bailable by sufficient securities, unless for capital offenses, when the proof is evident, or presumption great; and the privilege and benefit of the writ of Habeas Corpus shall be enjoyed in this republic, in the most free, easy, cheap, expeditious, and ample manner, and shall not be suspended by the Legislature, except upon the most urgent and pressing occasions, and for a limited time, not exceeding twelve months.

* * * * * * * * * *

The legislative powers are vested in a Legislature, consisting of two separate branches—a Senate and House of Representatives. The Representatives are apportioned according to the number of inhabitants. Two years' residence in the county which elects him, real estate to the value of one hundred and fifty dollars, and the age of twenty-three, constitute eligibility to the office of representative.

The Senate consists of two members from each county. No person can be elected to this office who has not resided three years in the republic previous to his election, who does not own real estate to the value of two hundred dollars, and who shall not have attained the age of twenty-five.

The supreme executive power resides in a president, elected by the people, and holding his office for two years. No person can be eligible who has not been a resident of the republic five years, who shall not have attained the age of twenty-five, and who shall not be possessed of real estate to the value of six hundred dollars. The duties of these several officers and bodies are similar to those in our own country.

The judicial power is vested in one supreme judicial court, and such subordinate courts as the Legislature, from time to time, may establish.

From the Inaugural Address of President Roberts.

The time has been, I admit, when men, without being chargeable with timidity, or with a disposition to undervalue the capacities of the African race, might have doubted the success of the colonization enterprise, and the feasibility of establishing an independent Christian State on this coast, composed of, and conducted wholly by, colored men; but, fellow-citizens, that time has passed. The American Colonization Society has redeemed its pledge; and I believe in my soul that the permanency of the government of the Republic of Liberia is now fixed upon as firm a basis as human wisdom is capable of devising. Nor is there any reason to apprehend that the Divine Disposer of human events, after having separated us from the house of bondage, and led us safely through so many dangers toward the land of liberty and promise, will leave the work of our political redemption and consequent happiness unfinished, and either permit us to perish in a wilderness of difficulties, or suffer us to be carried back in chains to that country of prejudices from whose oppression he has mercifully delivered us with his outstretched arm.

And, fellow-citizens, it must afford the most heartfelt pleasure and satisfaction to every friend of Liberia, and real lover of liberty in general, to observe by what a fortunate train of circumstances and incidents the people of these colonies have arrived at absolute freedom and independence. When we look abroad and see by what slow and painful steps, marked with blood and ills of every kind, other states of the world have advanced to liberty and independence, we can not but admire and praise that all-gracious Providence, who, by his unerring ways, has, with so few sufferings on our part, compared with other states, led us to this happy stage in our progress toward those great and important objects. And that it is the will of Heaven that mankind should be free, is clearly evidenced by the wealth, vigor, virtue, and consequent happiness of all free states. But the idea that Providence will establish such governments as he shall deem most fit for his creatures, and will give them wealth, influence, and happiness, without their efforts, is palpably absurd. In short, God's moral government of the earth is always performed by the intervention of second causes. Therefore, fellow-citizens, while with pious gratitude we survey the frequent interpositions of Heaven in our behalf, we ought to remember that, as the disbelief of an overruling Providence is atheism, so an absolute confidence of having our government relieved from every embarrassment, and its citizens made respectable and happy by the immediate hand of God, without our own exertions, is the most culpable presumption. Nor have we any reason to expect that He will miraculously make Liberia a paradise, and deliver us, in a moment of time, from all the ills and inconveniences consequent upon the peculiar circumstances under which we are placed, merely to convince us that He favors our cause and government.

* * * * * * * * * *

I ask you to join with me in supplications that He will so enlighten the minds of your servants, guide their councils, and prosper their measures, that whatsoever they do shall result in your good, and shall secure to you the peace, friendship, and approbation of all nations.

From another Address by the President.

The following passages are selected from the first message (after the adoption of the present Constitution of the republic) to the national Legislature:

"Our situation, however, for forming a political society, and erecting a free government, is more favorable, in many respects, than that of any people who have preceded us. We have the history and experience of all states before us: mankind have been toiling through all ages for our information, and the philosophers and learned men of antiquity have trimmed their midnight lamps to transmit to us instructions. We live, also, in an age when the principles of political liberty and the foundation of government have been fully canvassed and fairly settled.

"With these lights before them, our delegates have given us a Constitution founded, not upon party or prejudice, not for to-day or to-morrow, but for posterity. It is founded in good policy, because, in my humble opinion, it is founded in justice and honesty. All ambitious and interested views seem to have been entirely discarded, and regard had only to the good of the whole, in which the situation and rights of posterity are considered, and equal justice has been done to every citizen of the republic. And the highest respect has been paid to those great and equal rights of human nature which should forever remain inviolate in every society. Proper attention has also been given to the separation of the three great powers of the state. Indeed, it is essential to liberty that the legislative, judicial, and executive powers of the government be, as nearly as possible, independent of, and separate from, each other; for, were they united in the same persons, there would be wanting that mutual check which is the principal security against the making of arbitrary laws and a wanton exercise of power in the execution of them. If these three powers are united, the government will be absolute, whether they are in the hands of a few or a great number. The same party will be the legislator, accuser, judge, and executioner. What probability, then, as I have heard it remarked, will an accused person have of an acquittal, however innocent he may be, when his judge is also a party?"

Having shown the wisdom of the Convention who adopted the Constitution of the republic in their careful provisions to keep distinct and independent of each other the three great departments of the government, President Roberts adds:

"But, gentlemen, it is to be remembered, that whatever marks of wisdom, experience, and patriotism there may be in our new Constitution, like the just proportions and elegant forms of our first parents, before their Maker breathed into them the breath of life, it is yet to be animated, and, until then, may indeed excite admiration, but it will be of no use; from the people it must receive its spirit, and by them be quickened. Let virtue, honor, the love of liberty, and science be and remain the soul of our present Constitution, and it must, it will become the source of great and extensive happiness to this and future generations."

One other paper from President Roberts merits insertion here, as it indicates a firm determination on the part of the Liberian government to uphold the principles of freedom for all Africans under its protection. The fact that from subjects of Great Britain such violation is now feared, is curious, and should be carefully investigated.*

* From an article on "Slavery in Disguise," written by Rev. J. Morris Pease, nd published in the June number of the "Colonization Herald," we gather that a London company is actually engaged in bargaining with native chiefs of the Kroo tribe in Africa for *men, women, and children,* which this company have

A Proclamation by the President of Liberia.

Whereas Messrs. Hyde, Hodge, and Co., of London, contractors with her Britannic majesty's government to furnish laborers from the African coast for the West Indies, have sent some of their ships to the coast of the republic, offering an advance of ten dollars for every person who may be induced to emigrate; and whereas the extinction of the slave-trade has left large numbers of predial and other laborers in the possession of the chiefs and principal men of the country, while the offer of ten dollars each is nearly equivalent to the amount formerly paid for slaves during the prevalence of the slave-trade, and which operated mainly in producing and sustaining the wars by which the country was distracted;

And whereas certain refractory chiefs are reported to have engaged with the agents of said company to furnish a number of laborers, and are further known to have in concealment, near Grand Cape Mount, a number of unhappy victims of their predatory excursions; and whereas complaint has been made to the government that persons are held to be sent off without their voluntary consent, or the consent of their natural guardians; therefore, to prevent the abuses and evils which might otherwise result from the enterprise,

contracted to deliver to agents in British Guiana and Jamaica, to be employed as laborers. Mr. Pease quotes from the report of Mr. Hamilton, an agent of the British government, sent to negotiate with the negro chiefs for "laborers," as these forced emigrants were styled, showing that the people are under the absolute control of their chiefs, and *must* go when sent or sold. Mr. Pease thus concludes his article:

"It will be seen, throughout the whole of the agent's reports, that the parties with whom they invariably put themselves in communication were the chiefs, and not the people; and they always assumed the right of these chiefs to control their movements. To dignify such a mode of obtaining emigrants as free, is a delusion and a mockery. We close with the remark, that for any individual, parties, or government to negotiate with the Kroo, or any other African chiefs, for the labor or services of their people for periods of years, is really to sanction the principle of slave-trading, and to open the way to the revival, in new forms, of a traffic against which humanity revolts, and which the religion of the Gospel condemns."

Be it known by this proclamation, to all whom it may concern, that the law regulating passports must be strictly observed—that vessels carrying, or intending to carry away emigrants, must come to this port with their emigrants on board to obtain passports—in order that an opportunity may be presented to the government to ascertain whether the emigration be free or constrained. Every violation of the law regulating passports will be visited with the utmost penalty of the law, in that case made and provided.

Done at Monrovia, this twenty-sixth day of February, in the year of our Lord one thousand eight hundred and fifty-three, and of the republic the fifth. J. J. Roberts.

Flag and Seal of the Republic of Liberia.

The following Flag and Seal were adopted by the Convention, as the insignia of the Republic of Liberia, and ordered to be employed to mark its nationality:

Flag—six red stripes, with five white stripes alternately displayed longitudinally. In the upper angle of the flag, next to the spear, a square blue ground, covering in depth five stripes. In the centre of the blue, one white star.

Seal—a dove on the wing, with an open scroll in its claws. A view of the ocean, with a ship under sail. The sun just emerging from the waters. A palm-tree, and at its base a plow and spade. Beneath the emblems, the words Republic of Liberia; and above the emblems, the national motto, THE LOVE OF LIBERTY BROUGHT US HERE.

The Twenty-fourth of August.

The twenty-fourth day of August, 1847, was the day appointed for raising the flag of the new republic, and its happy dawn was announced by the thunder of cannon. At an early hour were seen groups of citizens gathered here and there, with a joyful smile lighting up every countenance. Old men seemed to have renewed their youth, and youth itself moved with a more buoyant and elastic step. At nine o'clock, the governor and his staff, with the military, assembled at the court-house. At the same time, people from all quarters were pouring toward the Government Square. At eleven, his excellency was escorted opposite to the Government House, where he was met by a band of ladies, bearing the flag of their country. On receiving it from Mrs. Lewis, accompanied with a short speech, he unfurled it amid the cheers and hurras of the assembled multitude. The troops then marched up to the Central Fort. At twelve, the first gun of the national salute pealed over the waters, when the flag was seen majestically arising, and from its lofty height soon floated on the breeze, the herald of a brighter day for poor, benighted Africa. At the same moment, a responsive gun was heard from Signal Hill, as if the mountains echoed the jubilant shout of freedom. A salute of twenty-one guns followed, when the procession marched to the Methodist church, where were holden exercises appropriate to the occasion.

* * * * * * * * * *

It was a day which will be long remembered. During the ceremony of presenting the flag, many eyes were suffused with tears. And, indeed, who that remembered the past could forbear to weep? Who that looked back to America, and remembered what he saw and felt there, could be otherwise than agitated? It is, indeed, a great undertaking; but that Almighty Being who hath conducted us thus far, can and will conduct us to the goal at which we aim.—*Liberia Herald.*

Hymn Sung on the Occasion.

Lines by H. Teague, of Monrovia.

Wake, every tuneful string,
To God loud praises bring,
  Wake, heart and tongue;
In strains of melody,

And choral harmony
Sing—for the oppressed are free;
  Wake, cheerful song.

See Mesurado's height,
Illumed with new-born light;
  Lo! the lone star;
Now it ascends the skies;
Lo! the deep darkness flies,
While new-born glories rise
  And shine afar.

Shine, life-creating ray—
Proclaim approaching day;
  Throw wide thy blaze:
Lo! savage Hottentot—
Bosjasman from his cot—
And nations long forgot,
  Astonished gaze.

Shout the loud jubilee,
Afric once more is free—
  Break forth with joy;
Let Nilus' fettered tongue,
Let Niger join the song,
And Congo's loud and long,
  Glad strains employ.

Star in the East, shine forth,
Proclaim a nation's birth;
  Ye nations hear—
This is our natal day,
And we our homage pay;
To Thee, O Lord, we pray;
  Lord, hear our prayer!

All hail, Liberia! hail!
Favored of God, all hail!
  Hail, happy band!
From virtue ne'er remove:
By peace, and truth, and love,
And wisdom from above,
  So shalt thou stand.

The Colonization Movement.

Thus far our appendix has shown the opinions of the colored people respecting Liberia, and what they have done there. Now we add a few pages illustrative of the feelings regarding colonization, which are influencing the minds, and calling forth the exertions of the best and noblest among the white race in America.

But, first, we will show, from the highest British authority, an acknowledgment of the failure of

West India Emancipation.

After a full trial by Great Britain of negro emancipation, the following article in the "London Times" should receive the discreet notice of those philanthropists who, in our country, are dealing so recklessly with the future happiness of the American blacks:

"Our legislation has been dictated by the presumed necessities of the African slave. After the Emancipation Act, a large charge was assessed upon the colony in aid of civil and religious institutions for the benefit of the enfranchised negro, and it was hoped that these colored subjects of the British crown would soon be assimilated to their fellow-citizens. From all the information which reaches us, no less than from the visible probabilities of the case, we are constrained to believe that these hopes have been falsified. The negro has not acquired with his freedom any habits of industry or morality. His independence is but little better than that of an uncaptured brute. Having accepted few of the restraints of civilization, he is amenable to few of its necessities; and the wants of his nature are so easily satisfied, that at the current rate of wages he is called upon for nothing but fitful or desultory exertion. The blacks, therefore, instead of becoming intelligent husbandmen, have become vagrants and squatters; and it is now apprehended, that with the failure of cultivation in the island will come the failure of its resources for instructing or controlling its population. So imminent does this consummation appear, that memorials have been signed by classes of colonial society hitherto standing aloof from politics, and not only the bench and the bar, but the bishop, clergy, and ministers of all denominations in the island, without exception, have recorded their conviction that, in the absence of timely relief, the religious and educational institutions of the island must be abandoned, and the masses of the population retrograde to barbarism."

The Virginia Law on Instruction of Colored Population.

A committee of the Synod of Virginia, consisting of Samuel C. Anderson, Esq., Rev. Peyton Harrison, and Mr. Winfree, were appointed to examine the acts of the General Assembly of that state, and report to the meeting what the law is touching the religious instruction of the colored population.

This committee subsequently reported, that it may be seen by reference to the Code of Virginia, chap. cxcviii., § 31, 2, pages 747–8, that there is nothing in the law prohibiting the owner of slaves, or any member of his family, with his knowledge and consent, to teach his own slaves, on his own plantation, in any subject and to any extent that may please such owner.

Southern Views of Liberia.

By Rev. J. Morris Pease.

From personal observation we know that the colored people of the South, both bond and free, are very far in advance of our colored people of the Free States in a correct knowledge and appreciation of the real character and condition of the government and citizens of Liberia.

From the first, the largest number of colonists, and some of the most distinguished citizens of that republic, have gone from the Southern States. From them thousands of letters have reached their friends left behind. All over the Southern States the colored people receive letters from their own dear friends in Liberia. We have known whole plantations called together to hear read letters from their friends or relatives residing in that country.

No people in the United States possess to-day a deeper, stronger, more thrilling and abiding interest in Liberia, or pray more earnestly for her prosperity, than do the colored people of the Southern States. Thousands of Christian servants, with the knowledge and consent of their masters, are in regular correspondence with citizens of that republic. Mothers have their sons, and sisters their brothers, who are missionaries of the cross of Christ in Western Africa. Many contribute liberally of their earthly substance to send the Gospel there, and to sustain the missions already established. Christian Liberia is their comfort and their hope. With her they sympathize! for her they pray, believing that at some day they may find their home in her bosom, if not for themselves, yet for their children. That republic, that prayer, that faith makes them better men—better Christians.

Besides, many Christian masters are educating and preparing their servants for freedom, in view of their enlarged usefulness in that interesting country.

We are not aware that these facts have been generally given in either the Southern or Northern press, though we are confident that the Christian people of the South, with but few exceptions, have a true religious interest in Liberia, and are ready to minister their aid in support of her claims.

Colonization Suppresses the Slave-trade.

From an Address by the Hon. Edward Everett.

I must pass to another very important object of the Colonization Society in establishing the colony of Liberia, and that is the effectual suppression of the slave-trade throughout its extent and within the sphere of its influence. It is grievous to reflect that contemporaneously with the discovery of our own continent, and from motives of kindness to its natives, the whole western coast of Africa was thrown open to that desolating traffic, which from time immemorial had been carried on from the ports of the Mediterranean, by the Nile, and along the eastern coasts of the continent. It is still more painful to consider that the very period at which the modern culture of the west of Europe was making the most rapid progress, is that at which Africa began to suffer the most from its connection with Europe.

It was the age of Shakspeare, of Spencer, of Hooker, and of Lord Bacon, of those other brightest suns in the firmament of England's glory, that her navigators first engaged in this detestable traffic, and vessels bearing, as if in derision, the venerable names of Jesus and Solomon were sent from Great Britain to the coast of Africa—at a time when some of the last remnants of the feudal system were broken down in England and France —when private war had wholly ceased—when men began to venture from the covert of the walled towns and traverse the high roads, and live in the open country in safety, these very states, the most civilized in Europe, began to struggle for the monopoly of that cruel trade, which was carried on by exciting the barbarous races of Africa to new fury against each other, and by introducing a state of universal war, not merely between nation and nation, but between tribe and tribe, village and village, and almost between house and house. In fact, it is not without example that these benighted beings have delivered their wives and children to the slave-dealers.

Thus, the western coast of Africa became, like the northeastern and eastern coasts, one great slave market, and so remained for nearly three centuries. It is now about twenty years since the powers of Christendom, excited to activity by philanthropic operations and benevolent individuals, began the warfare upon this cruel traffic. The American colonies, before their independence, passed laws for its abolition, which were uniformly negatived by the crown. The Revolutionary Congress, in the first year of its existence, denounced the traffic, and the Constitution of the United States appointed a date for its prospective abolition.

This example has been successfully followed by other states. The trade is now forbidden by the laws of every Christian and most of the Mohammedan powers of Europe and Asia. It still exists, however, to a frightful extent, and the more active the means used to suppress it by blockade and cruisers, the greater the cruelty incident to its practice, by crowding the slave-ships with a greater number of victims. Such being the case, many of those in England who have taken the greatest interest in the suppression of the traffic have seriously proposed to abandon the system of blockade and cruisers, and resort to other expedients; and of these, unquestionably, none can be compared for efficiency with settlement of the coast.

It is necessary only to look at the map to see what an important extent of country has been rescued in this way from the direst scourge which ever afflicted humanity. The last of the ancient slave-marts, Gallinas, has been lately purchased and brought within the limits of Liberia. Along a line of coast not less extensive than that from Maine to Georgia, from every bay, and within the shelter of every headland of which this traffic was carried on within the memory of man, the slave traffic has been wholly rooted out. What could not be effected by congresses of sovereigns at Vienna or Aix-la-Chapelle, by quintuple treaties, or by squadrons of war steamers, has been brought about by these feeble colonial settlements, of which that of Liberia has been obliged to struggle its way into permanence—drawing its supplies almost exclusively from the perennial fountains of Christian benevolence.

American Slavery has improved the Colored Man.

From an Address by Hon. Daniel Webster.

Gentlemen, there is a Power above us which sees the end of all things from the beginning, though we see it not. Almighty God is his own interpreter of the ways of his own providence; and I sometimes contemplate with amazement, and I may say with adoration, events which have taken place through the instrumentality of the cupidity and criminality of men, designed nevertheless to work out great ends of beneficence and goodness, by our Creator.

African slaves were brought hither to the shores of this continent almost simultaneously with the first tread of a white man's foot upon this our North America. We see in that, our short-sightedness only sees, the effect of a desire of the white man to appropriate to himself the results of the labor of the black man as an inferior and a slave. Now let us look at it.

These negroes, and all who have succeeded them, brought hither as captives taken in the wars of their own petty provinces, ignorant and barbarous, without the knowledge of God, and with no reasonable knowledge of their own character and condition, have come here, and here, although in a subordinate, in an inferior, in an enslaved condition, have learned more, and become to know more of themselves and of their Creator, than all whom they have left behind them in their own barbarous kingdoms. It would seem that this is the mode, as far as we can judge, this is the destiny, the rule of things established by Providence, by which knowledge, letters, and Christianity shall be returned by the descendants of those poor, ignorant barbarians who were brought here as slaves, to the country from which they came.

Who but must wonder, who can fail to see what appears to be so plainly the indication in the providence of God. He who now goes back to Africa under the auspices of this society is an intelligent man. He knows that he is an immortal man, what his ancestors hardly knew, except from that instinctive principle which pervades all human nature, that there is an hereafter. He has the lights of knowledge; he has the lights of Christianity, and he goes back infinitely more advanced in all that makes him a respectable human being than his ancestors were when they were brought from the barbarism of Africa to slavery in the United States.

Colonization an Act of Justice.

By Rev. John P. Durbin, D.D.

It was a stupendous public wrong to commence it (slavery);

it is a measure of public justice not only to put a stop to it, but to remedy the wrongs and evils which have flowed from it. These wrongs and evils, operating through a long series of years, have entwined themselves with the vast and complicated interests and institutions of a large portion of our country; and it will require a long series of years to accomplish the remedy effectually. But Providence allows time to work out the ends of public justice, and always seconds the efforts of man, if made sincerely, wisely, and patiently. Let us, then, do our part in setting on foot a system of public policy that shall safely, peacefully, and equitably render this great act of public justice to the millions of the exiled children of Africa.

But this act of public justice connects with the natural right of these people, and with the divine will not doubtfully expressed. In pursuance of the divine distribution of the earth among the different races of men, God gave Africa to the race from which our colored people come. The deed of distribution and the reason for it are found in holy Scripture, in these words: "God hath made of one blood all nations of men, for to dwell on all the face of the earth, *and hath determined the times before appointed, and the bounds of their habitation; that they should seek the Lord, if haply they might feel after him and find him.*" Who can doubt but the "bounds of the habitation" of these people are in Africa? Who can doubt but in that part of the world is their lot, in working out the wise designs of a Providence known to man only as God manifests them by the signs of the times? Perhaps this wise and mysterious Providence has permitted their bondage in order to prepare them to be the instruments of Christian civilization and religion to their vast and populous country. Had they remained in their own country, they would have remained pagans; in their slavery and exile they have become Christians in their ideas and feelings, and many of them truly experimental and intelligent Christians. Return them to Africa, and they will form a Christian republic whose light and civilization will illuminate and reform the western part of that great and gloomy continent. This single consideration is sufficient to move this whole country to action in favor of colonization. And if such be the designs of Providence, who shall estimate the guilt and punishment of our people if we refuse to send home these prepared missionaries, now that God, by the signs of the times, is intimating His will that we now enter upon the work?

Blessings of African Colonization.

From a Discourse delivered before the Louisiana State Colonization Society, by Rev. Dr. Scott, of New Orleans.

Another great blessing of the emigration of our free people of color to Africa, is that they carry with them the Gospel. This is the only practicable means that presents itself to the pious for the Christianization and civilization of that vast continent. How else can we hope to emancipate one hundred and fifty millions of people on that continent from ignorance, superstition, and paganism? What enterprise is more grand and noble, and worthy of our thoughts, prayers, and contributions, than the attempt to bring Africa under the influence of the Gospel? A wise and good man once said, if he were sure that he would die to-morrow, he would plant a tree to-day, whose shade or fruit might bless the coming generation. This man had a soul truly great, and in the likeness of the Creator. He looked forward to the future.

And if we look to the future of this grand movement; and seeing how the feeble beginning has grown into an independent republic, with seven hundred miles of sea-coast, and territory sufficient to accommodate all the black population of these United States, and country capable of raising all the leading and great products of the tropical climates, cotton, corn, rice, sugar, and coffee—who among us can look to the future of this grand movement? Who can read the microscope, or prophesy from the configuration of the planets, which presided over the birth of the free, independent, and Christianized Republic of Liberia, what shall be its history as it sweeps onward through the track of time, enlightening and redeeming that vast continent? The returning of the negroes of this continent to their fatherland, has made Africa the "land of promise" to the black man, as this country has become to the European Continent.

And when England asks in time to come, as she has often done heretofore, and not without a sneer, *What has America done for the negro?* we may gladly say, Look to Liberia, and see what America has done for the negro, for Africa, and for Christ. See there the only country on the globe in which the negro is a man, in full possession of all the rights of a man. See there a colony of intelligent, moral, and industrious people, grown already into a nation, carrying the English language, and science, and commerce, and arts, and the glad tidings of the Gospel, and of republican liberties, into the darkest regions of heathenism and slavery. And if fifty years hence England dares to ask again, "What has America done for the negro?" then all Africa will respond, saying, "The continent which England once robbed and ravaged, and from which she tore our bleeding sires, now smiles and rejoices in the light shed upon it by the sons of those exiles, returned to us ladened with Heaven's best blessings, through the Christian intelligence and philanthropy of America."

* * * * * * * * * *

I do not doubt but that the whole continent of Africa will be regenerated, and I believe the Republic of Liberia will be the great instrument, in the hands of God, in working out this regeneration. The colony of Liberia has succeeded better than the colony of Plymouth did for the same period of time. And yet, in that little company which was wafted across the mighty ocean in the *May Flower*, we see the germs of this already colossal nation, whose feet are in the tropics, while her head reposes upon the snows of Canada. Her right hand she stretches over the Atlantic, feeding the millions of the Old World, and beckoning them to her shores, as a refuge from famine and oppression; and, at the same time, she stretches forth her left hand to the islands of the Pacific, and to the old empires of the East, full of the blessings of the arts and sciences, of trade, civilization, and pure religion. And does not faith tell us that the lone star, that our example and benevolence has made to appear in the very central regions of African barbarism, shall become a mighty constellation, whose glorious light shall beam along the dark valleys of the Niger and Senegal, and make the Mountains of the Moon reflect the glory of the sun of righteousness, and that Africa redeemed, and having placed the topmost jewel in the crown of her great deliverer, shall sit with Europe, Asia, and America, clothed and in their right minds, at the feet of Jesus of Nazareth?

THE END.

Abbott's Mother at Home.

The Mother at Home; or, the Principles of Maternal Duty familiarly Illustrated. By J. S. C. Abbott. With numerous Engravings. 16mo, Muslin, 60 cents.

Abbott's Child at Home.

The Child at Home; or, the Principles of Filial Duty familiarly Illustrated. By J. S. C. Abbott. Beautifully embellished with Woodcuts. 16mo, Muslin, 60 cents.

Harry's Ladder to Learning.

With 250 Illustrations. 12mo, Muslin.

A Child's History of England.

By Charles Dickens 16mo, Muslin.

Evenings at Home;

or, the Juvenile Budget Opened. By Dr. Aikin and Mrs. Barbauld. With 34 Engravings by Adams. 18mo, Muslin, 75 cents; Muslin, gilt edges, $1 00.

The Juvenile Budget Opened;

being Selections from the Writings of Dr. John Aikin. Edited by Mrs. S. J. Hale. 18mo, Muslin, 37½ cents.

The Juvenile Budget Reopened;

being further Selections from the Writings of Dr. John Aikin, with copious Notes. 18mo, Muslin, 37½ cents.

Alice Gordon;

or, the Uses of Orphanage. By Jos. Alden, D.D. Engravings. 18mo, Muslin, 37½ cents; Muslin, gilt edges, 45 cents.

Elizabeth Benton;

or, Religion in Connection with Fashionable Life. By Jos. Alden, D.D. 18mo, Muslin, 37½ cents.

The Lawyer's Daughter.

By Jos. Alden, D.D. Engravings. 18mo, Muslin, 37½ cents; Muslin, gilt edges, 45 cents.

The Schoolmistress.

By Jos. Alden, D.D. 18mo, Muslin, 37½ cents; Muslin, gilt edges, 45 cents.

The Dying Robin, and other Tales.

By Jos. Alden, D.D. 18mo, Muslin, 37½ cents; Muslin, gilt edges, 45 cents.

Lives of the Apostles

and early Martyrs of the Church. Engravings. 18mo, Muslin, 25 cents.

A Hero,

Bread upon the Waters, and Alice Learmont. By the Author of "Olive," "The Head of the Family," "Agatha's Husband," "Ogil vies," &c. 12mo, Paper, 62½ cents; Muslin, 75 cents.

The Adopted Child.

The History of an Adopted Child. By GERALDINE ENDSOR JEWSBURY. Muslin, 62½ cents.

Eastbury.

A Novel. By ANNA HARRIET DRURY. 12mo, Paper, 60 cents; Muslin, 75 cents.

The Two Families;

an Episode in the History of Chapelton. By the Author of "Rose Douglass." 12mo, Muslin, 75 cents.

Balboa, Cortez, and Pizarro.

The Lives of Vasco Nunez de Balboa, the Discoverer of the Pacific Ocean; Hernando Cortez, the Conqueror of Mexico, and Francisco Pizarro, the Conqueror of Peru. 18mo, Muslin, 37½ cents.

Things by their Right Names.

By Mrs. BARBAULD. Edited by Mrs. S. J. HALE. 18mo, Muslin, 37½ cents.

The Child's Friend.

Being Selections from the Writings of M. BERQUIN. 18mo, Muslin, 37½ cents.

The Juvenile Companion

and Fireside Reader, consisting of Historical and Biographical Anecdotes, and Selections in Poetry. By Rev. J. L. BLAKE. 18mo, Muslin, 37½ cents.

History of the American Revolution.

Edited by Rev. J. L. BLAKE. Illustrated by Four Maps and Wood cuts. 18mo, Muslin, 37½ cents.

The Arabian Nights' Entertainments.

Translated and arranged for Family Reading, with Explanatory Notes, by E. W. LANE. Illustrated with 600 Engravings by Harvey. 2 vols. 12mo, Muslin, $2 75; Muslin, gilt edges, $3 00; Turkey Morocco, gilt edges, $5 00

Bunyan's Pilgrim's Progress.

The Pilgrim's Progress. By JOHN BUNYAN. With a Life of the Author, by ROBERT SOUTHEY, LL.D. Illustrated with fifty Engravings by ADAMS. 12mo, Muslin, 75 cents.

Home Influence.

A Tale for Mothers and Daughters. By GRACE AGUILAR. 12mo, Paper, 75 cents; Muslin, 90 cents

Miller's Boy's Own Book.

The Boy's Own Book of the Seasons. Comprising the Spring, Summer, Autumn, and Winter Books. Descriptive of the Season Scenery, Rural Life, and Country Amusements. By THOMAS MILLER. Embellished by numerous exquisite Engravings. 4 vols. in one. 12mo, Muslin, $1 75. 4 vols. separately, Muslin, 45 cents each.

Dickens's Christmas Books.

Christmas books. By CHARLES DICKENS. Comprising "A Christmas Carol," "The Chimes," "The Cricket on the Hearth," "The Battle of Life," and "The Haunted Man." Handsome Library Edition. Uniform with Dombey and Son. 12mo, Muslin, 75 cents.

Caleb Field.

A Novel. By the Author of "Margaret Maitland," &c. 12mo Muslin, 37½ cents.

Miss Edgeworth's Tales and Novels.

With Engravings. 10 vols. 12mo, Muslin, 75 cents each. The Volumes sold separately or in Sets.

I. Castle Rackrent; Essay on Irish Bulls; Essay on Self-Justification; The Prussian Vase; The Good Aunt.

II. Angelina; The Good French Governess; Mademoiselle Panache; The Knapsack; Lame Jervis; The Will; Out of Debt, Out of Danger; The Limerick Gloves; The Lottery; Rosanna.

III. Murad the Unlucky; The Manufacturers; Ennui; The Contrast; The Grateful Negro; To-morrow; The Dun.

IV. Maneuvering; Almeria; Vivian.

V. The Absentee; Madame De Fleury; Emily de Coulanges; The Modern Griselda.

VI. Belinda.

VII. Leonora; Letters on Female Education; Patronage.

VIII. Patronage; Comic Dramas.

IX. Harrington; Thoughts on Bores; Ormond.

X. Helen.

Evelina;

or, the History of a young Lady's Introduction to the World. By Miss BURNEY. 12mo, Muslin, 60 cents.

The Heir of Wast-Wayland.

By MARY HOWITT. 12mo, Paper, 37½ cents; Muslin, 50 cents.

Jane Bouverie.

By CATHARINE SINCLAIR. 12mo, Muslin, 62½ cents.

Children of the New Forest.

The Children of the New Forest. By Captain MARRYAT, R.N. 12mo, Paper, 37½ cents; Muslin, 45 cents.

The Little Savage.

The Little Savage. Being the History of a Boy left alone upon an uninhabited Island. By Captain MARRYAT, R.N. 12mo, Paper, 37½ cents; Muslin, 45 cents.

Moorland Cottage.

By Mrs. GASKELL, Author of "Mary Barton." Muslin, 37½ cents.

The Image of his Father.

The Image of his Father. By the Brothers MAYHEW. With Illustrations. 18mo, Paper, 50 cents; Muslin, 70 cents.

The Shoulder-Knot.

A Novel. By Rev B. F. TEFFT, D.D. 12mo, Paper, 60 cents; Muslin, 75 cents.

The Diary of a Physician.

By Dr. SAMUEL WARREN 3 vols. 18mo, Muslin, $1 35.

Boarding Out;

or, Domestic Life. By the Author of "Keeping House and Housekeeping." 18mo, Muslin, 37½ cents.

The Whale and his Captors;

or, the Whalemen's Adventures and the Whale's Biography, as gathered on the Homeward Cruise of the "Commodore Preble." By Rev H. T. CHEEVER. Engravings. 18mo, Muslin, 60 cents.

The Vicar of Wakefield.

By OLIVER GOLDSMITH. 18mo, Muslin, 37½ cents.

The Country Year-Book;

or, the Field, the Forest, and the Fireside. By WILLIAM HOWITT. 12mo, Muslin, 87½ cents.

Keeping House and Housekeeping.

A Story of Domestic Life. Edited by Mrs. S. J. HALE. 18mo, Muslin, 37½ cents.

The Useful Arts,

considered in connection with the Applications of Science. By JACOB BIGELOW, M.D. With numerous engravings. 2 vols. 12mo, Muslin, $1 50.

Nott's Counsels.

Counsels to Young Men on the Formation of Character, and the Principles which lead to Success and Happiness in Life. By ELIPHALET NOTT, D.D. 18mo, Half Bound, 50 cents.

Pursuit of Knowledge under Difficulties;

its Pleasures and Rewards. Illustrated by Memoirs of Eminent Men. By GEORGE L. CRAIK. 2 vols. 18mo, Muslin, 90 cents.

SAME WORK revised, with Notes and a Preface, by Rev. Dr. WAYLAND, President of Brown University. From larger Type than the foregoing Edition. Portraits. 2 vols. 12mo, Muslin, $1 50.

The Fireside Friend;

or, Female Student; being Advice to Young Ladies on the importan Subject of Education. With an Appendix on Moral and Religious Education, from the French of Madame de Saussure. By Mrs. A H. L. PHELPS. 12mo, Muslin, 75 cents.

The Complete Works of Hannah More.

Engravings. 1 vol. 8vo, Sheep extra, $2 50; 2 vols., $2 75.

The same Work, printed from large Type, 7 vols. 12mo, Muslin, $5 25.

Mrs. Sherwood's Works.

Engravings. 16 vols. 12mo, Muslin, 75 cents per Volume. The Volumes sold separately or in Sets.

I. The History of Henry Milner, Parts I., II., and III.

II. Fairchild Family; Orphans of Normandy; The Latter Days, &c.

III. Little Henry and his Bearer; Lucy and her Dhaye; Memoirs of Sergeant Dale, his Daughter, and the Orphan Mary; Susan Gray; Lucy Clare; Theophilus and Sophia; Abdallah, the Merchant of Bagdad.

IV. The Indian Pilgrim; The Broken Hyacinth; The Babes in the Wood of the New World; Katharine Seward; The Little Beggars, &c.

V. The Infant's Progress; The Flowers of the Forest; Ermina, &c.

VI. The Governess; The Little Momicre; The Stranger at Home; Pere la Chaise; English Mary; My Uncle Timothy.

VII. The Nun; Intimate Friends; My Aunt Kate; Emeline; Obedience; The Gipsey Babes; The Basket-maker; The Butterfly, &c.

VIII. Victoria; Arzoomund; The Birth-day Present; The Errand Boy; The Orphan Boy; The Two Sisters; Julian Percival; Edward Mansfield; The Infirmary; The Young Forester; The Bitter Sweet; Common Errors, &c

IX., X., XI., and XII. The Lady of the Manor.

XIII. The Mail-coach; My Three Uncles; The Old Lady's Complaint; The Shepherd's Fountain; The Hours of Infancy; Economy; Old Things and New Things; The Swiss Cottage; The Infant's Grave; The Father's Eye; Dudley Castle; The Blessed Family; Caroline Mordaunt, &c.

XIV. The Monk of Cimies; The Rosary; or, Rosee of Montreux; The Roman Baths; Saint Hospice; The Violet Leaf; The Convent of St. Clair.

XV. The History of Henry Milner, Part IV., Sabbaths on the Continent; The Idler.

XVI. John Marten.

How to Observe.

Morals and Manners. By Miss H. MARTINEAU. 12mo, Muslin, 42½ cents.

Letters to Young Ladies.

By Mrs. L. H. SIGOURNEY. 12mo, Muslin, 75 cents; Muslin, gilt edges, 90 cents.

Two Years before the Mast;

A Personal Narrative of Life at Sea. By R. H. DANA, Jr. 18mo, Muslin, 45 cents.

www.ingramcontent.com/pod-product-compliance
Lightning Source LLC
LaVergne TN
LVHW022039110826
845151LV00007B/863
* 9 7 8 1 4 2 5 5 3 0 9 4 5 *